IN THE DARKEST HOUR

ALSO AVAILABLE BY ANNA CARLISLE

All the Secret Places

Dark Road Home

IN THE DARKEST HOUR

A Gin Sullivan Mystery

Anna Carlisle

CROOKED
LANE

NEW YORK

Published in the United States by Crooked Lane Books, an imprint of The Quick Brown Fox & Company LLC.

Crooked Lane Books and its logo are trademarks of The Quick Brown Fox & Company LLC.

Library of Congress Catalog-in-Publication data available upon request.

ISBN (hardcover): 978-1-68331-731-9
ISBN (ePub): 978-1-68331-732-6
ISBN (ePDF): 978-1-68331-733-3

Cover design by Lori Palmer
Book design by Jennifer Canzone

Printed in the United States.

www.crookedlanebooks.com

Crooked Lane Books
34 West 27th St., 10th Floor
New York, NY 10001

First Edition: September 2018

10 9 8 7 6 5 4 3 2 1

1

"Nice job with Carolina today, Gin," Gordon Samson said, bending to retrieve a test tube that had rolled under one of the long lab tables in the seventh-grade science classroom at Shoney Middle School. "I think you're developing eyes in the back of your head. Which is absolutely a requirement of the job, if you haven't figured it out already."

Gin laughed, tossing the antiseptic wipe she'd been using to clean the lab tables into the trash. "I wish. That would certainly have come in handy in my old job, too."

"I still have trouble believing you left a career in the Chicago medical examiner's office to work with middle school kids in the middle of nowhere," Gordon said. "I mean, don't get me wrong—you're great at it. The kids love you, and though it pains me to admit it, you've managed to do the impossible and get them interested in the difference between qualitative and quantitative observations.

1

But if I'd spent all those years getting through medical school and a residency, I'm not sure I'd be so ready to trade it for a chance to work with a bunch of hormone-crazed adolescents."

Gin shrugged noncommittally, searching for a response that would satisfy her colleague's curiosity without getting into the details of her personal life. As much as she liked Gordon, who had spent more than two decades teaching science to the kids in Trumbull, Pennsylvania, she'd only recently begun volunteering in his classroom every Tuesday afternoon and was still getting to know the other teachers and staff. "I'll still have my consulting work. And the position would only be part time, anyway. If they even approve it." She grimaced at the thought. "I thought the red tape and institutional backlog were a challenge in the medical examiner's office, but it's nothing compared to getting things done in the school district."

"Yeah, I hear you. All kidding aside, though, I think you could really make a difference. Some of these girls—" A knock on the classroom door stopped him midsentence. "You might want to sneak out before one of the little darlings comes back to beg for more time to finish her lab report."

Gin laughed. "No, this is an opportunity for on-the-job training! Maybe I'll learn something from watching the master at work."

Gordon rolled his eyes good-naturedly and went to answer the door.

But it wasn't a seventh-grade student. Jake Crosby

entered the classroom, ducking to avoid a solar system mobile.

"Jake! What are you doing here?" Gin said, adding, "Gordon, this is my boyfriend, Jake Crosby. Jake, meet Gordon Samson, who heads the science department here at Shoney."

"Nice to meet you," Jake said, barely acknowledging the other man.

Recovering from the surprise of her boyfriend showing up at school, Gin noticed that Jake's jeans were streaked with white dust and his ball cap was splattered with paint, meaning he'd probably come straight from the job site.

"Is everything all right?"

"Gin, I'm sorry to bust in on you like this, but—are you about ready to go?"

"What's wrong?" Instantly on alert, Gin spoke more sharply than she intended.

"You weren't answering your phone."

It wasn't an answer to her question. "Jake, I can't have my phone on in the classroom!"

"Look . . . please."

Gin took in Jake's expression, his facial muscles tensed with some masked emotion, while Gordon did his best to pretend to be absorbed in the papers on his desk. She wouldn't get more out of Jake until they were alone. "Let me just grab my things."

After saying a terse goodbye to Gordon, she followed Jake out into the empty, echoing hallways of the school.

"What was so important that—"

Jake stopped her with a hand on her arm the minute

they were around the corner, in front of a row of lockers near the stairs. Gin had a sudden flashback to a time almost two decades ago, when she and Jake had been high school sweethearts just a couple of miles away at Trumbull High School. A lifetime ago.

"It's my mom." Jake swallowed.

"Your *mom*?"

"She's dead."

"Oh my God—"

"They found her in a motel room in Denton," Jake barreled on grimly as Gin blanched in shock. They want . . ." He stared at the floor while struggling to get his emotions under control. "Someone has to go identify her."

"Of course. I'll—I'll call and let them know we're on our way." Gin did her best to absorb the news as she fought to keep her own emotions under control. She had never met the woman who gave birth to Jake, but she could see in his eyes that her death had dealt him a harsh blow.

Her mind raced ahead, thinking through the task that awaited. As a consultant to the Allegheny County Medical Examiner's office, Gin had attended more than a dozen autopsies in their building near the Strip District of Pittsburgh, thirty miles away. She had learned the best routes when traffic was backed up, where to grab a cup of coffee or a quick lunch, and where to park when the visitor spaces were full.

But she had no idea how to conduct an identification when the son of the decedent hadn't seen his mother since he was an infant.

2

"When was the last time you had word of Marnie?" Gin asked carefully. They'd agreed to take her car; Jake's truck would be safe at the school until they could come back and pick it up.

"Jesus. Probably . . . at least ten years ago. Dad got a letter from her aunt when Marnie's mother died. Believe it or not, she thought Dad might be able to help them find Marnie."

Jake's parents had married impulsively, and his mother had been considerably younger than his father. She left before Jake was a year old to pursue a dream of acting in California. Lawrence Crosby, the Trumbull police chief until he passed away last year, had raised Jake by himself. By the time Jake and Gin started dating in high school, the hurt from his mother's abandonment had hardened into armor that was all but impenetrable. In the years she'd known him, Gin could count on one hand the number of times she had heard Jake mention his mother's name, and as far as she knew, they had never been in contact.

"Why would they think that?"

"According to her aunt, she actually contacted Dad every few years." The muscles in Jake's jaw twitched dangerously. "Wrote letters and stuff."

"And . . . he never told you?"

"No." Just the one syllable, hard and bitten off.

Gin knew better than to press Jake on the subject of his past, which had been a difficult one. After a stormy adolescence, in trouble more often than he was out of it—despite the fact that his father was the chief of police—Jake had settled into an uneasy truce with his hometown. He'd earned a solid reputation as a construction contractor, and steadily built his business until now he was building fine custom homes in several eastern Pennsylvania counties. But there were those who never forgot—or forgave—Jake's troubled history.

Sometimes the passage of time didn't mean much. Gin wondered what was going through Jake's head—if the pain of his mother's abandonment was as fresh today as it had been then.

"I . . . did do a little looking of my own," Jake conceded. "Online mostly."

"When was that?"

Jake shrugged. "After Dad got that letter. He told the aunt he couldn't help, but . . . well, I couldn't let go of it as easy as he did, I guess."

"What did you find out?"

Jake didn't answer for a moment, staring vacantly at the road ahead. "Nothing good. Records of her arrests—mostly petty stuff, check scams, shoplifting, drugs, a couple breaking and entering charges. She had a few different addresses, mostly around Trafford—she only lasted a couple of years in California, I guess. Never married again or anything. Never . . . had any more kids."

"Oh."

Gin's mind spun, trying to come up with something to say that would be a comfort. She'd known that Jake's mother had been troubled; she wasn't surprised to hear that Marnie had succumbed to drugs and minor crimes. But it hadn't occurred to Gin that she might have spent most of Jake's life living less than an hour away. She wondered if that was the most difficult thing for him to accept.

The hardest part of loving a man like Jake Crosby wasn't his solitude, or his habit of keeping his deepest hurts to himself.

The hardest thing was watching him suffer and being unable to help.

But there was one small thing that Gin could do: She could make the next hour of Jake's life a little less painful than it would otherwise be.

"Stephen's going to meet us in his office. We'll go together."

She got only a grunt in response, but she was sure that her friend and colleague Stephen Harper, the staff pathologist whom she'd worked with on several cases, would treat Jake's situation with compassion.

Traffic was light, most of the commuters heading home in the opposite direction, and they found a parking space right behind the modern concrete- and- glass building Gin used her ID to enter the quiet, nearly empty building. They found Stephen in his office, working at his computer.

"Jake. I'm very sorry for your loss," he said formally, rising and offering his hand. Jake mumbled a greeting.

"Let's sit for a moment before we go see her." They took the guest chairs, and Stephen pulled his own chair around his desk so that the three of them could confer more informally. "Can I get you some coffee? A soda?"

"No thanks," Jake said. "Look, Stephen—I never knew my mother. I literally have not laid eyes on her since I was a baby. So you don't need to spare my feelings here."

Stephen glanced at Gin, and she shrugged almost imperceptibly. Despite Jake's words, both she and Stephen had years of experience with the families of the dead, and knew that the emotional response could not be easily predicted. Even in a situation like this, when family members were estranged, confronting death could bring up a host of buried emotions and experiences.

"I understand," Stephen said kindly. "Then, let me tell you what we know. Marnie Bertram was found by a motel maid this morning at a little after eleven o'clock, when the maid entered her room to clean it. She found Marnie lying in bed, unresponsive, and called the police. When they arrived they determined that Marnie had been using heroin, based on various items they found near her body and also the condition of her body. The coroner confirmed her death at 2:18 PM and she was brought here. Tox results won't be available for several weeks, of course." He paused, seeming to search for the least painful way to deliver the news. "Multiple, unhealed injection-site wounds on her body suggest that she was a habitual user, and imply that this was an overdose."

Jake briefly covered his face with his hands, but when he had composed himself his eyes were dry. "Intentional?"

"I'm sorry, Jake, it's hard to know when heroin is involved. We'll know more with further testing, of course, but these overdoses are tragically common, as the street product is completely unregulated, so people can't know what they're getting."

"Yeah. I watch the news." Jake sighed, and sat up straighter in the chair. "Okay. Well, let's get this done."

He stood, and Gin and Stephen followed suit. Stephen led the way to the morgue, stepping aside so the others could enter. Only one body was waiting on one of several steel tables lined up in the middle of the room, draped in a white sheet. All the other bodies were stored in a state-of-the-art, high-density cold chamber that topped four thousand square feet. The entire facility had been built only seven years earlier, a showpiece of current forensic technology that was the envy of pathologists around the state, if not the country.

Gin had been here dozens of times, and while she always maintained clinical detachment when working, she had once come into this room to identify a loved one of her own: her only sibling, her sister Lily, who had disappeared at the age of seventeen. Her body had been discovered many years later, buried near the creek where she used to go with her friends.

Gin counted herself lucky to have been able to help track down Lily's killer, and the investigation had begun right here. But that was later. In the first seconds—the same seconds Jake was about to experience—there was nothing but the confrontation with death, the fragility of the assemblage of tissues and bones that had once laughed, cried, loved, raged, and experienced both joy and pain. A human life was so much more than the sum of its physical parts, but in the silence of the morgue, the body waited to tell its story.

Stephen stood at the head of the table and gently grasped the sheet. Glancing up at Jake to make sure he was prepared, he raised his eyebrows questioningly. Jake nodded and Stephen pulled back the sheet.

The body of the woman lying underneath seemed impossibly delicate and small, but Gin knew that it was partly an illusion, the contrast between the unaccustomed stillness of the form against the stark, steel surface. Marnie Bertram's face was weathered and aged beyond her sixty years. Her staring eyes were bloodshot and sightless; her skin purpled and sunken. Chapped, pale lips parted over broken and missing teeth. Her hair was thin and greasy and lay limply around her wrinkled neck and bony shoulders. A long, relatively recent gash near her collarbone had healed poorly, evidence of infection in its angry, swollen ridge.

Stephen drew the fabric away from one arm, while keeping her torso covered. The arm lay with the hand palm up, half a dozen red welts on the pale inner flesh. Track marks—Gin had seen more of them in her career than she ever would have wanted.

"I don't know what you want me to say," Jake said roughly. "The only photos I've seen of her in the last twenty years are the mug shots that came up when I searched her online."

"Of course," Stephen said, pulling the sheet gently back in place. "This is mostly a formality."

The forensic technicians would have taken fingerprints as part of the intake process, and given Marnie's criminal history, the print match in AFIS would provide the necessary proof of identity.

"There is, however, one thing that I thought you might like to see," Stephen added. "If I may."

He went to the other side of the table, and lifted the sheet to reveal the other arm. "Ms. Bertram was right handed, so the injection sites are, predictably, mostly on the left side of her body. But on her right shoulder, if you take a look . . ."

Jake bent down, obstructing Gin's view, and made a sound that was a cross between a curse and a strangled gasp. He backed away from the body, and Gin could see what he'd been looking at.

On his mother's shoulder, faded with time and inexpertly done, was a tattoo of a heart surrounded by roses.

In the middle was the name "Jake."

* * *

"You're sure you still need to go tomorrow?" Gin asked for the second time, standing in the doorway to their bedroom with a mostly untouched glass of wine in her hand. She was watching Jake pack, as she had every Tuesday night for the past month. Jake's firm had begun construction on his most ambitious project yet: a conference and retreat center commissioned by a Philadelphia pharmaceutical company. Because it was to be built on a wooded hillside two hours to the north in the tiny town of Tionesta on the edge of the Allegheny National Forest, Jake had arranged to be on-site Wednesday through Friday of each week to supervise the work of the local crew that he had hired. The rest of the week he spent on local projects, including the framing of a complete internal remodel of a downtown Trumbull restaurant—the project he'd been working on earlier today when he got the news.

"I'm fine," Jake said. "I already told you that. Marnie Bertram was a junkie who died a junkie's death. She doesn't have anything to do with me other than getting knocked up by my dad and giving birth. And that happened a long, long time ago, Gin."

Gin thought of the tattoo, the bluish, faded design against the pale, waxy skin. The face that bore the ravages of bad decisions and worse luck. The pain that the woman who had given birth to Jake had carried.

"I understand," she said. "But in my experience, it wouldn't be surprising if you had a . . . response to what you saw today. It might even hit you later, when you've had a chance to—"

"Drop it, Gin," Jake snapped. "Okay?"

He tossed a pair of jeans roughly into his duffle, and threw in a belt. Then his hands stilled, and he sighed. "Look," he said, in a considerably gentler tone. "I know what you're trying to do and I appreciate it. I do. But I don't need you analyzing me, and I don't need to be treated with kid gloves. The best thing for me to do is get back to work. I'll make some calls tomorrow—I'll make sure that my mother is given a proper burial. But that's where my obligation ends, and I hope you can understand that and let it go."

Gin nodded. She'd said her piece and now she needed to respect Jake's wishes. He might even be right; people handled grief in many different ways, and even if Jake was more affected by the death of his mother than he was letting on, it was unlikely that he would seek professional help.

If Gin had learned one thing in her career, it was not to anticipate—or try to change the course of—the recovery process of the families and loved ones of the dead.

"Okay," she said, aiming for a lighter tone. "We've got the dinner party on Saturday night, though. Are you still up for that? Or I could reschedule it for another time . . ."

"No, that's fine," Jake said. He attempted a smile. "It'll be nice to see everyone. I'll help you get ready when I get back."

"That's okay," Gin said. "I'll get the shopping and the prep done on Friday, and then when you get home we can just relax."

"That sounds good," Jake said. He zipped the duffle closed and slung it over his shoulder. "I'm going to throw this in the truck and then I need to take a look at that engineering report."

"Oh," Gin said, disappointed. "I thought maybe we could enjoy our wine and finish that show we started."

"You go ahead without me, okay? I might be up for a while. They've found dry rot in the internal structure. I need to figure out how extensive it is."

He touched her arm as he passed her, headed for the stairs. It wasn't much, but it would have to do for now.

3

Gin woke the next morning on the living room sofa, tucked under a wool blanket. For a moment she was disoriented. Not only could she not remember having fallen asleep there, but she didn't remember fetching the blanket or the pillow under her head.

Then it all came back to her: the news about Jake's mother, the visit to the morgue, the tense conversation with Jake. She'd restarted the show that she and Jake had begun watching earlier in the week, hoping that he would finish his paperwork and join her. Instead, she'd fallen asleep in front of the television, something she almost never did, and Jake must have covered her rather than waking her to come up to bed.

But that meant that she also had slept through her alarm. She could hear the faint tone of her phone alarm upstairs, a series of serene chords. She sat up and threw off the covers, stretching, and glanced over at the kitchen.

Jake's coffee mug was sitting on the counter; the lunch he'd packed the night before was gone. Judging from the angle of the sun, it was already well past dawn, and Jake was probably halfway to the job site already.

Gin tried to stifle her disappointment. She'd hoped to have another opportunity to talk to Jake this morning about his mother, after he'd had a chance to let the news sink in. She understood his desire to put it all behind him—but even the simplest burial required myriad decisions: the selection of a plot, a headstone, a casket; conferring with the cemetery staff; scheduling the interment, even if there was to be no service.

There was also the matter of the expense. A simple burial could cost thousands of dollars. Jake's finances, never completely secure in all of the years that she'd known him, had suffered a setback last year when a job he'd sunk all of his savings into was struck by tragedy: a fire wiped out the nearly completed house, and the investigation into a body discovered on the property tied up the project longer than Jake could comfortably manage. As a result, he'd bid for the retreat center, despite its distance. The project carried a lot of prestige and promised significant financial rewards once it was completed, but the progress payments were barely covering his expenses.

Gin suspected that Jake had no idea of the high cost of the burial. She would be more than happy to make a loan from her savings, but Jake had made it clear before that he didn't want to accept any money from her. Any support she hoped to give—financial or otherwise—would have to be offered with great sensitivity. It wasn't the sort of thing she could discuss with him on the phone, which meant that it would have to wait until the weekend.

"Damn it!" Gin exclaimed as she folded the blanket. She had gotten into the habit of talking to Jake's elderly dog when she was alone in the house, but Jett's health had declined precipitously last winter and they'd made the difficult decision to put her down once she lost her appetite and couldn't rise from her bed without pain. Since then, Gin had felt Jett's absence keenly; since she worked mostly from home, she missed the companionship.

What should we make for the dinner party? She would have asked the old dog. Since moving in with Jake nearly a year ago, she had slowly grown comfortable enough to add her own touches to the place, to hang a few pieces of her own art and mix her playlists in with his. Though Jake had been a bachelor for many years and had come to enjoy cooking, they fell into a comfortable routine of taking turns. Until now, though, Jake always took the lead when company came over. This weekend would be the first time Gin would be in charge.

The invited guests had been her friends first: Rosa Barnes, an old schoolmate with whom she'd renewed her friendship last year, was coming with Doyle Grynbaum, whom she had been dating for several months. And Brandon Hart, the widower of one of Gin's childhood friends, was bringing his girlfriend Diane.

Gin scrolled through recipes on several cooking websites before deciding on a menu to showcase the flavors of spring: eggplant parmesan, a salad of baby lettuces and herbs and peas, and strawberry shortcake. Nothing too ambitious, and if she ran into trouble, she could always call her mother. In addition to being the mayor of the town of Trumbull, Pennsylvania, Madeleine Sullivan was an accomplished hostess and cook.

Gin wrote up a grocery list and planned her errands for the next few days: visits to the farmers market that her mother had launched in the town's revitalized downtown, a new little wine shop that offered tastings and local vintages, her favorite bakery for a savory tart to serve as an appetizer. Her enthusiasm grew as she looked forward to hosting the other two couples, who'd been introduced but didn't know each other well. With any luck, the evening would cement their friendship and kick off a summer of enjoyable social events.

Evenings such as the one she had planned were something she suspected other couples did routinely, but Gin had spent the last two decades pursuing an arduous education to become a pathologist. She'd then completed a demanding residency at the Cook County Medical Examiner's office in Chicago, before finally being hired on staff. As the years went by, Gin honed her skills and developed a specialty in advanced decomposition after doing two tours as a Red Cross volunteer, working to identify victims of war crimes in the mass graves in Srebrenica. None of that had prepared her for the social life that other young people took for granted, and other than a few fleeting romantic relationships that failed to flourish from a lack of attention, Gin had never had time for a large social circle.

With the shopping list complete, Gin stepped into the shower and took her time under the luxuriant spray. Jake had built this house himself, and had lavished attention on every detail—from the stone tile to the window that gave views onto the woods behind the house, the burnished fixtures, the falling-rain shower showerhead. When she was done, she dried off with a plush, oversized towel.

Her phone rang as she was slathering rich lotion onto her legs, inhaling the heady scent. She glanced over at the display screen, expecting her mother; instead, it was a number she hadn't seen in months.

Tuck Baxter, Chief of Police.

She hesitated before picking up the phone. Tuck had only taken the chief position last November. The position had been vacated earlier in the year when Chief Crosby—Jake's father—was killed in the course of the investigation into the death of Gin's sister, Lily. Perhaps because of the circumstances of Crosby's death, the department had been slow to welcome Tuck. But that hadn't stopped him from implementing tough new policies that were meant to raise the level of professionalism of the force. After Crosby's easygoing style, the changes weren't universally appreciated.

But that wasn't the only reason Gin had put some distance between her and Tuck. He'd been involved in the investigation of the body discovered on Jake's job site last fall—an investigation that had focused briefly on Jake himself. There was no love lost between the two men, even though Tuck hadn't hesitated to arrest the true murderer when her identity came to light, thereby exonerating Jake.

The lingering chill between them, Gin had to admit, was mostly because of her. And that was a matter on which she had some very mixed feelings—feelings she didn't like to examine too closely.

She shook her head, attempting to clear out the unhelpful thoughts, and picked up the phone. "Hello, this is Gin," she said, attempting to sound cool and professional.

"Hey Gin. Tuck Baxter."

"Tuck. Nice to hear from you. What can I do for you?"

Did she imagine it, or was there a hesitation before Tuck spoke again? "I'm actually just following up on the matter of Marnie Bertram's death. Everything I'm about to tell you, I already spoke to Jake about. He . . . ah, look, Gin, as you probably know, calling you like this is a bit, um, irregular. So I'd appreciate it if you could consider this just a casual call between friends, rather than any sort of official communication."

"Of course, Tuck." Gin was aware of the rules in place for protecting the confidentiality of matters relating to a death, even in cases where there was no investigation into cause.

"In the past, with someone like Marnie Bertram, with a string of minor offenses behind her and a documented history of drug abuse, we wouldn't bother with an autopsy.

20

But there's some evidence of an uptick in opiate-related deaths in the area. There've been fourteen overdose deaths in the county in the past five weeks, and Wheeler's leaning on Narcotics to find the source. She's assigned Reggie Clawitter to head up the investigation."

"I can't say I'm surprised," Gin said. The surge in opiate overdoses was a nationwide problem with no ready solution, and communities everywhere were desperately grappling with a threat that seemed to have exploded to the front lines. "I hear from my colleagues in Cook County that they're experiencing a similar surge."

"Wheeler's pretty worried about public perception. She doesn't want to appear unconcerned."

"Chozick has instituted changes in how we report overdose on death certificates," Gin said, referring to the Allegheny County Chief ME. "It used to be that you'd see deaths certified as simply acute or multi-drug intoxication. But now we're much more specific. We list everything—like 'acute intoxication due to the combined effects of diazepam, alcohol, and heroin'—as much detail as possible."

"Yeah, it's a hard truth," Tuck sighed. "Anyway, Wheeler's made it clear that every overdose needs to be investigated, and I'm pretty sure she's going to insist on an autopsy on this one."

"I'm sure you're right," Gin murmured, while wondering what this meant for her mother and for the town of Trumbull. As mayor, Madeleine was well versed in the inner workings of local politics—to some degree, at the county level and even beyond—as in the case of the upcoming election for Allegheny County Sheriff. Captain Maureen Wheeler hadn't gone public yet with her intention to run, as the election was still eighteen months away, but her ambitions weren't exactly secret, either. "She must be desperate to get a handle on this before it takes more lives."

"Yeah, no shit. Nobody wants to get labeled the next Fulton County." Philadelphia had long been known as the city with the highest death rate for opiate-related overdoses, but the sparsely populated southern county had recently edged it out as the crisis moved out of the cities and into rural areas. "I hate to say it, Gin, but Marnie Bertram's death is going to be getting a lot of attention. We'll keep it out of the media the best we can, of course, but inside the department—that's another story."

Gin had a feeling she knew what Tuck was leading up to. "You said you told Jake all of this," she ventured tentatively. "I haven't had a chance to talk to him today. He's working on a project up in Trafford—he's been staying up there three days a week."

"Yeah, that's what he said." There was another pause. Gin could picture Tuck gathering his thoughts; he preferred to speak with precision. "Jake tells me that he wasn't close to his mother. I understand they didn't really have much of a relationship. Nevertheless . . . he is her next of kin, so there is likely to be a need for his involvement, even if it's just for documentation and the eventual return of the remains."

"Let me guess," Gin said quietly. "He didn't want to hear that."

Tuck cleared his throat. "His exact words were, 'Send me a fucking bill.' I told him he'd have to make arrangements with the mortuary, but he made it clear he didn't want any more involvement than necessary."

Gin winced; she could imagine Jake saying it. "You've got to understand, Tuck, I think Jake's . . . working through a lot of anger."

Tuck's laugh was short and bitter. "That's one way to put it. Listen, Gin, I'm not without sympathy here. I figure Jake's entitled to feel whatever he wants about this. And I really am sorry that I can't keep him out of it entirely."

"I appreciate that. And . . . I think Jake does, too. Jake's not the kind of man to say it, but this is affecting him deeply."

"Yeah," Tuck said. "To be honest, I think I might handle something like this about the same way. Which is why I thought, well, I wondered if I could talk you into attending the autopsy. I know it's not your area, and you'd just be observing. No consulting obligation, obviously, especially since it's going to be pretty straightforward, unless there's something we've all missed."

"I'm not sure what I could add," she said carefully. "Any of the staff pathologists are likely to have as much, or more, experience as I do with drug-related deaths."

"Yeah, I get that. The truth is . . . it'd be a favor to me as much as anything. Bruce and Liam Witt caught the case and, well, you know how that's going to go over. Let's just say I was hoping your presence might smooth the way to interdepartmental cooperation again."

Senior Homicide Detective Bruce Stillman and his younger partner, Liam Witt, had been involved not only in the investigation that took place on Jake's worksite last fall, but also in the case of Gin's sister, Lily. It was the discovery of her remains that had prompted Gin to take the leave of absence from the Cook County Medical Examiner's office, which had eventually turned into her permanent move back to her hometown.

Wheeler had probably assigned the pair because of the experience they'd amassed in Trumbull, but the decision had a downside. From the start, Bruce had suspected Jake in Lily's murder, and had pursued his case relentlessly, right up until the true killer was identified. Despite establishing Jake's innocence in that case, Bruce pushed hard when evidence on Jake's job site pointed to his possible involvement—even when there were other, likelier suspects.

Now that Jake had been cleared twice, Gin hoped that Bruce would finally give him the benefit of the doubt. But nothing about the detective's typically boorish behavior suggested he'd be extending an olive branch any time soon.

"Jake's mother is *dead*," Gin said, tempering her exasperation. "Surely even Bruce will show some sensitivity in a case like this."

"Yeah, you'd think so." After a beat, Tuck added, "I hate to ask this of you, but the truth is that I need to get some wins on the board. As you know, not everyone was behind me for this job. Wheeler's been keeping pretty close tabs, and the post is provisional for six months. Which is coming up pretty damn fast."

"You really think there's any question that Captain Wheeler will make it permanent?" Gin asked, surprised. "I'm sure my mother would be glad to give you a glowing review. She was telling me that the city's crime statistics have improved since you got here. A twenty percent decline in violent crime? That's pretty impressive."

"Or it could easily be cyclical, or due to increased patrols, or any number of things." Tuck sighed audibly. "We both know that these things can be spun any way the brass wants to spin them. And I just thought that maybe, if you showed up on this one, you could keep the tone a little more professional and we could get all the moving pieces to keep moving. Anything we can do to speed up the tox reports, and show that Trumbull PD is taking this crisis seriously—I'll take it."

"Of course." Gin could do this, both as the favor Tuck was seeking, and because she knew firsthand how devastating in influx of heroin would be to Trumbull. She hadn't witnessed the gradual rebirth and renewal of her hometown, only to see it sink back into despair. "I have to admit, I'm glad to hear that you're willing to fight for your job . . . and by extension, for Trumbull. I take it this means you've been happy here these last few months?"

"Yeah, definitely." Tuck's tone relaxed. "Cherie and I have been settling in really well. One of our neighbors has taken a shine to her, and stays with her sometimes when I can't be home. She's sort of a grandmother to Cherie—something she hasn't really had before."

"Oh, I'm so glad to hear that."

"You know, I've missed seeing you since basketball season ended. Cherie says she sees you around school. She's been bugging me about some girls-in-science thing—that have anything to do with you?"

Gin laughed. "Um, I guess so—I've applied to lead an initiative at the middle school—it's called Girls Rock Science. It's meant to encourage girls to prepare for careers in the sciences. It's only part-time, a few hours a week in the classroom and then after-school programs that I would be responsible for developing and leading."

"Wow, it sounds like it's right up your alley. And if you're half as good at it as you were at coaching, well, I'd say they've got the right woman for the job."

"Tuck Baxter, if I didn't know better, I'd say you were trying to butter me up," Gin said. She'd grown fond of Tuck's daughter Cherie during the basketball season when she'd led her eighth-grade team to a dubious two-seven season. "It's okay—I already said yes to attending the autopsy, so you can drop the charm offensive."

"Hell, Gin, if charm worked on you, I'd already—hey, strike that," Tuck said. "Forgive me. No need to dredge up the past. I'm just glad you said yes."

"Me too," Gin said, feeling her face warm. It had undoubtedly been inadvertent, but Tuck had brought her back to some complicated memories; when they'd first gotten acquainted last fall, Tuck had expressed an interest in her that went beyond a professional relationship. He'd made it known that if Jake should ever be out of the picture, he wanted in.

And Gin had to admit that she'd had feelings for him as well. During that difficult time with Jake, she'd come closer than she should have to taking their relationship into dangerous territory.

"So you'll let me know when the autopsy's scheduled?"

"I can do you one better—I'll shoot you the details right now. I think it's Friday at nine."

"Got it. I'll see you there. And Tuck? Please give my love to Cherie."

"Will do."

After they hung up, Gin found herself staring out the window, thinking not-entirely-professional thoughts about the chief of the Trumbull police department.

4

On Friday morning, Gin was walking from her car to the ME building when she nearly collided with a tall, angular woman who was speaking forcefully into her phone with her head down, not watching where she was going.

"You can consider that my final comment," she was saying as she came barreling around the corner of the building. She shoved the phone into her bag just as Gin stepped awkwardly out of her way.

"Oh, I'm so sorry," the woman said, tucking her chin-length, gray hair behind her ear. Gin realized it was Captain Maureen Wheeler, as recognition dawned on Wheeler's face. "Gin! What brings you up here today?"

Gin hesitated—unsure whether anyone had informed her of Tuck's invitation to observe the autopsy—and wondered what Wheeler was doing there. The county police department was located across town on Penn Avenue, too far to walk. Gin had had perhaps three conversations with the captain, always at the station, and had always found her pleasant, if slightly detached. "I've been asked to sit in on the Marnie Bertram autopsy," she said, hoping Wheeler wouldn't press her on who'd made the invitation.

"Oh, no kidding? I didn't realize there was a decomp aspect to that case."

Though Gin had worked on all kinds of cases while working at Cook County, the Allegheny County Medical Examiner's office had no one on staff with as much expertise in decomposition, so her work focused on cases where bodies had been dead for some time before being found or, for other reasons, had been badly decomposed or damaged.

"Oh, there isn't, really." Gin cast about for a suitable excuse that wouldn't put Tuck in a bind. "I'm strictly an observer, and of course the department won't be paying for my time on this one—"

Wheeler snapped her fingers. "Wait. I just remembered, the victim was Jake Crosby's mother, wasn't she?"

"She—yes."

Wheeler shook her head, eyes troubled. "That poor man has been through a lot. Look, I stand by my guys, of course, but I'm not insensitive to the fact that Jake's found himself in the middle of a few cases, and I'm sorry it happened that way. Anything we can do to help out on this—well, I'm just glad the department can wrap this up quickly. And if we can get any information to help out Narcotics, I'll count that a huge win."

"Yes, of course," Gin said, relieved that she hadn't asked how the invitation came about. "I doubt I can add anything to Stephen's assessment, but I'll do my best."

"Okay, sounds good. Listen, I've got to run—I'm late for a meeting."

Gin said goodbye and walked briskly toward the entrance, checking her watch. The autopsy was starting in two minutes. She showed her ID and made her way to the rear of the building where the morgue was located. Washing and gloving-up as quickly as she could, she let herself into the examining room only to find a surprisingly large group of observers gathered.

Ordinarily, only a few people were present at an autopsy: the pathologist, trained technicians, and sometimes residents in training. In active police investigations, detectives sometimes attended, as well as crime scene investigators in certain circumstances, and occasionally a doctor who had treated the deceased requested permission to attend.

But in addition to Stephen Harper, Gin recognized Bruce Stillman and Katie Kennedy, a young crime scene analyst, as well as two officers she didn't know. There were also two autopsy technicians, preparing the rolling cart containing the instruments that Stephen would need.

"Hi, Gin," Stephen said, raising his gloved hand in a friendly wave. "Good to see you."

"Didn't expect you to be here," Bruce said, rocking back on his heels, hands resting on his paunch. "Thought you only came out for the crispy critters and fossils."

"But I do have a few other skills, Bruce," Gin said, attempting to keep her tone light even though his tactless comments grated.

She turned to the others and smiled pleasantly. "Hi, Lance. Hi, Violet, nice to see you guys," she greeted the autopsy technicians, who'd assisted on several of the cases in which she'd been involved. Then she turned to the unfamiliar officers. "I'm Virginia Sullivan. Please call me Gin."

"Reggie Clawitter, Narcotics," the tall officer said. "I'd shake your hand, but these damn gloves—"

"It's no problem," Gin assured him.

"And I'm Serena Chiu," his partner added. "I've heard good things about your work."

"So that's everyone, right?" Stephen said, looking around.

"Yeah, Liam's probably out back upchucking into the bushes," Bruce said. "No need to wait on his sorry ass."

There were a few grins, but nobody said anything. It was common knowledge in the department that autopsies were not Liam Witt's cup of tea. The young officer had famously thrown up during his first autopsy, and hadn't returned unless absolutely necessary.

But Gin couldn't help noticing that Katie was blushing at the mention of Liam's name. She'd heard rumors that they were involved romantically. Gin liked them both; the young crime scene tech had impressed her as meticulous and sharp, and Liam had taken pains to offset some of Bruce's more offensive comments with kindness during the investigations that had swirled around Jake. She hid a smile, grateful for the pleasant possibility in the midst of an otherwise depressing event.

Stephen started his digital recorder and began by naming all of those present and making note of the time and date. The autopsy technicians assisted in weighing the body, and Stephen made a methodical visual examination, noting all relevant physical evidence including scars and the partially healed gash in addition to the many injection sites along her arms, hands, and behind her knees. They ranged from nearly-healed red dots to more recent, irritated tissue to several swollen, pus-filled abscesses.

In addition to the tattoo on her shoulder, Marnie Bertram had a butterfly on her hip, and a design of a beaded anklet with a cross, none of them particularly artful. Somehow this seemed like the saddest detail.

Stephen picked up a scalpel and glanced at the narcotics officers. "Reggie, Serena, sorry to ask, but I haven't had the pleasure of your company in here before—you going to be okay?"

"No problem," Reggie said, a slight tremor in his voice indicating otherwise.

"I've been to half a dozen of these," Serena said breezily. "I used to work homicide in Butler County."

Stephen nodded and made the Y-shaped incision. Moving the flaps of skin aside, he used a rib cutter—a tool that looked much like a pair of pruning shears—to sever the ribs from the breastbone cartilage. Gin watched sympathetically as Reggie swallowed hard and focused on a point near the ceiling.

Next, the intestines were removed and placed on a scale. "Excuse me," Reggie said. "I—I just need a minute. Be right back."

"Wanna bet?" Bruce called after him. "Twenty bucks says you lose your lunch."

"Nice," Serena said sarcastically as the door closed behind him. "It's his first time, Bruce, cut him a break."

"If you don't mind, Bruce," Stephen said testily, "Lance and Violet's time is valuable. Shall we move on?"

With their help, he removed the organs in one group, a technique known as the Rokitansky method. Gin knew that Stephen preferred it, as it allowed one of the technicians to begin closing the body while the other assisted in examining and taking samples from the individual organs.

The inspection and sampling moved quickly, since there were no notable anomalies in Marnie Bertram's organs other than those expected with chronic heroin use, including mild edema of the lungs and inflammation of heart tissue. As Violet placed the samples in storage containers and Lance prepared the body cavity to be closed, Serena went in search of her partner, and Bruce and the others began to file out.

"See you on the other side," Bruce said, giving Stephen a mock salute.

"What does that even mean?" Stephen asked, sotto voce.

Gin managed a wry grin. "Well, it's probably safest to assume he meant it in a professional sense."

She exchanged a few words with Katie, and then it was just her and Stephen and the two technicians.

"Glad you could be here," Stephen said. "And I'm sorry about the circumstances. I hope you'll pass along my condolences to Jake."

"I will, and thank you."

"Listen, Gin, I'll see what I can do to get the preliminary tox done today. Not much I can do about the rest of it."

"Of course," Gin said. The basic immunoassay would show what drugs had been in Marnie's system, but details about the concentrations of each, in addition to the effects of their interactions, would require further testing at a remote lab. "I appreciate it, but I suppose we both know what it's likely to reveal."

Stephen nodded somberly. "These opiate deaths are the biggest crisis I've seen in twenty years on the job."

"So many lives needlessly lost," Gin said, shaking her head sadly. "When will our country finally understand that addiction is a disease epidemic and treat it accordingly?"

But there was no answer to the question. She said goodbye to her colleague and left him to the task of preparing one more victim of the epidemic to be laid to rest.

* * *

On the days Jake stayed in Trafford, he usually called Gin from his motel room after dinner. Occasionally he took guys from his crew out for a beer, and sent a text rather than calling if they got in late.

But Jake hadn't been in touch at all last night, and on Wednesday he'd only texted to say he was crashing early. Gin had tried not to read too much into his lack of communication. Jake was the sort of man who turned inward under pressure, and Gin guessed that the death of his mother was weighing on him more than he was aware.

She considered waiting until he arrived home to give him a summary of what she'd learned at the autopsy, but decided that it would be better not to keep him waiting. After leaving the county offices, she walked the short distance to the shops and markets lining the Strip District. She passed bins filled with fresh produce and meat, shop windows displaying cookware and handmade goods, as well as a dizzying variety of pasta and olive oil and other dry goods. Browsing the strip had always been a pleasant diversion for Gin, but today she barely noticed the colorful sights, picking up a sandwich for which she had little appetite. Before eating, she found a shaded bench in front of an old converted warehouse, and called Jake.

He picked up on the third ring, sounding out of breath. "Hello?"

"Jake, it's me. I'm just coming from . . . Marnie's autopsy." She stopped herself from saying "your mother," suspecting it would be best to be as clinical as possible. "I wanted to let you know what they found. I'll just say up front that there weren't really any surprises; everything we saw was consistent with opioid overdose."

Jake was silent for so long that Gin wondered if he was still on the line. "Jake?"

"I'm here. I just don't have anything to say. You're telling me that my . . . that Marnie got into the kind of trouble that people who make terrible life choices end up with."

Gin bit back the response she usually saved for people who used the "addicts get what addicts deserve" line on her. The belief she shared with Stephen and the rest of her colleagues was that addiction is a disease, just like any other disease of the body or mind, and its victims deserve compassion and treatment.

But it was more complicated than that, of course. Gin had known plenty of people who rose above the curse of addiction to lead good, productive lives. But for every one of those, there were others who turned to crime and self-defeating behaviors to satisfy their addictions. She was not naïve enough to deny the terrible strain on hospitals, prisons, and communities posed by addicts and those who supplied them.

"She would not have suffered," she said instead, changing the subject. "She likely lost consciousness slowly and painlessly."

"So when are they releasing the body?" Jake asked.

"As soon as tomorrow—you just have to let them know where to release her to. Have you, um, thought about who you want to use? Because I could make a few calls, if you like."

"I'll probably just use Crogan's," Jake said, naming the largest funeral home in Trumbull. "They'll hold her for a while until I figure out what to do—I called."

Gin was surprised; Jake had given no indication

that he'd done any research at all. Maybe he cared more than he was letting on. "I can get you some information about the various options . . . if you'd like to consider cremation or—"

"No need. I'll handle it."

"I—I was only trying to help," Gin stammered, stung by his harsh tone.

"It's okay," Jake said. "I'm sorry I snapped at you. Look, I *will* take care of it. But now's not the time, okay? If it can wait, it needs to, because we've got a big problem with some code issues—we're going to have to regrade thirty percent of the site. We're looking at one day of overtime this weekend, possibly two, because we need to have the work done by early next week when they come back to reinspect or we'll be slapped with a huge fine. In fact . . . I wanted to talk to you about that."

"About what?"

"I know I promised to help get ready for the party, but I don't feel right asking the guys to show up tomorrow unless I at least make an appearance. Look, I'm really sorry to do this, but I need to stay tonight and try to make sure everything's set for tomorrow. We can't afford to get this wrong."

"I understand," Gin reassured him. "It's all right—I've already picked up almost everything I need, and I can start cooking tonight. I'll even buy the wine."

"Oh, no," Jake said in mock horror. He had a fine palette, while Gin was a self-proclaimed beginner when it came to choosing wines. "Maybe you'd better leave that to me."

"Jake!" Gin scolded. It felt good to laugh. "I promise I'll have the guy at the shop help me."

"Make sure you do," Jake said. "In fact, ask him for a couple of bottles of that Borolo I got that time I made pheasant. He'll remember."

"Okay. Get back out there and do what you need to do."

She was about to add *I miss you*—but he'd already hung up.

5

"You call this a pepper?" Rosa Barnes said, holding up the vegetable in question and squinting at it comically. "My mother would have a fit!"

Gin laughed. It was a little after five o'clock on Saturday evening, and the rest of the guests would arrive in an hour. When Jake called around lunchtime to say that he was tied up at the site longer than he'd expected, she decided to call her friend to keep her company while she put the finishing touches on the meal.

Gin was pleased with how her first attempt at entertaining in their home was going. After giving the house a thorough cleaning last night, she'd arranged the stems she'd purchased from the flower market in a pair of hammered copper vases and set the table with Jake's simple stoneware, accenting it with new hand-dyed placemats and napkins that she'd found in a little shop on Penn Avenue.

After a morning spent prepping and assembling the

meal, all that was left was to put the eggplant parmesan in the oven and dress the salad.

"That's actually a friggitello," she said. "It was hard to find—serves me right for choosing a recipe that's way out of my league. The woman from the market knew exactly what I was asking for, at least—even if I pronounced it wrong. She says it will give a bit of heat to the dish."

Rosa laughed at Gin's attempt at an Italian accent. "Do you want to go change? I can make sure nothing burns."

"I'd better, or you'll get all the attention," Gin joked, gesturing at Rosa's soft, fitted pink sweater and flowing skirt, which set off her generous curves and dark curls. "Seriously, you look beautiful tonight. Are things going well with Doyle?"

Rosa's blush gave her away. "*Really* well," she said shyly. "I'm almost afraid to jinx it . . . but Gin, we've been dating for six months now, and we've never even had so much as an argument. He's just so sweet, you know? Always leaving me little notes, flowers almost every weekend. And he's so good with my mom and Antonio!"

"I'm really happy for you," Gin murmured.

"I mean, after my divorce, I never thought I'd find love again. I guess I gave up on there being any guys out there who would treat me so well. Who'd be so open about wanting to share what's important, you know?"

"I—I do," Gin said, turning away so that Rosa wouldn't see her tear up. "Be right back."

Upstairs, she splashed water on her face and dressed on autopilot, tossing her sweats in the hamper and putting on the outfit she'd laid out earlier in the day. Rosa's words echoed in her mind: sweet . . . positive . . . put a woman first. As happy as Gin was for her friend, her effusive praise for Doyle were not words that could be applied to Jake.

He *had* been sweet, once. Positive . . . well, that was another matter; Jake had always been moody, but it hadn't seemed important back when they were each other's rock. But if Gin was honest with herself, since reuniting they hadn't reached the same level of emotional intimacy that they'd had when they were teens. After Jake had finally gotten free of the murder investigation on his job site last fall, they both had tried to put more effort into the relationship; but as his business picked up again, Jake had become distant once more.

Doyle was a wonderful man, though he wouldn't be right for Gin. Was there something wrong with her, choosing a man with such a complex background, whose dark moods tended to take him away from her for days at a time? But there was so much she loved about Jake. He was a true artist, with the vision to create beautiful things on any scale, from the hand-carved wooden bowl he'd made her for Christmas to the breathtaking homes he'd built. Jake was passionate about his work, and—despite the trouble he'd been in earlier in his life—honest and ethical. And he was determined to care for her.

Enough, she scolded herself. Now was not the time to brood. Jake would be home any second, and the house would soon be filled with good friends.

She touched up her makeup and ran a comb through

her hair. As she came back downstairs she forced herself to smile, and in the kitchen, she did a little twirl for Rosa.

"Ooh la la! Jake's going to love those pants—your derriere looks great in them!"

"I certainly hope so," Gin said, keeping her voice light. "Anything to convince him to spend more time at home!"

* * *

Brandon and Diane arrived moments later, followed by Doyle, who brought a potted chrysanthemum for Gin and a single red rose for Rosa. Before long, everyone had a glass of wine in hand and conversation was flowing.

Gin glanced at the clock often as she served the appetizers.

"Any word?" Rosa asked quietly, helping slice and plate the asparagus and mushroom tart Gin had selected at the bakery this morning.

"I tried his cell again—he's not picking up."

"He's probably on the road," Rosa said. "I'm sure he'll be here soon."

"I just hope nothing else went wrong on the site," Gin fretted.

"Oh, honey. They know what they're doing. And you know that Jake would never cut corners or endanger any of his workers."

Gin nodded. "I've held off as long as I could—if I don't serve the eggplant soon, it's going to taste like shoe leather."

Brandon had come into the kitchen during this

exchange. "Couldn't help overhearing, Gin," he said. "Listen, don't be too tough on Jake. He's under a lot of pressure to stay on schedule. But when it's finished, the retreat's going to give him a lot of visibility."

Brandon and Jake had gone out for beers a few times, and Brandon had invited Jake to join his entrepreneurs' networking group. Gin had encouraged Jake to take Brandon up on the invitation. *I've never been a suit and tie guy*, he'd said.

"I'm sure it's fine," Gin said, handing Brandon dishes to carry to the table. "He wouldn't be this late if he didn't have a good reason."

Determined not to let her anxiety ruin the party, she enjoyed a slice of tart with her guests. Conversation and laughter filled the room as she served the rest of the meal. When everything was on the table, Gin raised a glass and looked around at her friends over the flickering candlelight.

"To good friends," she said huskily. "I know Jake will agree once he gets here . . . there is no one we'd rather have at our table."

Everyone clinked their glasses and dug in. The eggplant had turned out beautifully, and people helped themselves to slices of fresh, crusty levain to sop up every bit of the savory sauce. Talk turned to one of Gin's recent cases that had been in the news.

"How on earth did you figure it out?" Diane asked. "All they said on the news was that evidence from the autopsy led them to the wife."

"The family is quite wealthy," Gin said. "They probably put considerable pressure on the media not to release those details. They were, um, a bit unsavory."

"Oh, do tell!" Doyle said, spearing a large bite with his fork.

Gin explained how the death of the prominent pastor had at first been attributed to his fall onto a spiked ornamental fence on the grounds of the couple's stately home, which led to the puncture of several vital organs. During autopsy, however, it was found that there was insufficient internal bleeding to support that theory, meaning that he had been dead *before* the fall. Additionally, there was unexplained blunt force trauma to the skull. Eventually, the wife admitted to having fatally struck him with a crystal decanter, then dragging him outside and pushing his body onto the sharp spikes.

"That's downright amazing," Brandon said. "I have to say, Gin, your job is a lot more interesting than most people's."

Gin smiled. "Well thank you, but honestly, it's not nearly as exciting as you might think. When I was a full-time forensic pathologist, I spent far more time on paperwork than I did in the autopsy room. And I probably spent just as much time in the courtroom, testifying, which is also less exciting than you might think." She shrugged. "Then there's dealing with the families, which can take time too. What can I say? Take what you see on TV and add hours and hours of waiting around in the courthouse and filling out forms and trying to contact family members, then throw in some bad coffee and endless county bureaucracy, and you've got a pretty good picture of what the job actually entails."

"Don't take this the wrong way," Rosa said, "because you know I have so much admiration for you—but why would anyone do your job? I mean, why not open up a nice little family practice and deal with living, breathing patients and, I don't know, buy a sports car or vacation in Aruba?"

Gin took her time choosing her words, trying to craft the response that Rosa's question deserved. "I actually feel . . . *honored* to perform my duty to the dead," she said. "In my profession, you come to view death as being as natural as birth. You lose your fear of it, while at the same time recognizing that the deceased person's friends and family are experiencing a terrible loss. It's true that I often feel inadequate in the face of grief, but I know that I can make a real difference if I can give them the answers they need to understand what happened."

"But it's got to be depressing," Brandon said. "I mean, especially when it's people who've been in accidents, or the victim of crimes—one minute they're leading their lives, and then next they're lying on your table. Doesn't that get you down?"

"Honestly . . . I think that being forced to face my own mortality every day has been a benefit. I definitely experience gratitude for my life after seeing some of the misfortune that befalls others. And besides, there's a lot of satisfaction in solving the puzzle of what exactly happened to someone. It goes beyond our work with the courts and the police, especially because once we hand over our findings, we're often out of the picture. It's almost like—"

Gin hesitated, wondering if what she was about to say would sound too strange. "It's like I'm in conversation with the dead, and I'm honoring them by keeping them company on this final part of their journey, before their bodies are buried or cremated. I guess our job is to be a sort of . . . steward, between life and death."

"Please tell me to mind my own business if you'd rather not answer," Diane said, "but has your job changed your views of what happens after death?"

"If you're asking me if I'm religious—I suppose I am, in my own way. Or spiritual, at any rate. I grew up going to church every week with my parents, and I still go with them now and then. But what happens when the soul leaves the body is as much a mystery to me now as it was on my first day of medical school. I suppose I don't consider it part of our realm of study."

"That doesn't stop some of these guys you see on TV," Doyle quipped. "Call that eight-hundred number and for a small donation they'll make a direct call to God on your behalf."

The laughter around the table was interrupted when the front door suddenly flew open with such force that it banged against the wall. Two people stumbled in; in front was a young man with short dark hair, dressed in jeans and a gray hoodie too large for his slight frame. His clothes were dirty and he had a large red welt on his jaw, and one of his eyes was swollen almost shut. His arms were clasped behind his back—or no, Gin realized as he staggered into the living room, they were tied with a large black plastic zip tie.

And the man holding onto his collar, shoving him along, was Jake.

Jake was dressed for work in ripped and faded jeans, an old plaid shirt, and well-worn boots. His expression was hard and unreadable as he gave the young man's collar a savage jerk, stopping him short.

"On the floor," he snarled. "Face down. Don't move. Gin, call Baxter."

"What is going on?" Gin demanded, as the man sank wordlessly to his knees. "Who is this?"

"This," Jake said, prodding the man with his boot so that he fell forward on his face, "is my mother's killer."

6

Everyone was talking at once. The stranger lay face down on the floor, saying nothing, and Jake stood inches from the man's head with his arms crossed over his chest. Doyle stood protectively in front of Rosa, and Brandon was offering to help Jake, as if the task of subduing the underweight young man required two large, muscular men.

"What can I do?" Diane asked briskly. "Do you want me to call nine-one-one?"

"Let me handle that," Gin said quickly. She already had her phone out and was dialing Tuck's personal number. Since there didn't seem to be any immediate danger, maybe there was a chance to get ahead of the potentially disastrous consequences of Jake's actions. There would be time to ask him what he'd been thinking later. For now, she worried that Jake could be guilty of assault, since the young man on the floor was the only one who seemed to have sustained any injuries.

"Gin?" Tuck answered on the second ring. "Everything okay?"

"I—why do you ask?" Gin said, stalling while she tried to figure out how to describe the scene in her living room.

"You don't make a habit of calling me on the weekend. It's Saturday night, in case you haven't noticed."

"Oh!" Despite the circumstances, Gin felt herself blush. Had she interrupted Tuck on a date? "I'm sorry, but there's a . . . a situation here that I need, that, well, I'm not sure what to do."

"Yeah?"

"Jake, uh, brought a man home who he says sold his mother the drugs she overdosed on."

"*What*? How the hell did that happen?"

"I'm not really sure. He—they—just got here. And Tuck—" Gin drew a breath; there wasn't any other way to say it. "Jake's got him tied up. He's not exactly here of his own free will."

"Shit. What was he thinking? Okay, look, I'm on my way. I'm going to send an on-duty officer too; he might get there first. Are there weapons?"

"No, I don't think so—"

"Injuries?"

"He, uh, bruising and minor contusions. I think there was a, um, scuffle."

Tuck cursed. "You don't need me to tell you this, but

do *nothing* until we get there. Keep them apart. Who's there with you?"

"Just some friends. They were over here for dinner—"

"Jake brought this guy home for *dinner*?"

"No, he just—he was supposed to be here hours ago. I don't know what happened."

This time her words were met with silence. When Tuck spoke again his voice was clipped. "Leaving now. Remember—do nothing."

After Gin reassured the others that there was nothing they could do to help and that the authorities would soon be arriving, the dinner guests departed. Gin knew there was a good chance the police would want statements from them, but that would have to wait. Once the door closed behind them, Gin turned to Jake.

"Please tell me he didn't get those injuries from you."

"You've got to be kidding, Gin," Jake retorted. "This guy pushes poison. He's human garbage."

The man on the floor had started quietly sobbing. He had to be in pain, but he didn't fight.

"How do you even know he's the one?"

A knock at the door cut her questions short. She opened the door to find Tuck in a pair of basketball shorts and a T-shirt, flip flops on his feet. Something sparkled on his forehead—a tiny fleck of silver. There were more sparkles in his eyelashes, totally at odds with his glowering countenance. His "date," Gin realized, had probably involved a craft project with his daughter.

Beside him was a young officer who looked vaguely familiar to Gin. She read his nametag: Max Khatri.

"Please come in," she said. "Our guests have gone home, so it's just me and Jake. And, uh . . ."

"Back away from him, Crosby," Tuck said, flashing his badge, making sure the young man on the floor got a good look.

Jake did as he was asked, though he didn't bother to conceal his disgust. "This is the guy," he said. "I've got video."

"I'm going to untie you," Tuck said, ignoring Jake. "Get up slowly, keeping your hands where I can see them. Then turn and put your hands on the wall with your feet shoulder-width apart."

The young man complied, wincing slightly as Tuck sliced through the zip tie with his knife. He got to his knees first, rubbing the angry red marks on his wrists, then stumbled to his feet. Slowly, he turned around and shuffled to the wall, falling once more when he tripped over his own feet. Finally he managed to stand with his hands in place as Tuck had ordered.

"Go ahead, Max."

Officer Khatri conducted a quick, efficient search, coming up with nothing other than the phone and wallet that had been in the pocket of the young man's jeans.

"He's good, sir," Khatri said.

"Okay. What's your name?"

"Jonah. Jonah Krischer." His voice was reedy with fear.

Tuck turned to Jake. "Okay, Crosby, why don't you tell

us why you interrupted Jonah's evening. Don't leave anything out."

"I saw him selling drugs," Jake said angrily. "I've got it on video. On my phone."

"Where was this?"

"Convenience store over by the power plant in Denton," Jake said, with slightly less certainty. "Out back, by the dumpsters. There's a homeless camp or something in the abandoned house next door."

"I know the area," Tuck said. "That's not a homeless camp, it's a trap house. If he really was dealing, he picked a good spot."

"I took this off him," Jake said, digging in his pocket. He took out a large ziplock bag containing a dozen bottles of pills.

"Jesus, Crosby, even if what you're suggesting is true, you've completely contaminated it. It's going to be fingerprint soup on there."

Jake rolled his eyes. "What was I supposed to do, let him keep it?"

Tuck gestured at Khatri, who took the package from Jake.

"Bag that for forensics. Mr. Krischer, how about you tell me what happened this evening."

"You're going to listen to *him*?" Jake demanded incredulously.

"We'll get back to you in a minute," Tuck snapped.

"I, uh, came to see a customer of mine," Krischer said. "He'd called to ask if I had any hydrocodone. Which, I mean, I swear to you I started with Adderall. For real." He looked like he was about to cry. "I never meant to do more than that, honest. It just . . . it was a mistake, okay, a huge mistake and I'm sorry, but I don't—I didn't mean—"

"Just stick to the facts. You can save your editorializing for someone who'll care," Tuck said. "We've got enough to invite you down to the station for a visit. You too, Jake, since you're so eager to give me an earful."

Ignoring Jake's silent fury, Tuck turned to the young officer. "Khatri, why don't you give Mr. Krischer here a ride down to the station. And put the bracelets on him, just for fun." He scowled in Jake's direction. "Crosby, you can ride with me."

* * *

Once the two police vehicles had pulled away, Gin was alone in the house. The remains of the dinner party looked forlorn; her guests had left so abruptly that it was as if they'd simply vanished, leaving the meal half-eaten. There was wine in the glasses, and the candles still flickered in their copper holders. The cobbler Gin had picked up from the bakery sat untouched on the counter alongside the cups she'd set out for after-dinner coffee.

After snuffing out the candles, Gin checked her phone and found a text from Rosa.

CALL ME!!!!

She picked up on the first ring.

"Oh my God, honey, how are you doing? Are the police still there? Is Jake all right?"

"I'm . . . kind of numb," Gin admitted. "Earlier today, Jake told me he'd been detained on the job site. I never would have dreamed that he would have gone looking for his mother's dealer like that."

"Catch me up—all you told me was that she'd been found dead in a likely overdose."

Gin had been sparing with the details. Even though Rosa was a good friend, she knew that Jake was private about his life, particularly the more painful aspects of his past. Most people assumed that he'd lost both his parents; though there were still people in Trumbull who remembered that former Sheriff Crosby's young wife had abandoned both him and their baby years ago, Gin hadn't heard her mentioned in years.

"It's—it was a shock, obviously." Gin explained that Jake hadn't confided in her that his mother had been in contact with his father. "I assumed that she'd simply disappeared, that no one had ever looked for her. I suppose that was naïve of me—every child in Jake's shoes surely wonders about their birth parent."

"It must have been awful for him to know that she'd chosen to leave. He probably felt completely abandoned. At least Antonio has his *abuela* and his cousins and aunt and uncle."

Antonio was Rosa's seven-year-old son from her first marriage to a man who'd left them both. Gin knew how hard Rosa worked to make sure her son knew he was loved.

Jake's father had tried just as hard in his own way. But his job as police chief kept him away from home a lot, and there were no other relatives nearby to fill in the gaps. By the time Gin and Jake started dating in high school, the scars left by his mother's departure had scabbed over, if they'd ever even properly healed.

"I tried to talk to him about it," Gin fretted. "I suggested counseling—"

"A man like Jake would have a hard time accepting help, I bet," Rosa said. "He is a wonderful man, but I see the way he keeps his feelings stuffed inside."

"I'm afraid you're right," Gin agreed. "But going after her dealer seems reckless even for Jake."

"What is it?" Rosa said. "I can hear it in your voice— did something happen?"

"It's just that . . . I was thinking about something that happened when he identified her body. My colleague showed him a tattoo on her shoulder. The design contained his name, Jake. It . . . I could tell that he was shaken. I guess it tested his assumption that she'd never cared for him."

"Oh, that's even worse, somehow. To know that she'd had feelings, that there could have been a relationship, if things had been different . . ."

"Yes, that's what I thought. But he barely said a word when he saw it. I guess I read the whole situation wrong."

"But he didn't offer you any clues, either," Rosa pointed out. "From what you've told me, he acted like he didn't care at all."

"He didn't even want to make any arrangements for her body yet."

"Listen, do you think he could really be facing serious trouble over what he did today?"

"I'm not sure," Gin said. "Obviously, the worst thing would be if Jonah Krischer was innocent, not only of selling the drugs that Marnie Bertram overdosed on, but of any involvement with illegal substances. If that were true, then Jake may be guilty of assaulting an innocent man."

"But what about that packet of drugs Jake took off him?"

"I agree it looked pretty damning. But we don't know for sure what was in that bag, or what Jonah was doing there. After all, Jake was there too. It isn't a crime to be in the same place where drugs are sold. And until the video is reviewed, we won't know what Jake caught on camera, either."

"*Dios mío*," Rosa said softly. "What a mess! Why couldn't he just have called the police and let them take care of it?"

"You have to remember Jake's past," Gin said. "Asking him to trust the same police department that tried to implicate him twice for murders he didn't commit—well, I'm not surprised he took matters into his own hands."

"Then for his sake I hope that video is crystal clear. I mean, I understand that Marnie Bertram took those drugs of her own free will. But anyone who knowingly sells such an evil thing—they deserve to be locked up."

Gin's visceral response was to agree—not just because the world would be better off without dealers, but because Jake's reckless act would be much more defensible if Jonah was proved to be guilty. But then she thought of the young man cowering on the floor, writhing with pain as his arms were pulled in an unnatural angle. Stumbling as he tried to stand. He'd looked so young, and he was no match for Jake, who was over six feet and two hundred and twenty pounds of work-hardened muscle.

"I think we need to let the investigation take its course before we judge," Gin said, admonishing herself for letting her emotions cloud her thoughts.

"Of course, you're right. But Gin, call back any time. I'll keep my phone turned on. And Gin, if you don't want to be alone, come on over to the house. No matter what time it is."

"Thank you, Rosa," Gin said. Her friend's offer was tempting, but Rosa lived in a small house with Antonio and her elderly mother, who suffered from dementia. Gin wouldn't feel right disrupting their little household. "But I'll be fine. I'll keep you posted, all right?"

After she hung up, Gin started the coffee and began cleaning up the dinner. There was no way she would be able to sleep until she knew what was happening with Jake. She took her time, scouring every surface to a shine, covering the leftovers and stowing them in the refrigerator.

She was nearly finished when Jake came through the front door, looking exhausted. Before Gin could greet him, he said, "The video gave them enough to detain that little son of a bitch, but he's threatening to lawyer up. At least they got tired of asking me the same questions over and over and let me get out of there."

"I made coffee, or I could pour you a glass of wine—"

"I'm fine," Jake said, sinking into a chair at the scrubbed dining table. "Look, I'm sorry I ruined the party. And I'm sorry I didn't tell you what I was doing, but I knew you'd try to talk me out of it."

"Well, you're right about that." Gin knew she shouldn't push, but she couldn't help the wave of frustration and fear that threatened to overtake her. "Now you've opened yourself up to accusations of attacking that man without provocation."

"Whose side are you on?" Jake demanded. "One of the duty cops, the one who took the bag for evidence, said that it was mostly narcotic prescription medications in that bag. The bad stuff, Gin—the stuff that's killing people."

"He can't know that," Gin said in exasperation. "They have to test it. Without analysis, there's no way to know what's in those bottles." In Cook County, Gin had testified at half a dozen cases involving knockoff medications imported from China and Russia; while they were manufactured to resemble the real medications, the dosages and even component contents were often wildly different. "It was irresponsible of him to venture an opinion."

"Yeah? Well, your friend Baxter sure didn't hold back on the opinions," Jake said. "He let me know in no uncertain terms that he doesn't want me near the case."

"Jake, I can't believe you! You're lucky that he didn't arrest you. He was probably doing you a favor when he let you go."

"God*damn* it, Gin," Jake roared, pushing back his chair and getting up. He paced the kitchen like a caged tiger, his face twisted in anger. "That's twice. If you're so convinced I fucked up, why don't you just come out and say so."

Gin knew that Jake had a temper, but he'd never before lashed out at her that way. Pushing aside her hurt, she reminded herself that Jake was dealing with the loss of his mother, which was stirring up a hornet's nest of pain and buried emotion.

"I never said you were wrong to want to identify the person who gave your mother the drugs," Gin said carefully. "I understand your anger, I think. I would do anything to protect you if I could. I love you, Jake, and when I see you hurting, I hurt for you. And for that reason, I don't want you to do anything that's going to make it worse. You should be dealing with your grief right now, not risking your own safety and freedom."

"*Grief*?" Jake bellowed, clenching his fists. "Does this look like grief to you?"

For a moment neither of them said anything, as his angry words echoed around the kitchen.

"Actually . . ." Gin said softly, "to tell you the truth, I think it does. Let me help you find someone trained to help people who—"

"I don't need a shrink," Jake said. "I don't need this bullshit at all."

He went up the stairs, his footfalls echoing on the

hardwood floors overhead. Gin stood rooted to the floor, listening to him move around their bedroom, wondering if she should try to go to him and suspecting it would only make things worse.

In moments, he was back downstairs with a duffle bag over his shoulder. "Look, I think you and I need to take a break," he said, in a voice that was quieter but no less agitated. "I obviously have some things to work out. Things that don't have anything to do with you. I'm sorry, Gin, but there's no way you can understand any of this. You grew up in the lap of luxury. You had two parents who never let you want for anything. I can't—I can't be around you right now."

"Don't make this about us," Gin said, stung by his words. "You know I've experienced tragedy. I lost my *sister*. I've seen hundreds of people who've died by every conceivable means. Maybe I don't know what it's like to lose an absent parent, to never have the chance to know them—but I *want* to. I'm asking you to let me in, to let me help."

"You can't."

Jake turned away, hiding his face, and as angry and afraid as Gin was, she knew that underneath Jake's fury was a core of pain that he was terrified for her to see. Swallowing her frustration with him, she crossed the room and laid a hand on his arm.

He flung it off with such force that she nearly stumbled backward. When he turned to face her, Gin was shocked to see tears in his eyes.

"Just leave me alone," Jake said. "Give me a few days. I'll—I'll call you when this is done."

"Where are you going?"

He shrugged. "I don't know. I'll get a room."

"Don't do this," Gin pleaded.

But he was already gone.

7

Gin spent a restless night, tossing and turning in the bed she'd been sharing with Jake for the last eleven months. When the first rays of dawn seeped through the windows, she gave up and got dressed.

In the bathroom, she looked at her reflection in the mirror. She'd been too tired to take off her makeup the night before, and her mascara was smudged under her eyes, her coppery shadow faded to brassy streaks. She put her hair up in a ponytail and washed her face, then went back into the bedroom.

She stood at the foot of the bed, looking around the room. How could Jake believe that it was better for him to be alone at a time like this? His coldness was so at odds with the home he had made with his own hands. Gin ran her hand along the footboard, which he'd carved from trees felled on this land. Underneath her feet were the heart pine boards he'd selected for their grain. Out the window was the view that he'd designed the house around, setting it into the slope of the land so that it opened up onto the valley below.

She couldn't stay here without him.

A sob escaped her throat as it truly hit her: he didn't want her with him as he faced this loss. He had reverted to the person he'd been in high school, before they met: angry, unmanageable, reckless, rebellious. By the time Jake had been fourteen, he'd been suspended from school for every infraction he could think of. He'd fought other kids with the slightest provocation, and by the time he was sixteen, he'd barely avoided going to juvenile. His father had taken to bringing him into the station, as much to keep an eye on him as it was to try to set an example.

It was only when Jake Crosby set his sights on Gin Sullivan, daughter of the most respected and wealthiest family in town, that he'd cleaned up his act. Her parents were wary at first, but he'd worked as hard at convincing them he'd changed as he ever worked at anything. As for Gin, the attraction she felt was even more powerful because Jake had reformed, for *her*.

Until today, she'd believed that he'd changed forever.

But the man who'd stormed out of the house last night was more like the adolescent who took his pain out in every broken window, every shoplifted bottle of liquor, every fight he provoked, than the man she'd been living with.

Jake had become a stranger again.

And suddenly Gin couldn't stand to stay another moment in this house where she'd been so happy with him.

Better to leave and go somewhere where she could replace the hurt she was feeling with action, a plan to do whatever she could to help Jake avoid more trouble.

She wasn't even aware of the tears streaming down her face until she'd gotten her suitcase from the closet and had begun filling it. She took enough clothes for a week, and her computer and files. She hesitated before taking the framed photo of the two of them that held pride of place on the dresser, but in the end she slipped it into the suitcase along with the carved wooden bowl he'd made for her for Christmas.

In the kitchen she took a moment to look around. Twenty-four hours ago, she'd been arranging flowers and setting the table, looking forward to Jake returning home, to sharing a meal with their friends.

It had been a dream. A dream that was now shattered.

* * *

On the short drive downtown, Gin barely registered the balmy breeze coming through the windows of her old Range Rover or the sun dappling the trees lining Hornbake Avenue, which had burst into bloom seemingly overnight. She found a parking space in front of the municipal building and hurried to her mother's office, hoping not to run into anyone she knew.

Madeleine's door was open, and she was just finishing a call.

"Hi, sweetheart," she said, hanging up.

"Listen, Mom, I was wondering . . . I was hoping I could come home for a bit."

"Home?" Madeleine repeated. "You mean, with me and your father?"

"Well, since you've lived in the same house my entire life, I guess that's the one," Gin said, making a weak attempt at a smile. "It's just temporary. I hope."

"Oh, honey, did you and Jake have a fight?" Madeleine asked, scooting her chair around the desk so that her knees touched Gin's, and reaching for her hands. "I know he's distressed about his mother, but—"

"Jake did something he shouldn't have," Gin said. She gave her mother a summary of what had happened yesterday, leaving out the worst of the scuffle and making it sound like Jake had offered to go to the station to give his version of events, rather than being compelled to.

"What was he *thinking*!" Madeleine exclaimed nevertheless. "That part of town is dangerous. He's lucky he escaped without being mugged, or worse."

"He's just . . . I think his mother's death is affecting him more than he realizes."

"I've got some excellent resources," Madeleine said briskly. "There's a therapist in town who specializes in trauma. It would probably be wise for Jake to take some time to examine his past, before he even attempts to make sense of what has happened in the last few days. Let me give you some numbers."

"Mom, believe me, I'd like nothing more," Gin sighed.

"But unfortunately, Jake's not willing to entertain the idea of counseling right now."

"Did he ask you to move out?" Madeleine asked. "Or was it your idea?"

"Actually, he left. I don't know where he went last night. I figured . . . given everything he's dealing with, he should be at home, where at least he's in a familiar setting."

"Perhaps you're right," Madeleine mused. "Though I must say, that's very generous of you, given everything he's done in the last twenty-four hours."

"Mom—I love him," Gin said simply.

Madeleine nodded. "Well, I guess that's all I need to know. Of course you can come home, honey. Dad will be thrilled. Maybe in a day or two, Jake will have come to his senses."

"Maybe," Gin said.

But somehow she suspected that it would take longer than a couple of days to heal the hurt inside him.

* * *

Gin was unpacking her clothes and putting them into the painted dresser that had been hers as a child when her phone rang. She grabbed for it, her heart pounding, but it wasn't Jake.

It was Tuck Baxter.

Gin stared at the screen, torn between conflicting emotions. Tuck had the power to make life easier for Jake—or more difficult. So far, he'd apparently chosen the former. But why would he be calling Gin now? Was he bending the rules—and his own personal code—to give her information about Marnie Bertram's death? Or had Jake done something else in his mistaken quest to avenge his mother's overdose, and ended up on the wrong side of the law again?

"Hello," she answered briskly.

"Gin. Hey. It's Tuck."

"Yes, I do have caller ID. How are you?" Gin heard the note of formality in her voice and felt ridiculous. After all, she and Tuck were professional colleagues. Yes, there'd been an attraction back in the summer when they first met, but they'd confronted and discussed it, and put it behind them.

"Been better. I have to tell you, Gin, I stuck my neck out for Jake last night. Not that he cares, or hell, maybe he doesn't even realize how much trouble he could have been in, especially when Krischer's father showed up and started threatening lawsuits."

"Oh, no."

"Yeah. He's a real piece of work. Turns out Jonah only turned eighteen two months ago. He's still in high school, getting ready to graduate. The dad actually tried to tell us Jonah was still a minor."

"I thought he looked young, but—"

"Yeah, well, fooled me too. I didn't pick him for a local, honestly. Most of these guys, they're coming in from the city, expanding their existing territory. But a kid? Anyway, to tell you the truth, I was on the fence about what to do about Jake until Dr. Krischer showed up. But that pretty much tipped the scale—I'm not about to do one damn thing for that S.O.B. if I can help it."

"We're talking about the suspected dealer's father, right? He's a physician?"

"Yes. That's one of the reasons I'm calling, actually. Apparently Krischer sees patients a couple days a month over at the surgery center. He's some sort of specialist. Anyway, I thought your dad might know him. I think he's mostly blowing hot air, but if he's really going to bring a suit against the department, I'd like to get in front of it. I just thought—obviously I can't give you any more information about the case than you already know, but if you could get a sense of this guy from your dad—well, I'd appreciate it."

"I'll be happy to see what I can do," Gin said. She wondered what Tuck would have to say about the way Jake had reacted when he'd returned home—and that she'd moved out as a result. "I'll be seeing him later today."

"Okay. Thanks, Gin. Look, I know Crosby thinks I've got him in the crosshairs, but the truth is that I'm not entirely unsympathetic to him. Not that I'm endorsing what he did, obviously, and I'm not putting up with any vigilante justice on my watch. But this overdose epidemic . . . well, I don't mind telling you that it scares the shit out of me every time it gets closer to Trumbull."

"I've seen what it does to a city firsthand," Gin said. "When I left Cook County, we were literally dealing with hundreds of heroin overdose deaths a year."

"So that brings me to the other thing I wanted to talk to you about. Two things, actually. One is—and this is a professional courtesy, meaning keep to yourself—the initial screen came back and Marnie Bertram had cocaine, alcohol, traces of MDMA, and oxycodone in her system."

"I see." Gin felt her shoulders sag. It wasn't surprising, of course, but it eliminated any doubt as to whether his mother had been using.

"The medication Jonah was selling included Vicodin, which is hydrocodone. At least, that's what the pills look like. We have to wait on confirmation from the lab."

"What else was Jonah carrying?"

"Adderall, mostly, which is an amphetamine. So maybe he was telling the truth about that. And Ativan, which is a benzodiazepine." He waited for his words to sink in.

"All prescription medications. Are you suggesting Jonah might have gotten it from his father?"

"I'm not suggesting anything at all, Gin. I'm just laying out what I'm working with. See, Jonah made us a very interesting offer. Waited until his dad was out of the room to do it, too."

"He made *you* an offer? Isn't it usually the other way around?"

"Yes, though I'm not sure we would have offered him much of a deal given that we've got him on video in the trap house literally listing everything he was selling, like he was reading from the menu from a Chinese restaurant. But it turns out that young Jonah's even more precocious than I would have guessed."

"I'm afraid I don't follow."

"Okay, I'll lay it out straight for you, but only because this might involve you. What I'm about to tell you is absolutely off the record. If you repeat it, I'll deny it."

"Tuck, I get it. Look, I'll do whatever I can, especially if it might help Jake."

"I understand that. But this isn't really about Jake." He drew an audible breath. "Jonah says he can lead us to a body."

"A . . . body? What does that mean?"

"He says he came across human remains just outside the city limits, but he hasn't given up the exact location yet. His father's lawyer is making noises about us giving him immunity on the drugs—but it's pretty clear the kid wants to talk. Thing is, Gin . . . I actually believe him."

"I still don't understand. How did he happen to stumble across these remains? And why didn't he come to you right away?"

"He's not saying. Not until we agree to the lawyer's terms, anyway. So look . . . I'm leaning toward doing it. We've got him on possession easy, we've got a good case for intent to deliver, and we can keep an eye on him easily enough. With a lawyer like the one he has, though, I wouldn't count on us holding him for long. Guy made a point of telling me he's going to Penn State this fall."

"But Tuck, if Jonah was really peddling powerful opiates—with everything that's been in the news—even a kid would have to understand the dangers."

"You think?" Tuck's mouth was set in a grim line. "I'm

not so sure. You may be overestimating the teenage brain. I'm not sure they're really all that good at connecting the dots, especially when it involves their own behavior. They tend to believe what they want to believe—even Cherie."

Tuck's daughter Cherie had been born with fetal alcohol syndrome and faced various cognitive and social challenges. She'd made tremendous progress since moving to Trumbull the prior November, and she'd enjoyed enrichment activities like the after-school basketball team Gin had coached, but she still required special attention in the classroom and at home.

"I do remember being a teen myself, Tuck," Gin said. "So I guess I'll grant you that. And the latest research on the adolescent brain indicates that it continues to develop until at least the age of twenty-five. Still, it seems like a stretch that he wouldn't have grasped the potentially disastrous consequences of his actions."

"I get that, but it's possible it got ahead of him, like he says. He says that he got started with Adderall. Even the honors kids use it—it's wildly popular with the college-bound crowd, so Jonah had the perfect audience at his private high school. Fifteen bucks a pill, apparently."

"So why didn't he just stick with that?"

"Not clear. Honestly? I think he only got into opiates because he was trying to get in with the popular crowd. I mean, you saw him—scrawny kid, doesn't have a lot going for him in the looks department. His parents probably push him hard academically. Maybe he saw an opening, or a kid he admired asked him to get something for him.

And look—obviously we're going to drill down all the way on this. I've got a team going around trying to trace every prescription that his dad wrote in the last six months. We'll know more soon."

"But what if he's lying? Are you willing to guarantee him immunity from more serious charges if it turns out that he made up this whole story?"

"In the first place, I personally can't guarantee him anything—that's up to the DA. All I can do is make a recommendation. And in the second place, if there's no body, there's no deal—I made sure the lawyer understood that. Frankly, he expected it, I'm sure."

"Well, I guess you don't have a lot to lose then."

"Exactly. So the thing is . . . Jonah didn't know how long the body had been there, only that it was—in his words—'messed up.' Given your expertise, I wondered if you'd mind coming with me. If this really pans out, I'd like to get your take before County gets there."

"You're saying that until you confirm there's a body, you don't have to let them know?"

"That's what I'm saying. There's some that would call this a gray area . . . hell, I'm sure a lot of people would say I'm out of line not passing this along right away. But, I guess you can figure I've got my reasons."

Gin was pretty sure she knew what he was referring to. At the time of Tuck's appointment to Trumbull police chief, rumors abounded that he'd been forced out as a senior detective on the county force. Speculation was that he'd been given the choice of banishment—which some viewed a small-town posting to be—or resignation. As for the cause, there were plenty of unsubstantiated theories—everything from a corruption charge to sexual harassment to a rumor that he'd gotten in a physical fight with the county superintendent.

"All right," Gin said, her mind racing to figure out if this would help or hurt Jake. In the end, though, it didn't really matter. Gin really was the county's best resource for decomp cases, and she wouldn't decline if her skills could help.

"Great. Pick you up in fifteen minutes."

"Wait, Tuck?" Gin considered asking if she could just meet Tuck at the station, but she didn't want to risk leaving her car there in case Jake happened to drive by. It would be easy enough to explain what she was doing with Chief Baxter—if he'd pause long enough to listen, which seemed unlikely right now.

Which left one option: the truth. "I'm staying at my folks' place. Can you pick me up there?"

"Everything okay with Richard and Madeleine?"

"Yes, everything's fine."

"Oh . . . okay. See you soon."

8

S he waited out front, perched on the iron bench under the portico, and experienced a strange moment of déjà vu: this was where she had waited countless times for Jake to pick her up for dates their senior year and the summer that followed.

They'd been so sure of themselves and their relationship back then. They were planning to attend college together—they'd both been accepted to Ohio State—and then they'd come back to Trumbull and begin their life together. Kids. House. Maybe a dog.

But that was the summer that Gin's sister Lily disappeared, her body not to be found for seventeen years. Shattered by the loss, isolated from her grieving parents, Gin had grown distant from Jake. They split up; she attended Ohio State in Columbus and he went to a satellite campus. Gin found herself drawn to studying medicine, and as time went on without her sister's case being solved, she accepted deep in her heart that Lily was probably dead.

She started medical school and the first time she'd entered the morgue, the hushed, reverent theater where they'd learned the secrets of the dead, she knew she was where she needed to be. Many years later when her sister's body was discovered, Gin was able to assist in the case, and without her help it might never have been solved and the killer never identified.

A chilly breeze ruffled her lightweight blouse, and Gin shivered. Since the end of that case, she'd surprised herself by having no desire to return to her job in Chicago. She felt no regret at stepping off the career ladder and leaving behind the pressures of her staff position.

Instead she'd found a niche for herself here, a much less demanding role as a consultant to the county office on cases of decomposition. While volunteering with the Red Cross in Srebrenica, Gin had helped identify the remains of hundreds of men and boys killed in the conflict and buried in mass graves, and during that time had confronted horrors—the likes of which most of her colleagues would never see. She'd written scholarly articles on the techniques she and her colleagues had developed as well as testified at The Hague. Gin was proud of the work she'd done, but she didn't seek attention for it; she'd felt uncomfortable with the praise that inevitably came her way after every article or speaking engagement or conference.

Gin was fond of her colleagues in Chicago, and she

counted herself lucky to have worked under Chief Medical Examiner Reginald Osnos, an exceptional teacher and mentor. She had a warm relationship with the entire staff, even if it rarely extended to socializing outside of work.

But in the end, she always did her best work when she was alone with the dead.

She spotted Tuck's SUV heading up the hill, and gathered her purse. He pulled into the circular drive and leaned out the window, his tanned, well-muscled arm resting on the sill.

"All set?" he asked. "I should have told you to wear clothes you don't mind getting dirty. The location Jonah identified is set back in the woods. It's some sort of hunting cabin."

Gin looked down at her simple black skirt and silk blouse. "Can you give me a few minutes? I'll just throw on jeans."

"Sure."

"Come on in. Mom's got tea in the fridge, you can help yourself."

"Well . . . okay, I guess. If you're sure she wouldn't mind."

"No, it's fine." Gin led the way into the house, wondering if Tuck was remembering the only other time he'd been here, when he'd come to arrest her father. Richard had been caught in the crossfire of the investigation into Lily's death and had briefly been a suspect. While the two men had a civil relationship, it had understandably been strained by Richard's arrest.

"My parents are both out," she said. "Mom's at work and Dad's gone to Johnstown for the day. He's been working on his coin collection, and the dealer called about some rare item he's thinking of buying."

"Didn't know Richard was a philatelist," Tuck said.

"I'm surprised you know the term."

"Gin, why do I always feel like you think I've got lead between my ears?" Tuck's tone was teasing, but Gin paused with her hand on the newel post and turned to face him.

"You know that's not true. I have nothing but respect for you and the work you've done." She could feel her face warm with embarrassment.

"Yeah, that's the problem," Tuck laughed. "Nothing but respect. I mean, don't get me wrong, I'm glad you think I'm doing a decent job."

Gin gave him an uncertain smile. He wouldn't be flirting this way if he knew that she and Jake had hit pause on their relationship—even though he'd let her know that he'd like to take things further with her, if Jake was ever out of the picture.

"I'll be right back," she mumbled, racing up the stairs, pushing those thoughts out of her head. The fact that she might actually be single again was too much to consider right now.

She rifled through the drawers of her old dresser, looking for jeans, and not finding them. She'd been distracted when she unpacked. Giving up, she dug out a pair of running tights and a moisture-wicking pullover that she often wore for early morning runs along the hills above town. She kicked off her heels and pulled on her running shoes.

She headed back down the stairs and found Tuck standing in the hall that connected the kitchen to the butler's pantry, looking at the collection of framed family photographs that her mother had hung there after remodeling the downstairs several years ago.

"She looked so much like your mother," Tuck said softly.

Gin looked at the photo he was examining, and realized with surprise that her mother had added new photographs to the collection. There was one of Lily at age fifteen, holding a paintbrush and mugging for the camera with a smudge of paint on her cheek, back when she'd worked on the sets for the school musical. Her mother had always loved that picture of Lily, but after her disappearance nearly every photo of her had disappeared. It had been too painful for her parents to look at them day after day.

Now they were back, a palpable symbol of their healing. Somehow, that made Gin feel even worse about the problems with Jake—as though her parents had moved on without her.

"Everyone always said so," she said wistfully. "My mother was something of a famous beauty, at least around here. Her debut made the society pages all the way to Philadelphia."

"Your mom was a debutante?" Tuck shook his head, bemused. "I'm way out of my league. I wasn't born with any silver spoons—more like a wrench."

"Shall we get going?" Gin asked, anxious to reel in the direction of the conversation. She followed Tuck out to the car. Once they were on their way, he filled her in on the conversation with Jonah.

"He says he comes out here sometimes to run. I checked—he's been on the cross-country team since his sophomore year, so that makes sense. His event is the mile. His coach confirmed that he puts in a lot of work on these roads."

"Wow, you've already done a lot of background," Gin said.

Tuck glanced at her, taking his eyes off the road for a second. "Gin . . ."

"I know, I know, you're a professional. Look, Tuck, I don't doubt your dedication. Anything you've got going on with County—well, you don't have to explain yourself to me." She paused. "I mean, unless you want to."

"I'll take that under advisement. Anyway, Jonah sketched out a loop that's roughly seven miles that he says he does during training. It goes up along the ridge above Canterbury Estates, along Baker Road toward Route 51. There's a path for most of it, and he says that where the path disappears—where it dips down to Saylor Creek—he'd run in the creek bed when it was dry, or up along the banks when it wasn't. He said he'd been by the spot he told me about often enough that he noticed that someone or something had dug up an area a dozen yards from where he ran, but he wasn't sure until after the rains last month. They washed away some of the dirt and branches that had been dragged over the site."

"Have you already been there to check it out?"

"No, not yet. I wanted to avoid bringing Jonah unless necessary. Obviously if we don't find anything today, we'll have to, but I'd rather have you take a look and maybe you'll come up with something that gives me some leverage with him. Assuming there really is a body."

Gin gazed thoughtfully out the window at the passing scenery. There was a weak sun obscured by thin clouds, giving the view of the modest homes lining both sides of the road a dispirited quality. "You believe him, then?" she finally asked. "Earlier, you said that he might have been looking for a way to fit in with the cool crowd. Did you get the impression that he struggles socially?"

Tuck shrugged. "Who can say? Hell, all I know is what I see. I mean, as someone with a special needs kid—there've been kids who've gone out of their way to be kind to Cherie. And there's others who've been downright cruel. I guess I'm saying that every kid is different. But he doesn't have the swagger, you know?"

"Yes . . . I know." Gin thought of Jake at that age—all attitude, with the reckless energy to back it up. Other boys at school had both feared and emulated him; girls couldn't resist him. He'd had the kind of charisma that can't be faked, though plenty of kids had tried. "And I also know how powerful the drive to fit in can be."

"Yeah. I'm hoping I can spend some more time with him before County gets involved. If there is a body, I'm going to end up with Bruce and Liam on my ass, and once again, I'll be persona non grata in my former department.

And the way things stand with Wheeler, I'm fresh out of favors I can call in."

"I didn't realize it was that bad," Gin admitted.

In Allegheny County, law enforcement at the local level was limited to minor crimes. Anything on the level of a major crime—including murder, violent assault, drug trafficking, and arson—was turned over to the county. Specialized services, such as crime scene investigation and forensic support, explosive ordnance disposal, SWAT, and cold case investigations also fell under the county umbrella.

When Jake's father had been chief of police, he'd managed his officers with a casual approach. It had worked well enough with the old guard of the county officers. The lines between the departments had been blurred, and Lawrence Crosby had been involved with any number of cases in which the county took the official lead.

When Tuck took over, he'd made it clear that his would be a more disciplined department, with greater accountability and a clear chain of command. There had been some grumbling from the old guard, but in the months since then, Tuck had managed to win over his staff by being consistent, fair, and generous in giving credit to those who'd earned it.

But even as Tuck had tightened things up in Trumbull, the county officers were becoming more possessive of their cases. At least, that had been Gin's experience with the homicide detectives with whom she regularly interacted with in the course of her consulting work. Bruce Stillman, the senior detective, was rude, possessive, even combative.

And his partner Liam Witt was still too junior to override his partner's actions. So Gin could understand the urgency Tuck felt to make some progress before he was ousted from the case.

"Why do you care about this one?" she asked quietly. "I mean . . . on behalf of Jake, I'm glad that you're taking this seriously, rather than dismissing his mother's death as just one more victim of the epidemic. But I don't understand why you don't just kick the can up the chain and let someone else pursue it."

"Because it happened on my watch. And before you say it, Gin, *I* will—this place has gotten under my skin, okay? This is our home now, mine and Cherie's. She's finally settled in here. And the day's going to come, sooner than I'd like, probably, when I'm not always going to be able to be there to make sure she's making the right choices. She's growing up, just like every other kid. I don't need to tell you she's vulnerable. And so when somebody—even a goddamn kid—starts handing out this shit like lollipops, I take it pretty fucking personally."

"I understand," Gin said quietly.

"Anyway . . . this is our turn, according to the directions Jonah gave me," Tuck said, veering onto a rutted road that led past farms on either side into a gentle, wooded valley. After a moment he added, "Sorry if I got a little heated there. It's not you, believe me."

"I know," Gin said. "I'd probably feel the same way. I actually, um, admire you. As a parent, I mean."

"Okay." He stared straight ahead, but the atmosphere

in the car seemed suddenly charged. Complimenting a man's relationship with his child hardly constituted flirting . . . but it did highlight the differences between Tuck and Jake, who answered to no one but himself. Tuck was singularly focused on making Trumbull safe for his daughter, as well as the rest of its citizens; Jake traveled an orbit around his own past hurts and grudges and losses. He wasn't a selfish man, but his focus sometimes didn't leave room for anyone else. And while he'd endured a great deal, Gin was starting to wonder if he would ever find what he was looking for—if there would ever be room in his life for more.

For *her*.

"Hey, can you check the route?" Tuck asked, breaking into her reverie. "I can't read my goddamn notes and drive at the same time, and the phone's GPS is completely worthless out here."

"Sure," Gin said, glad for the distraction. She scanned the page of notes on yellow legal paper that was stained with a coffee ring. "Tuck . . . is this even in English?"

He scowled. "Very funny. Penmanship has never been my strong suit."

"I'll say. Okay, according to this you either turn past the gray storage shed . . . or maybe it's the gray stargaze ship."

It took twenty minutes, and several false leads and treacherous U-turns on the narrow dirt road, but finally they pulled up to a rustic cabin nearly hidden by the overhanging branches of a stand of tall evergreens. This was the densest part of the forest that hugged the creek on either side; further up the valley, the rich bottom land was farmed for grain.

"Our neighbor used to hunt somewhere near here," Gin said, as Tuck pulled the SUV up in front of the cabin and killed the engine. "Judge Viafore. He's elderly now, but I think he hunted pheasant."

"Yeah, that would make sense," Tuck said. "That and deer. Over there—see that rope up in that tree? With the rusty metal thing with the hooks? That's somebody's hoist and gambrel system for skinning and dressing deer. But given its condition, it's been a while."

"Oh." Despite the nature of Gin's work, in which she was accustomed to seeing human bodies with clinical detachment, she didn't like imagining the beautiful animals hung from the tree and was not a fan of the hunting of animals for sport. She changed the subject. "Do you still want me to try to interpret your chicken scratch? If there's any hope of us finding the spot, maybe it's better if you look at your notes."

Tuck merely grunted in response, taking the sheet of notes back from her. Gin followed him around the back of the cabin, down a gentle slope to the banks of the creek. There was a slow, lazy flow of water from the recent rains; rushes and water weeds grew abundantly along the banks. Unfortunately, the storms had also washed trash into the creek, and as the waters receded, it ended up on the banks. The soda bottles, food wrappers, and bits of plastic marred the otherwise pristine natural beauty. The buzz of insects filled the air as they waded through the dense undergrowth. Gin's shoe caught on a root and she nearly stumbled. Tuck grabbed her arm to prevent her from falling.

"Steady there. No sense having you out for the season with an injury." He grabbed her hand. "Just hang on. It should be up ahead past that sand bar."

As he helped her over the uneven creek bank, she was acutely aware of his touch, her hand enveloped in his large one. When he helped her over a fallen tree blocking the path, her hand rested briefly on his shoulder before she leapt down, and she could feel the warmth of his skin under his shirt. When she turned to make sure he'd made it over the tree, she caught him staring and blushed, regretting her choice to wear the form-fitting athletic tights.

Or . . . perhaps the emotion she was feeling wasn't regret, exactly. But dwelling on it probably wasn't a wise idea, especially given the nature of their errand.

"Are we close?"

"Yeah. Matter of fact . . ." Tuck went past her, picking his way through a stand of alder trees up a gentle slope to a small clearing where there was a depression in the earth. Behind a rock outcropping there was a patch that, unlike the ground around it, was bare of weeds and shrubs, a muddy area of about five feet across was partially covered with branches and fallen limbs. As Gin examined it more carefully, it was evident that the brush and branches could easily have been dragged there on purpose.

Tuck started clearing the branches, tossing them to the side. "Here, give me a hand with this big one."

Together they lifted several of the larger branches, and it was obvious that the soil underneath had been disturbed. The dirt was raw and muddy; dead leaves and withered roots were the only evidence of the plants that had grown there. Gin lifted an especially leafy branch, and gasped: underneath, obscured by the mud and foliage, was part of a large black plastic trash bag.

And protruding from a long gash in the side . . . a human arm. At least, Gin thought it was an arm, though it was difficult to be certain because the hand had been hacked off, leaving a ragged stump with dirt and debris clotting the ragged and torn tissues.

Tuck whistled. "Guess our boy wasn't bullshitting us after all."

Gin froze, taking a deep breath to compose herself. It wasn't the presence of the corpse that had unsettled her; she'd been around the dead nearly every day of her life for decades. But encountering a body away from the bright lights of the morgue, tossed haphazardly like garbage, took her back to the difficult days when she'd helped exhume the mass graves.

There had been no plastic bags then, no order to the remains, which were piled as many as four deep. Many of the bodies had been moved at some point after their initial burial, and as the excavating crew had done their heartbreaking, painstaking work, she'd stood shoulder to shoulder with her colleagues and had attempted to make sense of the nearly unrecognizable pieces of the decomposed bodies that had been torn apart.

Even now, her mind was adjusting to the scene in front of her, adjusting to what she was seeing, switching into analytical mode. The edges of the torn flesh of the exposed wrist had dried and stiffened, curling away from the muscle and splintered end of the bone. The tissue ranged from pale and waxy with yellow and purple undertones to grayish shades.

Gin pushed the remnants of her memories away and focused on what was in front of her. "So what happens now?"

"I'll call County. Get the CSI team out here." Tuck's picked up a stick and lifted a corner of the black plastic. "It'll take them at least an hour to get here. We'll take a look in a second."

Tuck pulled out his phone and dialed. As he was waiting to be connected, he bent down and picked up a stone and tossed it into the creek. While he gave the dispatcher directions, he watched the surface of the water where the stone had gone under.

As if he were deep in concentration. Or . . . prayer.

Where had that thought come from? Gin shook her head in an effort to clear her thoughts as he walked back toward her.

"Okay, they're on their way. And yes, we drew the lucky card, as usual—Bruce and Liam are coming too." He scowled. "They'll probably get here first, just so Bruce can have the satisfaction of taking the case off my hands in person."

Gin didn't relish the encounter any more than Tuck did. "Won't they question why I'm here?"

"Hell, he questions everything I do, so I don't know if it matters. But if it makes you feel better, I'll just tell him the truth—that I had a questionable lead from a suspect in another case. These interview-room 'confessions' often don't lead to squat, and Bruce knows that. No way he can fault me for not calling them in and wasting resources before we knew if there was anything to get excited about. And as for you—I don't have a single person on staff who grew up in this area, so I was forced to rely on you to help me find the location."

"Even though you found it yourself, with hardly any trouble."

Tuck shrugged. "We don't need to share that fact. Besides, why wouldn't I bring along the departmental expert, since we had lunch plans anyway?"

"We . . . did?"

"We did. We do. Unfortunately, I don't think either of us is going to make it, given our little buried treasure. But at least we can take a look while we're waiting."

"I'm not sure I can tell you a whole lot until CSI gets here," Gin said. She knew that the body would have to be photographed before it was disturbed in any way. The area around it would be considered part of the scene as well; samples would be taken from the soil, the foliage, and any dead insects or larvae.

Tuck cleared his throat. "Absolutely. Although, since according to Jonah, he already looked in the bag, and since I had to unearth it to determine that there was anything worth our time, I don't see that it will harm anything to take a quick look—from a safe remove, of course."

He picked up the stick again, and used it to gently prod the bag down and away from the body, uncovering the head and torso, down to the hips—and once again Gin slipped into her analytical mode.

In trying to describe the process to a group of students years earlier, she'd used the metaphor of a camera's shutter clicking at a rapid speed, taking a series of impressions so quickly that she was barely aware of the whole being comprised of the parts. It wasn't a perfect analogy, but she had no better way to describe her process of taking in the whole and then breaking down the details into smaller and smaller segments—sometimes, until she was literally examining tissues at the cellular level.

The body lying at her feet was naked, the skin pale and tight with patches of mold here and there. The eyes were shut and the gray hair was shorn close to the scalp. As Gin scanned the exposed flesh, her eye caught on a flash of orange, bright against the mottled gray skin.

"This body's been embalmed, Tuck."

"Yeah? How can you tell?"

"Well, the easiest way is this," she picked up a stick of her own and used it to point at the orange plastic screw embedded about two inches from the navel.

"What is it?"

"Trocar screw. It seals the hole after the fluid is drained from the organs. Also, here—" She nudged the plastic bag away from the inner thigh, where there was a small suture—"this is where the blood was drained and replaced with embalming fluid. Also, those rosy cheeks are the result of makeup, which is part of the embalmer's job."

"Jesus. I never really thought about what happens in between an autopsy and the funeral. Anything else?"

"Well, there's likely to be plastic caps between the eye and lid to help hold the eye's shape. And there'll either be a mouth form or sutures, or a combination, to keep the mouth looking natural. There's other things, too, but . . ." Most people didn't want to know about the steps taken to prevent leakage from the body's orifices.

"I'll take your word for it," Tuck said quickly. "Even I have limits."

"Well, you're doing pretty well, given the body's condition."

"What else can you tell me?"

"Just from what I can see? The hands were most likely severed post-mortem. No embalmer would leave them like that."

"If he was embalmed, why isn't he better preserved?"

"Embalming doesn't last forever," Gin said. It was one of the most common misconceptions about the process. "It only delays decomposition, usually just for the few days needed for the viewing and burial. Judging from what I see, death occurred no more than a few months ago. Of course, it's hard to be more precise without knowing how long it was here, and how much moisture it was exposed to."

"So why would someone embalm a body, just to dump it?"

"Could it have been buried first, then removed and relocated?" Gin knew of cases where graves had been tampered with in an effort to steal jewelry and even tooth fillings, but she'd never heard of the body itself being stolen.

"I guess so. Can't imagine why, though." Tuck used his stick to move the plastic bag back as it had been before. "So, fingerprints are out, obviously. Maybe we can do something with dental impressions. What about DNA?"

"Might be able to get a usable sample from a follicle, though with decomp, the best bet is to use the long bones like the humerus or femur. But I hate to draw any conclusions before the official autopsy."

"Okay. Might as well get comfortable."

Tuck sat down with his back against the trunk of a large tree, and patted the ground next to him. "Here, I'll share my backrest with you."

She sat down next to him with her legs out in front of her, aware of their hips and shoulders touching. They sat without speaking, each of them lost in their own thoughts.

After a while Gin heard people coming toward them through the woods before she saw them. She shielded her eyes from the sun filtering through the branches overhead and peered through the trees, which created a natural screen between the creek and the land further uphill where the cabin was situated.

"So much for our little party," Tuck said, getting to his

feet. He offered his hand to help Gin up. "Guess word got out that it's the hottest ticket in town."

Three people came single file through the trees. Gin recognized Katie Kennedy's long dark hair and trim figure. Right behind her, in shirtsleeves and shoes that weren't meant for hiking, were Bruce and Liam.

"Thanks for making time in your busy day," Tuck deadpanned. Gin cut him a look, wondering why he couldn't resist taunting the detective. "Traveling solo today, Katie?"

"Paula will be along in a minute," Katie said. "She's, um, not feeling well."

"That's what happens when you let women into the field during your childbearing years," Bruce said. "Whose idea was it to let the two of you partner up, anyway? Next thing you know, you'll get knocked up too. And then what are we going to do, give your camera and kit to the janitor and let him take over for you?"

"Wow," Katie said cheerfully. "That was incredibly insensitive even for you, Bruce. Ever hear of affirmative action?"

"Don't let him get under your skin," Liam said apologetically, with a look of genuine chagrin.

A woman with close-cropped blonde hair and stylish red glasses came through the clearing, her complexion pale. Her windbreaker hid any indication that she was expecting, but Gin had spoken to her last week and knew she was nearing the end of her fourth month of pregnancy. With any luck, the nausea would abate soon.

"What did I miss?"

"Not much," Bruce said. "I guess they asked us here to shoot the shit."

"Damn," Paula said. "I was afraid you might have started without me."

She unzipped the bag slung around her neck, while Katie knelt on the ground to open her own kit.

"I don't know how you do it," Liam said. "I've thrown up twice in the field, but I don't have the excuse of being pregnant."

"This doesn't bother me," Paula said. "The smell of Jenkins heating up his breakfast burrito in the microwave—that's what did it this morning. It was a relief to get called out."

Tuck went over what they knew so far, including an abbreviated account of Jonah's offer. "Kid says he stumbled on this while he was out running. Didn't disturb the branches covering the body, but as you can see, we moved a few to get access. If we hadn't come out here, some dog or day hiker was bound to find this before long."

"You're a runner, aren't you, Gin?" Liam asked. "Do you ever come out this way?"

She shook her head. "I prefer more established paths— I'm always worried I'll twist my ankle, or worse. But I'm considerably older than Jonah Krischer. When I was his age I probably would have."

"The two of you can stick around if you want," Bruce said. "But we've got this from here. Mind staying outside the perimeter?"

Gin simmered with irritation. Bruce was obviously pulling rank, but she and Tuck were well versed in evidence-preservation procedures and didn't pose a threat to the scene.

"It seems likely I'll be asked to consult on this one," she snapped, even though she had gotten all she needed from the scene until the CSI team's report came back. "I don't see how it can hurt for me to participate."

"I'd welcome that," Katie chimed in mildly, not looking up from setting out the various supplies she'd use to bag and label the evidence she would collect. "Paula's got her hands full, and I could use a little help."

"That works for me," Liam said.

"That's just great," Bruce fumed. "Do any of you remember who's in charge here? Oh, yeah, that would be me, the senior officer on scene. I'll let it slide that you're all ganging up on me, but don't think I won't remember this at review time."

Tuck's cell phone rang, preventing him from adding fuel to the fire. He squinted at the screen, then answered tersely.

"Baxter. Hey. Fine." As he listened, his expression hardened. "Yeah . . . no shit. Had a feeling we hadn't seen the last of that guy. Okay, put him in three. Tell him I'm on my way. Owens? You mean his attorney? Uh-uh. He can wait out in the lobby, unless he's got new information directly related to the case . . . I understand. Remember, though, you're the one with the badge, right?"

"Having trouble with your direct reports, Baxter?"

Bruce smirked. "Guess it's not as easy to push people around out in the sticks."

Tuck ignored the comment. "Sorry, Gin, but I've got to head back. Want to catch a ride with me, or stick around?"

"We can give you a lift if you want to stay, Gin," Katie said. "Long as you don't mind riding in the back of the van."

"Thanks, Katie, but I'll let you guys work in peace," Gin said. It was unlikely that Katie and Paula would be finished documenting the scene and collecting evidence for several more hours. "Listen, you're going to get soil samples, right?"

"Of course. But you're not thinking Sarcophagidae, are you? I mean, since he was embalmed—"

"Right, no. I thought if there were Pilophilidae, we could look at colony density."

"Oh, right, to see when he was moved here. Makes sense."

"Hang on," Liam said. "The two of you were both thinking . . . sarco-what?"

"Sarcophagidae and Pilophilidae," Paula chimed in, pausing between shots. "They're insects. Sarcophagidae feed on blood, which our friend here doesn't have, since he was embalmed. But a cheese skipper feeds on decaying flesh, so we can see how dense they are in this location to help estimate how long the body has been there."

"Er . . . cheese skipper?"

"Because they jump. And cheese, like . . . well, you know. Dead flesh."

Katie giggled, and Liam looked disgusted. "Honestly,

I've never met anyone like the three of you. Didn't anyone ever buy you guys a Barbie? Or even a football?"

"I asked for a microscope for my eleventh birthday," Paula said.

"I nearly blew up my parents' microwave up trying to form plasmoids from an old candle," Katie added. "You should talk to Gin—she's spearheading this new program to get more girls interested in science in the middle school."

"I wish we'd had that when I was a kid," Paula sighed. "Let me know if you ever want me to come in and talk to the kids, Gin."

"I'll definitely take you up on that," Gin said. "Maybe I could invite both of you. It could make a great impression to present a team of women, to combat the idea that you're still a token presence in the field."

"Oh, great," Bruce said. "You mind reminding your girlfriend that she's on the clock, Witt?"

Katie blushed and bent down to her work, while Liam glared at Bruce. Gin knew the pair had been trying to keep their romantic relationship discreet; leave it to Bruce to turn it into a crude joke.

"I'll call you this weekend to discuss the program," she told Paula kindly.

"Now that we've got that settled, I'm going to want everything you've got on your witness," Bruce called after Tuck. "I'll want to interview him again as soon as possible."

"I'm sure he'll be delighted," Tuck said archly. "Why

don't you ask his dad to come up too? Charming guy. Real fan of law enforcement."

Gin said her goodbyes and followed Tuck along the path back toward the cabin.

"Well, that went well," he sighed when they were out of earshot.

"Katie and Paula are good at what they do," Gin reassured him. "I doubt there's anything we could learn by sticking around that we won't be able to confirm later, either from the evidence or in the autopsy."

"You seem pretty confident that you'll be asked to help," Tuck observed. "I sure hope you do, or we lose any leverage we have for insider access to the case."

"Captain Wheeler has gone out of her way to thank me lately," Gin said. "Do you have any reason to think she wouldn't bring me in?" Too late, she remembered Tuck's comment about friction between him and the captain.

Tuck shrugged, but didn't answer. They'd reached the cabin, and he veered toward it. "Just give me a minute here," he said. "It won't hurt to keep Dr. Krischer waiting a few more minutes."

He stepped up on the cabin's rough wooden porch and peered through the dusty window, using the cuff of his sleeve to rub a small circle of grime away. Gin followed him, being careful not to disturb anything.

"Doesn't look like anyone's been here in quite some time," Tuck said. He pointed to the door handle, which was coated with dust and had an intricate spider web stretched across the door jam.

"Did Jonah say if he knew whose cabin this was?"

"No. Just called it a 'creepy' cabin. I got the impression he avoided coming too close."

"You'll need to establish whether the body was on land that belonged to the owner of the cabin, for notification purposes," Gin pointed out. "Although they'll probably see it on the news."

"Yeah, maybe not," Tuck said. "I kept the details off the radio, and hopefully Bruce and Liam won't leak anything until they know a little more. At this stage there's nothing to be gained from those parasites showing up here today. We don't need another protest march in Trumbull."

During the case last fall involving Jake's job site, a body had been discovered that was suspected of being a civil war soldier. The media and the reenactor community had come out in force, convinced that the body's presence meant that the land should be designated and protected as a site of historical significance. They'd managed to halt construction completely while they staged protests, putting Jake's livelihood in jeopardy until Gin was able to prove that the body had died much more recently.

"I agree. Hey, check that out."

In the corner of the porch, dangling from a nail pounded into a splintered post, was a filthy, matted beige and brown pelt.

"Guy get tired of his dog?" Tuck suggested sarcastically.

"No . . . probably a coyote. Hunters around here sometimes hang them up as a deterrent."

"No kidding?" Tuck said. "Does it work?"

Gin shrugged. "I've never hunted so I can't say for sure. But most mammals are a lot more cavalier about death than humans, so probably not."

Tuck looked over his shoulder, through the trees to where the others were at work on the crime scene.

"Maybe I ought to try stringing one up outside my office. See if it gets people to leave me in peace."

9

They were halfway back to town when Madeleine called. Gin considered letting the call go to voicemail, but since she was now living in her parents' house, she supposed she owed her mother the courtesy of answering.

"Do you mind if I take this?" she asked Tuck, who'd been uncharacteristically quiet.

"Knock yourself out."

"Hi, Mom."

"Hi, honey," Madeleine's voice was brisk, as usual. "Finding everything you need at the house?"

"Yes, of course. And I wanted to say thanks again for, um . . ." Gin didn't want to discuss her current situation in front of Tuck, so she settled for saying ". . . everything."

"Absolutely, honey. Listen, I wanted to give you a heads up on a bulletin we received this morning. It's going to be in the news later today, so I'm not breaking confidentiality."

"Of course not," Gin said drily. Her mother was discretion personified; she took her job as mayor extremely seriously. Madeleine was the third generation of her family to live in Trumbull, and was determined to restore prosperity to the town and reverse its long decline following the collapse of the steel industry.

"Captain Wheeler's going to do a press conference announcing the gun amnesty program."

Gin was familiar with the program, which encouraged owners of unlicensed or unused guns to turn them in with no questions asked and incur no penalties for unlawful ownership. Modeled after successful programs in larger cities, the Allegheny County police department was hoping to reduce the number of gun injuries and fatalities. Chicago had seen fantastic results at its own gun buy-back events, and Gin hoped the trend would grow; she'd seen too many deaths from accidental shootings, many of them involving children.

"Anything we can do to remove guns from homes is a good idea," she said.

"Yes. Well . . . unfortunately, this isn't exactly coming out of the blue. There's apparently been an investigation going on internally for almost a year. Guns taken off the streets can end up in a variety of places, but some of them have been disappearing. And it's looking like it might be someone in the department."

"Wait, I don't understand. What do you mean, 'a variety of places'? And how do they know they're missing?"

"I'm just learning this myself, but when a gun is seized by police, it's checked against a theft database and can be returned to the owner after the case is over. They check with a crime weapon database next and if it was involved in any crimes, then it's handed over to whoever's working on that case. But if nothing's found, and it's not needed for evidence, then it's supposed to be destroyed. Only in the last year or so, there's no record of them having actually made it to the facility where they're destroyed."

"And they only figured this out now?"

"I don't think so—no one's coming out and saying it, but this seems to have been under investigation for a while. They're not giving us a lot of details yet. Maureen's remarks are going to be fairly brief, but reading between the lines, I think she wanted to keep a lid on the investigation until she had identified who was responsible. Unfortunately, someone leaked it, and now she has no choice but to try to get in front of it."

"Okay," Gin said cautiously, glancing over at Tuck. What, if anything, did he know about all this—and could it be related somehow to his transfer to Trumbull last year, the details of which had been vague? Surely Tuck hadn't been involved with the disappearance of the seized weapons. Gin chastised herself for even considering it, but then again . . . it wasn't outside the realm of possibility. When it came down to it, all she had to go on where Tuck was concerned was his word . . . and the confusing emotions he stirred within her.

Which didn't add up to any sort of defense against the possibility that he'd been guilty of wrongdoing while working for the county.

"What does this all mean for me?" Gin demanded, more roughly than she'd intended. "I assume there's a reason you're giving me this heads-up."

"Not just you," Madeleine said, "our whole family. Maureen's asking for support from local townships, so I'll need to make a statement. Your father's going to turn in that old WWII pistol that belonged to his uncle. I'll be working with Chief Baxter to set up an intake booth at the station and maybe do a little local outreach. And Gin . . . now might be a good time for Jake to think about getting rid of his rifle."

"Mom," Gin said, suddenly wishing she'd waited until later to have this conversation. "I can't ask him to do that."

"I understand the two of you are working through some things. But you have to remember that both of you have been in the public eye quite a bit. And you've got additional visibility as the mayor's daughter. I'm sorry to say it, honey, but Jake can't simply decide not to be in the limelight any more. But don't immediately assume that this is a bad thing—he could turn it to his advantage, generate a little good publicity."

"He doesn't even use the rifle that much," Gin said. Jake kept it locked in a safe in the garage, and had used it only twice since Gin moved in—both times when squirrels were digging under the foundation of his shed.

"All the more reason to turn it in. Look, I'd ask if it was licensed but I figure I already know the answer."

Gin sighed, massaging her temple with her fingertips. If only Lawrence Crosby had run the department a little more like an administrator and a little less like the old-school lawman he'd been at heart. "Jake will never give it up, because it was his father's. Now if you want him to get a license for it—that's another story. But I'm not the one to ask him, given . . . our situation."

"All right. I understand. Do you have a problem with me contacting him myself?"

The twinge threatened to turn into a blazing headache. "I guess I can't object to that," Gin said. "May I ask why this is such a big deal?"

"Melanie Carter is sitting outside my office right now, with her cameraman in tow," Madeleine said crisply. "She's been keen on finding an angle ever since the Morgenson case."

Melanie Carter was a reporter for a Pittsburgh station who'd covered the civil war reenactor protests last fall. It was widely known that she'd hoped her coverage might attract national coverage and possibly award consideration—only to suffer embarrassment when it came to light that the man buried on the land had died only three years earlier, not during the war. "Surely she doesn't hold *you* responsible for her story being a bust?" Gin asked.

"No. That would be Jake. Apparently he had some choice words for her crew."

"I was there, Mom. I practically had to hold him back from tossing the camera over the cliff—the cameraman, too."

"So you see the problem. If she can discredit him, she will—and she's not above going through me, or Tuck, to do so."

"God, what a nightmare," Gin sighed. "I should tell you, Mom, I'm with Tuck now."

"Oh, really? Why?"

"I may be . . . consulting on a new case. I can't say more now, but I should warn you that it's likely to be newsworthy, too."

"Maybe you should give Melanie the scoop, get her off my back," Madeleine suggested.

"Very funny. Okay, well, I'll see you back at the house, okay? Shall I pick up something for dinner?"

"There's no need, honey. I can take something out of the freezer."

"No, let me do it," Gin said, warming to the idea. "I'd like to contribute, as long as I'm staying there."

"All right then, I'll look forward to it. Dad's having lunch with a friend after his appointment with the coin dealer, so he probably won't be home until late afternoon."

"Okay. See you soon."

Gin hung up and blew out a breath of frustration.

"So," Tuck said, glancing at her out of the corner of his

eye. "I wasn't eavesdropping, but it sounds like there's trouble in paradise."

"Tuck. It's really none of your business."

"Didn't say it was. Only, when a woman discusses her love life in the front seat of my car, I can't exactly unhear it. You need me to beat anyone up?"

Gin couldn't help an exasperated laugh. "You don't need to pretend we don't both know who we're talking about."

"That was some tangled grammar, especially from you."

"Can we talk about the gun thing instead? Mom says you're going to have a collection to coincide with the county's effort."

Tuck was silent for a moment. "Guess so," he said shortly.

"Isn't that . . . a good thing?" Gin asked, surprised by the terseness of his response.

"Yes, in general, getting guns off the street is a good thing. But there's angles to this thing that . . . look, can we go back to talking about Jake, please? Or, I don't know, the Pirates. Or politics. Or hell, lip gloss for all I care."

"You're not making a whole lot of sense right now," Gin said, uneasy that he was avoiding the subject. "Also, you just passed my turn."

"Shit." Tuck smacked the steering wheel with his hand.

"But tell you what, I need to pick up a few things for dinner, so I'll just ride to the station with you and walk home. That way I can stop at the market."

"If you're sure . . . and hey, I wanted to ask you about that. It's looking like I'm not going to make it home on time. Is there any chance that Cherie could stay with you after school for a few hours? I hate to ask, but I think I'm about to walk back into a shit storm, and then I've got to prepare all the paperwork for County on this new vic."

"Of course. I'd love to have her." Gin decided to put her misgivings about the gun buy-back conversation aside. After building a warm relationship with Tuck's daughter during the basketball season, Gin had watched Cherie after school from time to time when Tuck had to work late. Occasionally, Brendan's daughter, Olive, came over too. Gin hadn't examined too closely how much she enjoyed these afternoons, not wanting to dwell on the unexpected stirring of maternal urges. "She can help me make dinner— Mom and Dad will be thrilled. In fact, come on over whenever you get free, and join us."

"That's awfully generous," Tuck said, pulling into the municipal parking lot. "I can't predict when it will be, though."

"That's okay, we'll keep a plate in the oven."

Tuck parked and looked at Gin. "You're bailing me out again," he said quietly, a rare note of seriousness in his voice. "It's becoming a habit."

"Yeah, okay, call it payback for saving my life," Gin said, avoiding his gaze. During the Morgenson investigation, Tuck had come to her aid when she'd been the target of a killer who thought she'd come too close to the truth.

"Listen, woman, I'd save you any day of the week."

Gin was trying to craft a response when someone knocked on Tuck's window.

He opened the door and got out, breaking the tension. Gin followed. One of the staff police officers waited, looking abashed.

"Saw you pull in, Chief. Just wanted to give you a heads-up—that lawyer's in there making all kinds of threats. He won't leave the duty officer alone."

"It's okay, Hammond. He can threaten all day long—he's just trying to stir things up. There's nothing he can do here."

"Dr. Krischer is in Interview Three like you asked."

"Okay, got it."

But at that moment, the front door of the station was flung open and a tall, balding man in a button-down shirt and loosened tie came striding toward them.

"Shit," Officer Hammond said.

"It's okay, I got this," Tuck said. "Dr. Krischer. I understand you want to speak to me."

"You were just about to duck out, weren't you?" Krischer said. "You can't hide from me forever. My lawyer's going to slap you with wrongful arrest."

"I'm not ducking out of anything, Doc," Tuck said mildly. "I just arrived, as a matter of fact."

"Who's she?" Krischer shot Gin a glare. "Departmental lawyer? 'Cause you're going to need one."

"I'd watch your tone. This is Dr. Virginia Sullivan, a forensic anthropologist who consults for the Allegheny County Medical Examiner's office. If your son is telling the truth, she may hold the key to exonerating him, so you might not want to piss her off."

Krischer appeared visibly taken aback. "So—you found it, then. A body."

"You know I can't comment on that. But I can't help noticing that you seem surprised. Which makes me wonder—maybe you didn't believe your son's story?"

"I—of course I do," Krischer said. "Jonah's a model student. He earns excellent marks. He doesn't deserve to be impugned by this department and if you don't remove the cloud of suspicion over his head immediately I'll—"

"Calm down, Doc," Tuck said, clapping him on the shoulder. "Tell you what, let's get a cup of coffee and talk this out. You can invite your lawyer buddy along if you want. We'll make it a party."

"I don't know what you're trying to—"

"It was nice meeting you," Gin said pleasantly.

"Wait a minute," Krischer said, snapping his fingers. "Sullivan? You're the one—your boyfriend attacked my son and took him to your house against his will. You can tell him he'll be hearing from us, too."

"Dr. Sullivan is under no obligation to talk to you, or to convey any messages to Jake Crosby," Tuck said. He seemed to be enjoying this interaction. "But since the county police is getting involved, you'll have plenty of opportunities to complain about her to the detectives."

He guided Dr. Krischer into the building, ignoring his protests. Officer Hammond followed with an awkward wave at Gin.

She didn't envy Tuck the conversation he was about to have. She'd been the target of angry family members in the past; in the grip of high emotion, they sometimes lashed out at her because there was no one else onto whom they could vent their grief. She did her best not to react, to simply let their harsh words roll off.

Tuck seemed to have a gift for not engaging. He was almost preternaturally "chill," as Olive liked to say, an excellent quality for a man in his position.

As Gin headed toward the organic market, enjoying the sunshine, she tried to put her troubling thoughts aside.

Tuck had been very keen not to discuss the gun collection effort. He either didn't want to participate, which seemed unlikely, as such programs had virtually no downside, or there was more to the investigation into the missing weapons—and Tuck's involvement—than he was admitting.

But either way, there was nothing more that Gin was going to learn from him, at least for now.

10

Gin picked Cherie up after school and had just arrived back at her parents' house when she got a call from Stephen Harper letting her know that his boss, Chief Medical Examiner Harvey Chozick, had secured approval from Captain Wheeler for Gin to consult on the new case. She went out onto the screen porch so that she could speak freely, after making sure Cherie was settled with an after-school snack at the kitchen table.

"I'm happy to help out, Stephen. Has the body been brought in yet?"

"Just arrived half an hour ago. It's being processed now. And before you ask, your buddy Bruce has already weighed in with his opinion that you're not needed on this one."

Gin sighed. "Always nice to know one has the support of one's colleagues."

"Well, *I'm* your colleague," Stephen laughed, "and I

very much support the idea of you being there. These decomp cases are out of my wheelhouse."

"You're developing a real expertise with cytogenetics," Gin pointed out. "That article you wrote on molecular mutation analysis is getting a lot of praise. I even heard from my old boss, Reginald Osnos—he wanted to know if I'd met the author and if he might be willing to consult from time to time for Cook County."

"No kidding?"

"No kidding." Gin smiled to hear the note of pride in Stephen's voice. "Has the autopsy been scheduled yet?"

"I wanted to check with you on availability." Stephen paused. "I, um, apologize in advance if this is out of line, but I understood that there are some . . . changes in your personal life. I wasn't sure if your schedule was impacted."

Gin was dismayed that the news had spread so quickly. "I appreciate your concern, Stephen, but everything's fine. I'm staying with my folks for a bit, that's all. Do you mind me asking—how did you find out that Jake and I are, um, taking a break?"

Stephen sounded even more embarrassed. "Katie said something. Look, I know she didn't mean to be spreading rumors. She was just—well, I think she admires you, and she was telling me that things had gotten tense out at the scene today—what else is new—and then she said that she was glad you were with Chief Baxter, and then I think she realized that she'd implied something and was trying to back up from it. Really, she was just tripping over herself trying to make it right, so I hope you'll forgive her."

"Of course," Gin said, inwardly cringing. When would she ever learn that ME offices were like small towns—there were no secrets. "Look, I'd appreciate it if you could keep it to yourself, as much as possible. I mean, I am hoping that this is a temporary thing and—well, and it's just happened so I'm still trying to adjust. I'm just putting one foot in front of the other for now."

More cringing—she sounded like a self-help book.

"Good to keep busy," Stephen agreed. "And no worries—I'll guard your privacy with my life." He chuckled awkwardly. "Or at least with a skull chisel."

"Thanks, Stephen," Gin said. "I really appreciate that."

"And for what it's worth—I really hope you guys work it out. I think—Jane and I think—you're really great together."

Gin felt tears unexpectedly prick her eyes. Stephen was a kind man, a good friend—and she'd very much enjoyed meeting his wife Jane at their holiday open house. Their young children were adorable, "helping" out by serving the refreshments and making paper chains to send home with the guests.

They were the sort of family that Gin, deep in her hidden heart, longed to have someday.

"I—I need to go, Stephen," she blurted, afraid that if she didn't get off the phone—and think about something else—the floodgates were going to open. "Schedule the autopsy for the soonest you can fit it in and I'll be there."

"Of course. It'll probably be Thursday, but I'll text you a confirmation. Take care, okay?"

After Gin hung up she took a moment to compose herself before going back into the kitchen, where she'd left Cherie with her snack of cut-up peaches and a dish of pretzels.

But Cherie wasn't alone. Sitting across the table from her was Richard Sullivan.

"Dad!" Gin said. "When did you get back? I didn't hear you come in."

"About ten minutes ago. And imagine how delighted I was to discover that we have such a charming visitor."

"Doctor Sullivan says I'm a good eater," Cherie beamed, picking up her plate to show Gin that she'd finished her peaches. "I'm going to be a healthy grownup!"

"That's right," Richard said, winking. "I told her that as a reward for good behavior, I'd let her watch golf on television with me."

"Ick!" Cherie said, then dissolved into a gale of giggles.

"Cherie here tells me that she wants to be a professional golfer when she grows up," Richard continued.

"I do not! I hate golf! Golf is stupid!" Cherie yelled, as Richard pretended to be shocked, then pantomimed crying.

Gin was reminded of the way her father used to tease her and Lily in this very kitchen, so many years ago. Lily, like Cherie, loved nothing more than this game of reducing Richard to pretend tears, while it had made Gin anxious. She'd never had the gift of theater and whimsy that her father and Lily shared; she'd been more like her mother, pragmatic and practical.

But seeing Cherie enjoying their game made her suddenly miss Lily with an acuteness she hadn't felt in months, not since the days after her sister was finally put to rest next to her grandparents' graves.

And that somehow worsened the ache of Jake's absence. He'd been so kind to her during those difficult days, eager to offer comfort, whether it was a meal he'd prepared, a drive in the country, or simply holding her at night.

It was unthinkable that she might never have that again.

"Dad," she said, more sharply than she'd meant to. Her emotions were being stretched to breaking today. "I wonder if you could hang out with Cherie just a little bit longer while I make one more call for work? And then when I'm done, we'll start dinner."

"Great," her father said with an exaggerated grin, rubbing his hands together in pretend glee. "We'll work on our form so that Cherie can be a golf champion."

"No! Let's play Barbies!"

Gin went back out on the screen porch and forced herself to focus on the case. She checked her phone and saw that a text had arrived from Stephen:

Autopsy Thursday 9:00am. Hang in there

She texted back assuring him that she'd be present, and then called Katie Kennedy, who answered on the first ring.

"Gin! Oh my gosh, I'm so sorry, you have every right to be furious with me—"

"It's fine, Katie," Gin reassured her. "Truly. I just hope I didn't let my personal issues interfere with the investigation today. I should have kept that to myself."

"Oh, no, not at all. I really meant it when I said I was glad to have you there. I've been trying to take on a little extra to give Paula some relief. She's really had a tough time with this one."

"Pregnancy isn't for the faint of heart," Gin agreed. "Too bad certain men can't seem to understand that."

"Yeah, no kidding. Sometimes I wonder if Bruce thinks he arrived on earth by divine intervention or something. Can you even imagine him as a toddler? I bet he was a handful!"

Gin smiled. "Pity his poor mother. Listen, I was just calling to see if you turned up anything interesting after I left. The autopsy's going to be on Thursday, and I'll be consulting."

"Yeah, I heard. I'll try to be there, but just in case I can't, I'll be sure to send you my notes. We've got soil samples out for analysis, and obviously that won't be back yet. We did find a few fibers and I can probably get you some information on that before Thursday. I don't expect much from them, though—looks like we've got some cotton and wool blends, all contemporary. I also bagged some fly larvae and casings. That's about it for now."

"Okay, if I don't see you on Thursday, let's get together for coffee soon, all right?"

"I'd love that," the girl said shyly. "And thanks for, you know, being so cool about this morning."

Gin took a deep breath and tried to clear her head before going back into the house. She found her sixty-year-old father sitting cross-legged on the floor, a blond-haired doll in his hand. Cherie was holding a brunette doll, moving her arms while she "talked" to the other doll.

"Dr. Barbie is a doctor just like Dr. Sullivan," she said gravely. "Vice-President Barbie has a broken arm, and Dr. Barbie is going to make it all better."

"Luckily, she has these excellent bandages to work with." Richard held up a small band-aid imprinted with a popular cartoon character.

"Where on earth did you get that, Dad?" Gin laughed.

"Cherie's dad packed them in her backpack," Richard said, "along with about half a dozen pairs of tiny plastic shoes and a whole Tupperware full of Barbie outfits. Got to say, that man has a whole side to him that I'd never have guessed."

"My dad's very brave," Cherie said stoutly. "But he's also a super good dad."

"That," Gin said, feeling something in her heart give way, "may be the understatement of the year. Now, I guess I'll have to go make the cookie dough all by myself since the two of you are having an office visit."

"Vice President Barbie's all better!" Cherie said, jumping up and dropping her doll on the floor. "I want to help!"

"Sounds like a plan, but let's help clean up first." She gave her father a smile. "Even doctors have to clean up after themselves, you know."

* * *

After a simple meal of roast chicken, rice pilaf, and salad, Gin let Cherie take her cookie into the family room to watch an episode of her favorite program. The excitement of the visit had tired her, and Gin suspected that she would fall asleep in front of the television.

"I wonder what's keeping Tuck," Madeleine fretted.

"He texted half an hour ago saying he'd be here soon," Gin said. "I bet he just got stuck finishing up paperwork."

There was a knock at the door. "See? There he is." Gin opened the door and her smile faltered: it wasn't Tuck, but Jake Crosby standing on the front porch.

"Hi, Gin," he said uncomfortably. "I was wondering . . . could we talk? Just for a minute."

Gin looked behind her. "I—yes, of course," she said. "But I don't have much time. Cherie Baxter's here, and her dad's going to be here any minute to pick her up."

"That makes this even more important. Look, I only need a few minutes." He touched her arm. "I know I owe you an apology. More than an apology. I . . . you were right. I'm not taking my mother's death well. It turns out that, well, I underestimated how much it would affect me to know that I'll never . . ."

His voice went hoarse, and he cleared his throat. Gin battled an urge to put her arms around him and offer him comfort. "All right. Let's take a walk. I'm sorry I only have a few minutes now, but we can meet to talk again."

They set off down the street. Hyacinth Lane dated back

to the heyday of the steel industry, its five large mansions built for the managers of Trumbull's steel and coke plants. The Sullivans' house was the grandest of all, designed by Gin's grandfather, who had presided over one of the largest operations on the Monongahela River.

No streetlights had ever been erected on the street, the better to enjoy the glittering lights of the town below. Gin and Jake had walked along the ridge a hundred times before, holding hands, under a million stars and a gentle moon.

Tonight, however, they did not hold hands. Jake's posture was rigid and he walked like the damned, headed for an execution.

"So you were saying—"

"I wanted to let you know—"

They spoke unison and then each awkwardly paused. "No, go ahead," Gin said.

"It's just that . . . I, well, I've contacted a psychotherapist. I'm going to give counseling a try." He raked his hands through his hair. "Probably something I should have done a long time ago."

"Jake . . . I think that's a really good idea." *I'm proud of you*, Gin wanted to add, but she feared that it would sound patronizing to his ears.

"Thank you. But that's not all. I've decided to stay up in Tionesta full-time for a while. At least until this job's done. Things are a little chaotic there right now anyway— the engineering report required us to go back to square one on the drainage plan for the north side of the site. And if I don't pull something out of a hat, we're going to miss the completion deadline, and Asher's offered a huge bonus if we hit that target."

Gin stopped walking, trying to absorb Jake's words. They had reached the end of the guardrail that divided the end of the street from the sheer drop-off to the spectacular view. She stared out at the town, the river snaking along its edge, a band of black in the night. Far in the distance she could see the clusters of lights that were the towns of Clairton and Lincoln.

"You're moving away," she said woodenly.

"Not forever. Probably. I'm going to have one of my guys move into my house here and keep an eye on it. Asher's agreed to let me use his corporate apartment up there for now. Look, Gin . . . I'll be the first to admit that I don't have any idea what I'm doing. But I ran this by my therapist at my first session and he said it didn't sound like a bad idea. Given . . . the past, and the way I've dealt with it."

"But what about Jonah Krischer? And—the rest of it?" She'd been about to say *what about your mother's remains?*—but she realized that Jake was handling her death, and everything associated with it, the best way he knew how.

"I talked to Baxter on the way down here, actually. I'm sorry I didn't say that before. I called to see if there was anything new in the investigation into Marnie's death, and he told me he'd give me time to talk to you before he came to get Cherie." He stared down at the ground.

"I'm going back up there tonight. I only came back to tell you."

Somehow, that was the worst thing of all—that Jake would drive so many hours just to give her this message. It made it seem more real.

It made it seem final.

"Baxter told me that they cut a deal with Krischer. He told me about the body." Jake jammed his hands in his pockets and finally turned toward her. He looked exhausted in the moonlight. "Whatever they decide to do with the kid, it doesn't have anything to do with me. I'm just the guy who accidentally set it in motion."

"What if you have to come back to testify?" Gin asked. She felt like she was grasping at straws—searching for something, anything, that would be a reason for him not to go, to realize that he belonged here. She was terrified that this was the end of their relationship—a loss she wasn't prepared for, one that threatened to tear her heart in two.

"Then I'll come back. I've lived with—with not knowing what happened to my mother for almost thirty-nine years. I can live with it a little longer. Look, Gin, I don't expect this to make sense to you. But for as far back as I can remember, I've felt like my life was dragging me around. I want to change that. I want to feel like I can choose how it affects me." He swallowed. "I want to see if I can find some fucking peace."

"Jake—" Gin's voice threatened to break. "You make it sound like this is more than a temporary separation. Like you're—" She couldn't bring herself to say the words *you're breaking up with me.*

"I'm sorry," Jake said quietly, but he didn't meet her eyes. "I wish I could do better by you. That I could be what you need. But I can't—not now."

Gin choked back a sob, frantic to find the words to change his mind, when headlights flashed across their legs as a car made the turn. No—not a car, but a police SUV. Tuck had arrived.

"Please, don't leave like this," she pleaded. "Take some time to think about it, to—"

"I just want you to know that I love you," Jake said with an air of sad finality. "Always have. Always will. Until the day they put me in the ground."

Gin backed away, tears nearly blinding her—and then she was running, running as fast as she could away from the pain of losing him.

Toward the house, her family, the future she couldn't yet imagine.

* * *

Gin managed to get her emotions under control by the time she walked into the house. She heard voices in the kitchen—Cherie excitedly telling her father all about the afternoon she'd spent with Gin and Richard.

"He was going to make me do putt-putt!" Cherie exclaimed merrily.

Richard laughed. "I was actually going to let her use my lucky putting iron," he said.

"But we did Barbie hospital instead. Vice President Barbie broke her arm! And Doctor Barbie fixed her!" Cherie's voice trailed into a huge yawn, and Tuck gathered her against him in a hug. At nearly fourteen, she was too big for him to carry, but she loved to snuggle against her father. Given her developmental delays, it was sometimes hard to remember that Cherie was on the verge of puberty.

"Hello, Gin," Tuck said evenly. "Those were some mighty fine cookies you ladies made."

"I helped," Cherie said sleepily.

"I know you did, punkin. Okay, let's let these fine folks get some sleep, just like you're going to the minute we get home."

"Not tired," Cherie mumbled as her eyelids drifted closed.

Richard walked them to the door, and Gin could hear the two men talking. She started to help her mother clear the dishes, but Madeleine stopped her. "Are you all right? Of course you're not all right. Look at you, honey."

She held out her arms, and Gin walked into them and allowed her mother to hold her. "He's moving to Tionesta," she mumbled against her mother's shoulder. "At least until the retreat center has been completed." She explained that he was seeking counseling to deal with his mother's death.

Madeleine nodded. "And the death of his father last year. Don't forget that. He's had a lot to cope with. Honey . . . this might not be forever. In fact, maybe it will end up even better than before, once he's worked through these issues."

"Maybe," Gin snuffled, but her heart wasn't in it.

Richard walked back into the room. "Cute kid," he said heartily. "She can come back any—aw, hey, sweetie, are you okay?"

Gin pulled away from Madeleine and wiped her eyes. She didn't think she could bear any more kindness just now. "I'm fine," she mumbled. "I want you guys to know that I really appreciate you letting me stay here."

"This is your home," Richard said. "Always will be."

11

On Thursday morning, Gin left early to try to beat the worst of the northbound traffic. She made excellent time and arrived early enough to treat herself to an espresso and a biscotti on the Strip before heading back to the morgue for the autopsy.

Stephen and Harvey Chozick, the chief medical examiner, were chatting in the break room. Gin set down the white pasteboard box, tied with a bright yellow ribbon, that she'd purchased at the bakery.

"Try some—they're from Nina's Biscotti," she said, untying the bow and lifting the lid. "Best in the city."

"I take back everything I ever said about you, Sullivan." Bruce came into the break room and helped himself to a chocolate-drizzled pastry. Spotting his partner in the hall, he called, "Saw you pull up in Kennedy's car this morning. Guess you were taking advantage of the *benefits* part of your friendship last night eh?"

"Detective Stillman, please keep the locker room humor out of my office," Chozick said wearily.

"This is the break room," Bruce pointed out around a mouthful of crumbs.

"Since everyone's here, let's get started," Chozick said, ignoring him. "I'm sitting in on this one, given the likelihood of media scrutiny. We'll want to make sure we cross every T and dot every I."

They scrubbed and gloved up, and trooped into the morgue. The body looked quite different laid out on the steel surface than it had two days earlier in the black plastic garbage bag. It had been washed by the autopsy technicians and looked much less jarring. The man's graying hair had been combed away from his face, and it was easy to guess that he'd been a striking man, with a strong jaw and pronounced cheekbones.

One week earlier, they'd been in this very same room, examining the body of Jake's mother. It felt like a lifetime ago, and Gin forced herself not to think about Jake, a hundred and thirty miles away on the job site. She took a step forward, better to follow along as Stephen began recording his observations.

He made a thorough visual examination of the exterior of the body, confirming that embalming had taken place by the hole made by the trocar. He noted nothing extraordinary until he came to the wrists. When Stephen probed the ragged right stump, something inside Gin skidded. Not quite a jolt, more like a . . . memory.

She gazed, transfixed, at the damaged, abraded flesh

and mangled tissues, trying to understand the almost nauseating flash of emotion that had flashed through her and just as quickly, dissipated. Something about the past. Something about . . .

She blinked, an image transposing itself for a split second over what was right in front of her—a dusty, sepiatoned memory from the past; and Gin suddenly knew exactly what it was and why it had come back just now. It was the eerie similarity between the body in front of her and one she'd encountered in her first days in Srebrenica, when everything she confronted was unfamiliar, shocking, confounding.

In time she would learn to discipline herself against the horror, to put clinical distance between herself and the pits filled with bones, to treat the task as a series of quantifiable steps, nothing more. But that day she'd been supervising two young men dressed in white coveralls and blue gloves who were gingerly bagging body parts at her direction, when they'd cleared a new area and come across skeletal remains that were nearly intact. It was the shock of seeing the remains of a man positioned as if he'd just been napping, his clothes dirty but whole, his arms cradling his head—except that his hands had been hacked off. She had let loose a cry and stumbled, twisting her ankle on a clod of dirt and nearly fell. She'd tried to brush it off as mere surprise, but in the young men's eyes was a dull familiarity just short of sympathy.

It was far from the last time she'd see such unimaginable cruelty, but it was the first, and while she thought she'd healed from the trauma of the mission, her reaction just now was proof that it still haunted her, deep in her unconscious mind.

"Gin?" Stephen prompted, concern in his voice. She blinked and shook her head.

"Sorry, I . . . sorry."

"No problem. I was just saying that these multiple parallel lacerations suggest a series of hacking blows," Stephen said, pointing to the jagged, mutilated flesh above the severed edges of the skin. "I note crushing of the carpal bones and the carpal tunnel itself."

"Looks like someone threw up in there," Bruce said.

Ignoring him, Stephen probed gently with a small steel instrument; following his movements intently, Gin's concentration returned, and she relaxed slightly.

"Muscles are densely packed here, and given the damage it is difficult to identify . . . but I think this is the extensor carpi ulnaris. And on the other side here, the abductor policis longus. There is extensive damage to the tendons, the ligaments, the medial nerve." He looked up at Gin.

"I concur," Gin said stiffly. She was determined not to let her colleagues see how shaken she was. "Also, see the plastic deformation of the bone—I think it's too pronounced for ante- or even perimortem amputation."

"English, please," Bruce demanded.

"Living bone has a certain degree of elasticity," Stephen explained, pointing at the splintered bone protruding from the arm. "After death, the bone dries out. Trauma to living bone generally leads to an irregular or radiating 'butterfly' type of fracture, rather than jagged edges like these. So we would conclude that this injury happened after death."

"But what about the blood? When I saw him at the scene, before you guys cleaned him up, I thought I saw dried blood on the, uh, where it got chopped off. And people don't bleed after they're dead, especially if they've been embalmed."

"What you saw was probably a dried mixture of embalming fluid and bloody residue. That's why we drew our conclusions from the condition of the bone, not the absence of blood," Gin said.

"Still, the bone wouldn't dry out right away," Bruce said. "So can you tell how long this guy was dead by the way the bone broke?"

"Not really, unfortunately," Gin said, warming to the subject as she regained her composure. "There are many factors that contribute to the rate of drying of the bone. In an earthen grave, that includes soil moisture, of course, as well as the water table, precipitation history, the mineral content of the soil, and other things. We can deduce that this amputation occurred after a significant amount of time had passed—weeks, at least, to dry to this extent, and that would probably not have been at the site where the body was discovered, because of the proximity to water and the dampness of the soil."

"So you're saying our dude had to be somewhere else— like a nice dry coffin—for at least a few weeks."

"I can't make such a specific conclusion, but that's the general idea, yes."

"Any idea what was used to chop that hand off?"

"I would say something heavy, with a sharp blade. With a blunt-edged weapon, we'd see more of a depressed fracture; we would expect to see bone fragments driven inward. But the splintering is more uniform, and the skin laceration was fairly clean."

"So an axe, then."

"I wouldn't be that specific. Cartilage can occasionally retain tool marks, which can tell you if a blade was serrated, for instance. And sometimes microscopic examination of bone can reveal striation or gouge marks. But in this case there's simply too much damage."

Bruce shook his head. "Sometimes I wonder why we even bother to get you guys in here, at your pay grade. I could have guessed everything you've said so far—*some* guy used *some*thing to hack off this dead guy's hands, and he made a hell of a mess in the process."

"Sorry to disappoint you, Bruce," Stephen said sarcastically. "And we're not done disappointing you yet."

"What's that supposed to mean?"

Stephen walked to the head of the table, where he used his metal probe to part the lips, revealing even white teeth beneath.

"Identification through dental records isn't going to be possible," he said. "The deceased had full implants."

"Aw, *hell*," Bruce said. Gin almost felt sorry for him.

"That's rather unusual," Chozick said. "Estimating his age at between thirty-five and fifty-five, he would have been quite young to get them. Most people lose a tooth or two eventually—to injury, decay and gum disease, illness—but complete edentulism occurs rarely outside of the geriatric population."

"How did you guess his age? Not that a twenty-year range is any help."

"True," Chozick said. "Without odontological and osteological methodology—determining age through teeth and bones—I'm really just making a visual assessment."

"I agree with you, and I'll go a bit further," Gin said. "He has a significant amount of gray in his hair. Also, the skin tells us a lot. Over time, the four Ds—deterioration, deflation, discoloration, and descent—show evidence of age. We can't really do much with color at this point, but I see lines and evidence of sun damage on the face and neck that occurred over time. Other changes include the hollowness under the eyes, the sagging of the eyelid, the loss of fatty tissue in the cheeks, the sagging of the jaw—as well as the effects of sarcopenia, or the loss of muscle mass. I'd actually estimate his age at between forty-five and fifty-five."

"How about that, Stephen," Bruce said. "She beat you by ten years. Okay, so we've got a middle-aged guy who lost all his teeth early. Great."

"I do have one other . . . thought," Gin said cautiously. "You see the unusually large forehead, jaw, and nose, and possible skull bossing—the protuberance of this bony ridge below the brow? I think he may have suffered from acromegaly, which is a disorder characterized by excess growth hormone after the growth plates have closed. We would expect to see unusually large hands, which we can't confirm, of course, but these craniofacial abnormalities would be consistent with such a diagnosis."

"What happens to people who have it?"

"To be honest, it's often diagnosed in middle age, because people aren't even aware of it. Symptoms include headaches and vision problems, so sometimes that causes people to seek help. Joint pain, too. And if it's not treated, it can also lead to complications—high blood pressure, sleep apnea, type two diabetes."

"Nothing that would have killed him, in other words. And there's no way to use this condition in any of our search databases, especially if they don't even know they have it." Bruce looked at his watch. "Well, this has been a truly epic waste of my time."

"Sorry we couldn't be of more help," Stephen called after him as he headed for the door. "Sometimes the dead are just assholes that way."

At Gin's startled expression, Stephen shrugged. "What can I say? I think he's starting to rub off on me."

* * *

On her way out, Gin decided to drop in on the forensic lab to visit Katie. She found the young technician bent over her microscope, classical guitar music playing softly in the background.

"Gin! How did the autopsy go?"

Gin gave her a brief summary, including her suspicion that the dead man suffered from acromegaly.

"I did notice those facial anomalies, but honestly, I just

though he had what my mom always called 'strong features.'" Katie shrugged. "I actually thought he must have been handsome. I mean, for an old guy."

Gin laughed. "I won't tell Liam."

"God, that sounded a little creepy, didn't it?" Katie took off her glasses and stretched. "I think I've been spending too much time in the lab."

"You guys have been pretty busy, huh?"

"Well, honestly, we would have been anyway—we've lost two techs in the last few months. One went to grad school and the other's wife got transferred. And with Paula, some smells make her puke, so I've tried to take on some of her work too." She smiled brightly. "I hope someday I'll be able to call in the favor. You know, if I ever get married and have kids."

"That's planning in advance! Are things . . . moving that fast, with Liam?"

Katie's cheeks turned pink. "Oh, no, nothing like that. I mean, it's still early. But . . . I like him a lot."

Gin didn't want to embarrass her further, so she changed the subject. "Thanks again for being so understanding when Tuck got called in. I know you had a long afternoon ahead of you."

"Not too bad," Katie said. "We were done by four. Honestly, I wish Chief Baxter hadn't transferred. He was a lot easier to work with than certain other detectives I won't mention."

"County's loss is our gain, I suppose," Gin said diplomatically.

"It just doesn't seem fair. I mean, not that it's any of my business, but . . ." Katie looked worried. "Things are getting weird around here with that probe, and some people have suggested that Tuck might have been involved. Which is ridiculous, because, I mean, if Captain Wheeler thought he was crooked there's no way she'd transfer him. I mean, we tend to keep our head down in the lab, so you know it's bad when the gossip reaches all the way in here."

"This isn't really any of my business . . ." Gin said cautiously.

"Every bit as much your business as mine," Katie said. "Besides, this is just between us."

"I'm just wondering if Tuck really has a reason to worry," Gin blurted. "He's said a few things—nothing specific, just that he left County due to a difference of opinion." That wasn't quite right, but Gin couldn't remember the exact words he'd used. "Or a misunderstanding or . . . but he definitely gave me the impression that he hadn't done anything to merit a demotion."

"Maybe it was just a personality thing," Katie said. "I shouldn't be implying—I mean, he could have rubbed someone the wrong way."

"I guess. I mean, I'm only asking because it has a direct bearing on my work." It was the truth . . . just not the complete truth. But Gin wasn't about to tell Katie about the complicated attraction between her and the chief of police.

"Honestly, I don't know who's behind it," Katie said. She glanced out her office door, making sure there was no one in the hallway. "But Liam's got some theories."

"Oh . . . ?"

"He's convinced things are coming to a head with the IA investigation. Did you hear that Captain Wheeler's doing a press conference later today?"

"To announce the gun turn-in program, right?"

"Yes. And people are saying she's furious, that she wants to know who leaked it. That she thinks someone's trying to sabotage the investigation."

"Surely she doesn't think Tuck did . . ."

"No. But Liam thinks Tuck might know who's behind all of it."

Gin considered that for a moment. "Why does he think that?"

Katie frowned. "Look, Gin, this is all just theories, you know? Water cooler conversation."

"I understand. And it's totally fine if you don't want to talk about it—"

"No, that's just it. I *do*, I could really stand to vent to somebody. But I can't really talk to anyone around here because—well, there's this whole atmosphere of mistrust, because everyone has theories about who's behind the missing guns. Anyway, you're probably the *only* person whose name has never come up when people are speculating about who it is."

"That's got to be tough on morale," Gin said.

"Yeah, especially since it's been going on so long."

"Really? I thought it was just the last few months."

"No, it's just been in the last few months that someone noticed the discrepancy between the storage logs and what's actually in impound. Wheeler was furious because some of the records have been destroyed. They're supposed to log everything using the computer, but for stuff that they don't have a code for, sometimes they put it in the paper log and then batch process it whenever the supervisor has time to figure it out. And apparently there are a bunch of pages missing from the log from last fall." Katie looked around the forensics lab, with its bays filled with high tech equipment, and cabinets and shelves full of storage and labeling materials. "I would *never* trust our evidence to a system like that."

"Maybe someone should put a scientist in charge," Gin suggested, only half kidding. "So no one knows how long this has been happening?"

"There's this theory going around, that the gun thing is just an escalation. Do you remember last fall when there were all those copper thefts from building sites?"

"Yes—Jake was really worried about it. He and his foreman were taking turns staying on site early mornings, when the thefts were happening."

"Right, I forgot it came up in the Sigal case. Well, the thing is, witnesses said they saw a police cruiser driving slowly by the site short before several of those thefts. Like they were providing cover for whoever was coming in and stripping the copper."

"Then couldn't they just check the logs to see who was on duty those nights?"

Katie was already shaking her head. "Plenty of officers take their cars home. Or they could be rotating them out of motor pool. And anyway, those thefts stopped right around the time the problem started showing up in the impound inventory. So the theory is that whoever is responsible for stealing the missing guns, was working the smaller con before."

"But how would that work?"

"Easy. Liam says all you'd need to do would be to identify the sites and provide cover, for a cut of the profits. Any off-duty cop could do it—he'd know exactly where the real on-duty patrols were and how to avoid them. And if someone happened to question them, they could just say they were responding to a report of someone breaking in."

"So the theory is that someone inside the department saw an opportunity to make some extra cash on the side, with the copper. Then it escalated—"

"Because they got greedy. You can sell a gun for a lot more than a bunch of wire. And now Wheeler's hired temps to help the clerks going back through to inventory *everything*—because if this extends to drugs, for instance, then she's got an even bigger problem."

"Because of a public perception that she's not doing enough to combat the opiate epidemic?"

"Exactly."

"I have to say, I don't envy her."

"Yeah, you can see why she's so desperate to figure this out."

"But you said that Liam has some theories? About who's behind it?"

Katie looked distinctly uncomfortable. "Gin . . .

everyone's got theories, depending mostly on who they don't like."

"So then Bruce must be the top suspect."

Gin had been joking, but Katie looked pensive. "The thing most people don't know? And Liam only found this out because they've been partners ever since he got promoted—that's a lot of time in the car together—but Bruce worked construction for his uncle before he entered the academy. And his uncle has been in trouble before— multiple lawsuits, shoddy construction and misuse of funds and all kinds of things. He eventually went bankrupt or Bruce might never even have applied to the academy. I mean, please don't say anything. Liam doesn't want to jeopardize his job."

"Maybe that explains some things," Gin said thoughtfully.

"Like what?"

"I'm just thinking out loud, but Bruce's always had a lot of animosity toward Jake. I've never understood why . . . but maybe he hated seeing Jake succeed in a business where he didn't?"

"And add to that that Jake is, well . . . *hot*, if you don't mind me saying so," Katie said, flashing a grin. "Bruce hates to be showed up by other guys. Have you noticed how he's always putting Liam down? It's like with Tuck— before he got transferred last year, people thought he might be in line for Wheeler's job, if she runs for sheriff. And Bruce *hated* him."

"Yes, I've noticed that they don't get along, to put it mildly," Gin said. "This is all very interesting."

She considered asking if Katie had any insight into why Tuck had been moved to Trumbull, but their conversation had already entered a gray area. "I'm sorry Liam has to put up with that kind of treatment," she settled for saying.

Katie shrugged. "He just sees it as paying his dues. He's wanted to be a detective his whole life—it's his dream."

Paula Burkett popped her head in the door. "Oh, hey, Gin, didn't know you were here. They're starting the press conference, if you guys want to watch it. Come on down to the conference room, we've got it on the big screen."

"Okay, be there in a minute," Katie said. "Come with us, Gin?"

"Sure, why not?" she said. "I don't have to be at the school for a couple hours."

The forensics conference room was only large enough for a six-seat conference table, but at least double that number of people were jammed in, watching the press conference get under way. As the three women joined the others in the room, Captain Wheeler was finishing her introductory remarks.

". . . do everything we can to put an end to gun violence. The Allegheny County police department is committed to doing everything within our power to reduce the number of unlicensed firearms in our community."

She briefly described the plans for the turn-in program,

saying that drop-off sites would be set up throughout the county, with local police coordinating.

"See our web site for full details about what we will accept, and proper disposal." She glanced down at the podium and squared her notes, before removing her glasses and gazing out at the reporters crowded around the large, upstairs conference room. "I'll take a couple of questions."

Several reporters started asking questions at once.

"Any news on the Internal Affairs investigation into crooked cops?"

"Is it true that drugs seized in raids are also unaccounted for?"

"Has anyone been identified in the corruption scandal?"

"Cooper," Wheeler said, pointedly ignoring Melanie Carter, who had pushed her way to the front.

"Cooper Kincaid, WTAF. Is it true that former county homicide detective, and now Trumbull police chief Tuck Baxter has been suspended? Is he the target of an Internal Affairs investigation?"

There was a shocked murmur throughout the gathered reporters, but Wheeler showed no emotion. "No charges have been brought against Chief Baxter at this time. I can confirm only that he will be on administrative leave until the investigation has been satisfactorily closed."

Everyone started talking at once.

"Was he under suspicion last year when he left Homicide?"

"Who will run the Trumbull department while he's one leave?"

"I've asked Westmoreland County Deputy Chief Morgan King to serve as interim chief. I'm afraid that's all the time we have. Thank you and good day."

Wheeler stepped away from the podium and made her way to the exit, clearing a path through the reporters. Inside the forensics conference room, it was pandemonium, with everyone talking at once.

"Did you have any idea?" one of the analysts asked. "Your mom's the mayor, right?"

"I—no," Gin stammered, reeling from the announcement. Tuck was being suspended?—but she'd seen him just last night, and he hadn't given any indication of what was coming. And what about her mother? Had Madeleine known? "I mean, yes, but I knew nothing about this until now. I need to go. Katie, thanks for everything. I'll call you."

She raced for the door and hurried down the stairs. Tuck at the center of the corruption scandal? Gin couldn't believe it. True, he had never told her why he'd been sent to Trumbull, only that he had 'pissed some people off.'

That he should have kept his mouth shut more often.

Gin got in her car and locked the doors before calling her mother. She got the answering service; Madeleine's office was probably being flooded with calls.

She hesitated for a moment and then dialed Tuck, but that call too went straight to voice mail.

Her fingertip hovered over the screen. She wanted to

call Jake—but what would she say? All she had at this point were the same rumors and conjecture that everyone else had heard. There was no love lost between Jake and Tuck; Jake might even be happy to hear that Tuck had been relieved of his duties.

Her phone rang in her hand, making her jump.

"Hi, Brandon."

"Wow, Gin, did you know that was coming?"

"Everyone's asking me that, but I'm as shocked as anyone."

"I can't believe it's true. Baxter seems ... but then again, you never really know anyone."

"I'll be seeing my mom tonight. Maybe she'll know something by then."

"Yeah, listen, about that . . . I heard you've moved back home."

Gin pressed a hand to her forehead. "It seems like everyone knows. The grapevine in this town works overtime."

"I just wanted to say I'm sorry to hear it. I really am. And that makes me feel even worse about asking you for a favor . . ."

"It's all right—just ask, Brandon."

"Are you going to be at the school today?"

"Yes, I'm just going to grab lunch and then I'm headed over there."

"Olive's clarinet lesson got canceled. I was wondering if there's any chance you could give her and Austen a ride home."

"Of course. It's no problem at all. They're welcome to come over to the house until you get out of work."

"No, Austen has to work on his report for Spanish. I'll try to cut out a little early."

Gin said goodbye and headed toward the exit. Not a moment too soon—reporters was beginning to stream into the parking lot, setting up to record on-air reports. Melanie Carter had spotted her, and was walking toward her faster than Gin would have thought possible in her towering heels.

As she pulled out of the parking lot, she felt like she was escaping a zombie horde. She was glad to be headed to the school as a distraction. With Tuck out of a job, and Jake having beat a retreat out of town, Gin was beginning to wonder if she understood anything about men at all.

12

Gin spent the afternoon alternating between assisting in Gordon's classroom and working on her grant proposal on her laptop in the faculty lounge, but she found it difficult to concentrate, staring at the screen and reading the same words over and over. She had a faint headache which she suspected was the result of stress caused by her flashback during the autopsy. It didn't help that no fewer than three teachers stopped in to ask her if she had any more information about why Tuck Baxter had been relieved of his duties. Opinions seemed split: while most people felt he hadn't been on the job long enough to make an assessment, Colin Izzo, the math department head, was vociferous with his condemnation.

"He came in here on a promise to clean up this dump. But there's still trash in the street—the human kind *and* the rest."

"Those boarded up businesses downtown are just an invitation for trouble," another teacher chimed in.

"What I'm talking about. I saw two gangbangers out front of the hardware store, looking at lawnmowers. You want to tell me what a ghetto hood needs a lawnmower for? They don't take care of their *own* property."

Gin bit back an angry retort; Izzo had been on the faculty back when she attended the middle school herself, and he was infamous for his inflammatory politics. He'd been reprimanded for sharing them with the kids in his class; now, apparently, he just vented to his colleagues.

"Well, I think he's doing a great job," Yvette Correa, the Spanish teacher, interjected. "So's the mayor. Your mom's done a lot for this town, Gin. The new restaurants, the farmers market and the maker faire—"

Izzo snorted. "A lot of hipster nonsense, if you ask me. I'd like to see what would happen if those snowflakes had to defend themselves. They'd fold like wet cardboard."

"Okay, Colin," Natalie Bohn, the assistant principal, said wearily. "If I'm not mistaken, period five will be starting in a few minutes. How about we get back to the business of educating the kids of Trumbull?"

The teachers filed out one by one, leaving Gin alone in the room with Yvette.

"How are things going on the Girls in Science initiative?" she asked.

"Really well, thanks. I've got more interest than I

anticipated—I'm putting in an interim request to increase resources for this school year, and then looking to double it for the pilot."

"That's fantastic! Anything I can do to help, just let me know."

Gin tried to work on the proposal for a few more minutes, but made little headway. She was gathering up her things, slipping her laptop into her messenger bag, when her phone dinged a text.

She checked the screen: *Tuck*.

Can you meet? It's important.

She texted back: where and when?

Now if you can. Come on over to my place.

Gin stared at the screen for a moment before answering.

Be there in ten.

Not her wisest move, Gin reflected as she hurried to her car. In the midst of controversy and accusations, all it took was a single text from the embattled chief and she dropped everything to meet him.

One of them wasn't being rational.

* * *

When Gin knocked on the cheerful red door of Tuck's rented house on the east side of town, Cherie answered the door.

"Gin!" Cherie threw her arms around Gin and hugged her hard. Then she grabbed Gin's hand and tugged her into the house. "Dad said you were coming over to help him with his homework! Want to see my homework?"

Tuck emerged from the kitchen, drying a dish, wearing a red apron emblazoned with the words "World's Best Dad." When Gin laughed, he looked down at himself, embarrassed. "Christmas gift from one of my cousins," he admitted. "I'm cursed with having all women cousins. They seem to think I need their help or something."

Laid out on the kitchen table were a tablet, a workbook, and a plate of graham crackers spread with strawberry cream cheese. Cherie pointed excitedly at the chair across from hers. "You sit there. Dad says I have to share my snack with you."

"Only if she wants some," Tuck said mildly, going to the fridge. "Or, she can have a grownup snack with me." Her pulled out a beer and held it up to Gin. "I've also got juice boxes and some iced tea."

"I think I'll have tea, thanks," Gin said with a forced smile. Seeing Tuck here—in his kitchen, in that silly apron, with his daughter and the snack he'd made with such care—it was impossible to believe that he was mixed up in a corruption scandal. And she couldn't very well talk to him about it, or anyone else, for that matter.

"Suit yourself. Okay, Cherie, you have five minutes to

show Gin your homework and then she and I are going to my study to work on my project."

"But Dad—"

"Five minutes." He pointed up at the kitchen clock with its large hands and numerals. "Where will the big hand be?"

"On the eight," Cherie said solemnly.

True to her word, Cherie spent exactly five minutes chattering about the writing homework, which she did using a special program on her tablet that used a picture dictionary and a talking spell checker. Armed with her growing knowledge about assistive technology, Gin recognized the value of the tool for students like Cherie.

"I hope you're going to join my science club at school," she said.

"When is it starting?"

"Not until next year," Gin said. "I'm going to spend the summer working on it. But I might get to use Mr. Gordon's classroom—won't that be fun?"

"Yes!" Cherie said, jumping up from her chair and spinning around. "Amanda is my partner. She likes planets!"

"Somebody's a little excited," Tuck observed. "Okay, missy, how about you get back to your work and after Gin and I are done, you can help me shuck the corn."

"I love shucking corn!"

Gin followed Tuck to the spare bedroom, which he'd furnished with an old, scarred wooden desk and a couple of rolling chairs that looked like they'd come from a secondhand office supply store. On the wall were family photographs, his diploma from Penn State, several awards from the County Police, and at least half a dozen framed pieces of colorful art that Gin assumed had been created by Cherie.

"She was considering being an artist," he said, following her gaze, "until you got her all stirred up on this science thing. Now she wants to do experiments."

Gin smiled, for real this time. She decided to follow her instincts, as she should have from the start. "You know, Tuck . . . that apron is appropriate. You really are an amazing dad. Especially considering you're doing it alone."

"I'd like to take credit . . . but the truth is there's a whole network of people looking out for Cherie. She's fine on her own for a few hours at a time, but Mrs. Hill comes three afternoons a week to keep her company and make sure she's doing her homework. And those meddlesome cousins of mine are constantly coming down on the weekends to make sure I'm not screwing up. And . . . there's you."

"I—I only do what any friend would," Gin stammered, as he gazed at her with an inscrutable expression. And then, because the conversation was leading into a direction she wasn't sure she was ready to go, she said briskly, "So that was some news conference today. Want to tell me what's going on?"

"Yeah, well, that's why I asked you to come over. Sorry about that, by the way—I would have asked you to meet somewhere more civilized, but Cherie—"

"No need to apologize," Gin said firmly. "You know I'm fond of her."

"Okay. Uh, well, I was hoping to get out in front of this with you—" Tuck glared past her at a fixed point on the wall, tipping back in his chair and crossing his arms over his chest. "And Wheeler was hoping it wouldn't come up, I mean, the part about me, which was probably naïve on her part—anyway, I would have rather been the one to tell you . . . ah, hell." He let the chair legs slam down on the floor in exasperation as Gin realized that he was *embarrassed*. Not an emotion she'd ever seen him display before. "This damn investigation. I didn't do anything wrong. And for some reason it's been really bothering me that you might think I had."

"Oh," Gin said. She wasn't about to admit that she'd wondered, not now. "Is there . . . anything more you can tell me?"

"Unfortunately not," Tuck said. "Truth is, I'm not surprised by the suspension. I figured it was just a matter of when. I was just hoping that it would all wrap up before it caught up with me."

"You're not making a lot of sense. The other day you said you felt like you were under close scrutiny by Captain Wheeler," Gin said. "But I thought you were just worried that you wouldn't make it past the six-month provisional period. And besides, if you haven't done anything wrong—"

"Yeah. Right. But that's the part I can't really discuss. So I guess admin leave is preferable to getting canned, since if—when—I'm reinstated it means I'm permanent." Tuck picked up his beer and took a long swallow. "Anyway, I can't say much more right now, not even to you, even though I'd like to. All I can say is, there's more to the story than what you're probably hearing. And I'd like to ask for your trust."

"Tuck—are you in trouble? I mean, leaving aside the question of what you did or didn't do, are you being forced out? Does someone have it in for you?" Gin knew she shouldn't ask—and that he wouldn't tell her anyway. But if he lost his job, that would mean he'd most likely move. Which was something she definitely didn't want to happen.

"Depends on what you consider trouble. I've still got a paycheck coming in, and if I end up getting let go, I've got some savings. And as far as public perception goes— well, I've never won any popularity contests. The people who think I'm guilty of something now, already thought so before."

"It's just that . . . I was talking to Katie Kennedy. She seems to think the IA investigation goes deeper than people think."

"Really?" Tuck asked impassively. "How so?"

"Well, she said there's a theory that whoever was behind the copper thefts last year might have been assisted by someone in the department. One of the officers. And that he got greedy and decided he could make more money by switching from copper to guns . . . and maybe even drugs." She adjusted her skirt uncomfortably. "Look, I'm not asking you to confirm that."

"Gin. Do you seriously think I could be involved with

all of this? I mean, I'll admit that the timing doesn't look too good for me . . . if I really was behind the copper thefts, or this gun business, but they couldn't put together the proof, it could have made sense for them to ship me out here to the hinterlands while they investigated. But I'm giving you my word."

"Hinterlands?"

"The more remote part of the county. Whatever. Look, that's all I'm going to say about it, for now. When I was up in the city the other day, HR had me sign all kinds of paperwork that I'm pretty sure forbids me from talking about anything to anyone ever again. I'm probably violating that by sitting here shooting the shit with you."

"Tuck!" Gin said, alarmed. Now that she'd made a decision to trust him, she wished he was doing more in his own defense. "You seem to be awfully cavalier about all of this. If talking to me could truly threaten your job, then—"

Tuck shrugged. "I can handle it."

Gin stared at him in disbelief. "How, exactly? I mean, I get that your charisma and charm have probably kept you out of trouble until now—"

"Hey," Tuck objected, his mouth twisting up in a grin. "No need for sarcasm."

"—but I do know something about local politics, and even Captain Wheeler won't be able to help if this goes too far. Not to mention she's got some pretty lofty ambitions. What makes you think you can count on her support if popular opinion goes against you?"

"I said I'd handle it," Tuck drawled, his jaw set.

Gin was all too familiar with the sort of male stubbornness that set in when some men felt cornered: like a trapped wild animal, they'd lash out at attempts to help while digging themselves further and further into trouble.

"No," Gin said, "that's ridiculous. I understand you can't tell me the details, but you *can* let me help. There's got to be something I can do to clear your name, at least in the court of public opinion."

"Ha. Yeah, well, I don't give a fuck what anyone thinks of me—all I care about is getting my damn job done. The longer I'm sidelined, the worse it's going to be for the department—we've already been playing catchup with the caseload since Sheriff Crosby's death, and an interim chief isn't going to help matters."

"You're going to have to trust Wheeler on that one," Gin said. "Mom says she has confidence in Morgan King. He can keep the admin side running while you're away. And as for your current caseload . . . well, maybe I can help."

Tuck raised one eyebrow skeptically. "Look, we always seem to get here—you defending Crosby after he brings trouble on himself. His mother's death is—sorry to say—pretty open and shut. It's the John Doe case that's really going to suffer. I'd like to pin this on Bruce, but the truth is that we've got so little to go on, with their backlog, it's just going to fall through the cracks. And I hate to see that." He blew out a frustrated breath. "Turns out I'm kind of attached to this place, and I'm pretty goddamn unhappy to have mangled corpses popping up, even if it isn't on my watch."

Gin rolled her eyes. "What did you think I meant when I said I could help?"

Tuck regarded her steadily. "Yeah? Why would you want to do that? Seriously, Gin, you did your thing, I'm sure you were thorough, but unfortunately whoever hacked up our guy is just a few steps ahead of you. But more importantly, why do you care? It's not like you don't have other cases of your own, other things to do with your time. And if I understand your contract, you get paid whether the killer's found or not."

"Humor me," Gin said in a steely voice, but as the silence between them stretched into a staring contest, she realized she was going to have to offer him a little more. Like the truth—at least part of it.

"Okay, you win," she said, relenting. "I have my own reasons for wanting to see this one through. Something happened when I was in the theater—when Stephen was making his examination. I had a—a—well, I guess you could call it a flashback of sorts. Without going into too much detail, the, uh . . ." For the second time in a day, her voice broke as she described the mutilated wrists, the moment it had brought back, from her time in Srebrenica. She tried to stay as dispassionate as possible, but by the time she had finished explaining in as few words as possible, Tuck had reached for her hand.

And she didn't pull away.

"I don't know how you got through it," he said hoarsely. "I can't even begin to tell you how I admire your guts. Your generosity."

Gin shook her head impatiently. "Then don't. Just trust me instead. I think what I need—what would help me the most—is to stay focused on finding out what happened to this guy. Because, see, the worst thing for all of us in Srebrenica wasn't dealing with the bodies." She closed her eyes, remembering. "It was the families who were desperate for answers. For closure. For a chance to bury their dead with all the love and respect they deserved."

Tuck said nothing; when she opened her eyes again, he looked thoughtful, his eyes clouded. "I don't have to tell you that you can never bring them back."

"No. But I can give the families—not what they want, nobody can do that. But maybe a little of what they need."

They sat in silence for a moment, Gin's hand cradled in Tuck's large one. Finally he cleared his throat. "Gin . . . I don't think—it can't be healthy, to keep reliving the trauma of losing your sister, over and over."

"That's not what I'm trying to do," Gin said sharply. Then she took a breath: he was only trying to help, and she knew that he couldn't—no one could—understand what she and her family had gone through: the years of torment and waiting, not knowing what had become of Lily. This was what she wanted to save other families from.

"I'm sorry I reacted like that," she said, trying again. "It's just that—look, I've seen more cold case victims than you ever will. As frustrating as it is to be unable to identify them or put together what happened to them when they wind up on my table, it's a walk in the park compared to what their loved ones are going through. I mean sure, there are people in this world who have no one—who die alone, with no friends or family to their name. But it also happens that people simply disappear, and that means that there are mothers and fathers out there, siblings and spouses, friends and children who will never know what happened." She swallowed hard. "It happened to us. So I know how it feels."

"Gin—"

"No, please let me finish," Gin said, not looking at him. "I thought I was doing good work in Srebrenica, trying to bring justice to those who were butchered. But I think the most important thing we did, looking back on it, was to bring the families a little peace. That John Doe on my table—maybe his family has no idea that he ended up like that. Maybe they're not even aware his body went missing. But if not, then they need my help. So I'm going to keep on this, whether you approve or not. But you might as well help me out. For both of us."

Tuck simply stared at her for a long moment. "Damn, girl," he finally said. "I think you're more stubborn than me. All right. I'm in."

Gin's shoulders sagged with relief; she hadn't been aware how invested she had already become. But before she could respond, Tuck held up his hand warningly. "Let's get one thing straight, though—no going off half-cocked on this. I may have my wings clipped, but I'm still a cop and you're still a headstrong woman who's as short on common sense as you are easy on the eyes. No offense. So the deal is, you don't make a move before checking with me. Got it?"

Gin knew he was baiting her, but she didn't miss the smile tugging at his mouth. He needed to be involved as badly as she did.

"I'm not making any promises," she said crisply. "But I will do my best to keep you apprised, as long as you do the same."

"No promises from me either," Tuck said, holding her gaze. "So I guess we're going to have to trust each other."

He reached for his laptop and spun the large screen on his desk so that Gin could see: an aerial view of a wooded area. He tapped the screen for emphasis.

"Okay, let's start with this. Bruce and Liam went out and interviewed the man who owns that cabin. Or rather, the cabin belongs to a Mortimer Walker, but considering that he's almost eighty years old, the guy Bruce talked to is more likely to be his son, Keith. He's a recreational hunter from Pittsburgh who mostly uses it on the weekends. Single guy, in his early forties, owns his own business. I looked him up and couldn't find any red flags: no priors, no outstanding parking tickets, lots of friends, active online—he even signed up for an online dating site using his real name. I mean, who does that? Guy's an open book. He was cooperative, apparently genuinely wanted to help, but he couldn't give them anything solid so they concluded it was a dead end. I learned all this right before I officially got escorted out, so as you can imagine, there goes any access I have to information."

"They've got the case now, and you're not even allowed on the sidelines . . . is that the deal?"

"Yeah. Bruce is probably sticking pins in his voodoo doll of me right now—best thing to happen to him all year, not having to give me anything. What we need is access to this guy—just a chance to feel him out, get a sense of what he knows. Only the minute I show up he'll know something's off, since they already talked to him. And if it got back to County . . ." He drew his finger across his throat.

"So you can't even talk to him informally, off the record."

"Uh-uh. And we're not likely to get anything else out of Jonah. As of eleven this morning, when I walked out the door with my ass handed to me, Jonah Krischer's father had threatened a lawsuit naming not just Jake, and me, and Garrett Liu, but everyone all the way up the chain including Wheeler herself. Nobody thinks he'd get any traction—that video Jake took was about as clear as it could be—but there's a chance the judge won't allow it in if this goes to trial. A pretty good chance. So now they're treating Jonah like a dead end."

"But his story doesn't add up all the way," Gin said, trying not to get stuck on the possibility that Jake was going to be involved in a lawsuit. "He says he was running down there and 'just happened' to find the body. But he would have had to have deliberately removed at least some of the branches to be able to even see it. Why would he do that?"

"He said he saw the plastic trash bag sticking out . . ."

"Yes, but that doesn't make sense. Why would that have caught his eye? It's black, it blends in with the dirt. And there was other debris in the creek, anyway. He was running along, passing food wrappers, water bottles, that broken tackle box, but none of that caught his attention. He didn't even mention it, right? So a piece of black plastic, that would have probably faded into the background even if the branches weren't there—I just don't believe it."

"It would if it seemed out of place," Tuck said. "A bag from a fast food joint, you'd expect to see that. But a large black trash bag? Why would it be out in the woods?"

"Tuck, I've run there dozens of times. You're moving too quickly to process or even notice something like that—unless he'd literally stopped long enough to search for something out of place."

"Are you suggesting that he put it there himself?"

"I'm only suggesting that he didn't find it the way he said. Beyond that—I've got no idea. But it's a loose thread that seems significant."

Tuck said nothing for a moment, frowning. "I'll give you that," he finally said. "It does seem unlikely. If it was me, I'd lean harder on the kid, maybe lock him in a room with nothing but a stack of religious tracts and the Dreamgirls soundtrack on an endless loop until he remembers something. But I doubt Bruce will make the effort. Listen, are you sure there was nothing else from the autopsy? Nothing that could give us a place to start?"

"Nothing stood out." She went over the main findings of the autopsy, including her opinion that the brittleness of the bones meant that the body had been in a dry environment for quite a while. "There were a few things that might point to a condition called acromegaly," she conceded. "But it's non-life-threatening and even if the John Doe had it, he may not have known."

"So, you got squat." Tuck got up from his chair and started pacing. "Which is even more reason to be following up other leads. I keep coming back to the guy who owns the cabin—maybe he saw something that he didn't think was important at the time, maybe he could take a look at the photos and see something that we're not."

Gin thought for a moment. "You can't talk to him," she said slowly. "But what about me? I could use an assumed name, so he couldn't trace it back to the department."

"Oh, right. You going to go knock on his door, pretend you're selling encyclopedias? It's a little harder than it looks, Ace."

Gin bit back a retort, but Tuck's casual dismissal had the effect of emboldening her. "You said he's dating, right? Well, I'm single. What site was it?"

Tuck raised his eyebrows. "Why, which one are *you* on? Never mind, forget I asked." He tapped at his keyboard for a moment, and a dating profile came up featuring a bearded man in a Pirates ball cap with laugh lines and an appealing smile.

"He doesn't look like a killer," Gin observed. "Okay, let's create a profile for me and see if I can catch his eye."

Tuck stared at her. "Are you serious? This isn't an

episode of Scooby-Doo, Gin. I agree there's nothing overtly threatening about him, but you're not even—"

"Are you going to do this, or do I need to go home and do it myself? It's just a date—in a public place, okay? A chance to feel him out, which is what you said you needed. And meanwhile you can take on the prescription drug abuse angle and see what you can turn up. And then we can meet back here at the clubhouse and compare notes."

"Clubhouse?" Tuck echoed, shaking his head, but he was already typing. "Do me a favor, send me a selfie—a sexy one, if you've got it."

Gin felt her face flame but thumbed through her photos until she found a flattering one her mother had taken of her and her father when they'd gone out for brunch. "You'll have to crop my Dad out," she said, texting it to him.

"No problem. Can you check on Cherie while I set this up?"

Gin left him to it and joined Cherie at the table. Twenty minutes later, after pouring her some more juice and helping her with her phonetics homework, she returned to the office to find Tuck with his feet up on the desk, grinning triumphantly.

"With this profile, you could get George Clooney to ask you out," he said, moving out of the way so she could pull her chair closer. "I should be a yenta."

"Sure, if this cop thing doesn't work out," Gin said, squinting at the screen.

"Better yet, Keith is online now, *and* you just winked at him. You also sent him a nice note complimenting his profile."

"I did?" Gin tried to hide the trepidation she felt; after chatting with Cherie, some of her determination had dissipated, replaced by second thoughts.

"Sure. In addition to hunting, Keith listed his interests as listening to live music, campfires, cooking together, and exploring the country in his RV. Hell, maybe *I* should date him."

"Is that right," Gin said, distracted by the profile Tuck had created for her. She had to admit that he'd done a remarkably good job in such a short time: under her photo, which he'd cropped and enhanced to bring out her smile, she read that Beth Conway was a thirty-two-year-old medical device consultant who enjoyed singing in her church choir and volunteering at the animal shelter. "What else did you learn about him?"

Before he could answer, a ping indicated a new message in "Beth's" inbox. "He took the bait!" Tuck exclaimed. "Let's see. 'Hello Beth, thank you for your note. I've looked at your profile and feel we have a lot in common. Would you be interested in meeting for coffee?'" He glanced at Gin, winking. "Coffee, eh? No sir, we don't have time for that . . ."

For the next few moments his fingers flew over the keyboard. Gin tried to read over his shoulder, but he batted her away.

"Tuck—come on, you have no idea how a woman

would respond." *That* came out wrong. There was another ding—Tuck and Keith Walker were apparently in a full-on conversation. Gin tried again. "What are you telling him? Listen, if you stray too far from the truth I'll never be able to—"

"Just give me a minute," Tuck said impatiently.

Gin gave up and let him work, sitting back in her chair and wondering if she'd taken leave of her senses. But in a few more minutes Tuck hit send and spun around in his chair, a grin on his face.

"You, Beth Conway, are meeting Keith for a drink tomorrow night. Your schedule was too full to do coffee this week and naturally the weekend was out of the question, because you're serving meals at a homeless shelter and going to a watercolor painting class, but luckily you had an opening tomorrow." Tuck gave her a wicked grin. "And just in case you're getting cold feet—you're single now, you should be getting yourself out there anyway."

"I think you're enjoying this way too much. Besides, Jake and I are—we're just taking a break." But her voice wavered on the words. "And I'll never be able to remember all those lies."

"Everyone lies on their profile," Tuck said. "No big. You should see some of the women I've met for coffee. Wouldn't have been able to pick them out of a crowd based on the photos they used—most of them seem to be twenty years out of date."

"But you told him I was thirty-two." Gin protested. "I'm thirty-nine."

"So? You could pass for ten years younger, not that it matters—I personally like some miles on a woman. Trust me, this guy is going to be counting his lucky stars and trying to figure out how he can get you over to his place."

"Ugh . . . is that your MO?"

"A gentleman doesn't kiss and tell," Tuck said. "But since we're being all touchy-feely here . . . the truth is that most women seem to find that they're too busy for a second date once they find out about Cherie. Their loss."

Gin didn't notice the faint hint of bitterness in his voice. How frustrating it must be—and what a mistake the women were making. Tuck's obvious love and devotion to Cherie were an asset, in Gin's mind. Once you got past his flippant, abrasive exterior, there was a kind, generous, dependable man . . . with a broad chest and rock-hard shoulders that didn't exactly hurt, either.

She cleared her throat. "The right woman won't be put off by that—she'll see you for what you are."

Tuck's gaze held hers, the unspoken question in the air between them: what did *she* see when she looked at him?

Another ding interrupted the charged moment. Tuck clicked on the inbox. "Great news . . . the gentleman suggests Drake's Tavern at seven. I hear they do a pretty good grilled snapper."

"It's just drinks," Gin reminded him. "So. I guess I should go home and, um . . ."

"Wash your hair," Tuck said wryly. "Shave your legs. Do your nails."

"All that, for a faux date?"

"You'll want to be convincing. Maybe you should buy a new dress or something. Something red and tight."

"I hardly think that's necessary when all I'm trying to get is an impression of Keith Walker."

"Yeah, use your feminine intuition. Is this a guy who could dig up a body and haul it back behind his cabin and bury it? Does he seem to have problems in other areas of his life—debts, gambling problem, grudges . . . that sort of thing. By the end of your date, I'd just like to be able to cross him off my list." He sighed. "Which we could already have done if Bruce wasn't too afraid of a damn pasty-ass doctor with a temper and a lawyer on retainer to conduct a proper investigation."

"Tuck . . ." Gin ventured, remembering her conversation with Katie. "Do you think Bruce . . . I mean, he's so scornful of people, even his closest colleagues. Every time I'm around him, he violates at least one HR guideline. I know you don't want to talk to me about what's going on in County, but I feel like it's not much of a stretch to think he'd see an opportunity to make some cash and take it."

"Bruce is a dick," Tuck said. "No doubt about it. And if it ends up to be him, I'll make a special trip up to the city just for the pleasure of watching him get taken away in cuffs. But I'm telling you the truth when I say I don't have any proof that it's him."

"That sounds like double-speak. What you're saying is that you don't have any proof that exonerates him either."

Tuck drank the rest of the beer and crushed the can in his fist, regarding her thoughtfully. "You're not very good at this game, Gin. You don't put all your cards on the table in the first round."

His voice had dropped, and his gaze drifted down to her neck, and Gin remembered the night last winter when, standing under a streetlight in the drifting snow, he'd almost kissed her.

Luckily, Cherie burst into the room, breaking the awkward silence. "Aren't you guys done yet?" she yelled. "Want to help with the corn, Gin?"

"I'd love to, Cherie, but I need to go home and have dinner with *my* parents."

"Oh," Cherie said seriously. "Do you have a mom *and* a dad?"

"I do," Gin admitted, hoping she hadn't brought up a painful subject. In a strange parallel to Jake's situation, Cherie's mother was an alcoholic who signed away her rights to her child after she was born and had no contact with Cherie or Tuck.

"I just have a dad. But he's twice as good as regular dads so it's okay!" She gave her father a high-five, and he pretended that it hurt, moaning and letting his hand flap uselessly.

"Don't forget," Tuck said. "Tomorrow night at seven at Drake's Tavern. Wear something pretty. And wear your hair down, with the curls or whatever."

"Are you going on a date with my dad?" Cherie asked, looking very surprised.

"No, not at all."

"She's going to meet a new friend. A man."

"Oh, okay. Maybe you'll marry him, Gin!

"Maybe," Tuck said, taking her firmly by the shoulder and steering her out of the room, "we should get started on that corn."

13

When Gin got home, Richard was peering over his glasses at one of Madeleine's old cookbooks. He'd only begun cooking recently, after Jake put him to work in the kitchen one night and taught him how to prep the ingredients, and Richard discovered that he enjoyed it.

"Boef bourguignon tonight, honey," Richard said. "You and your mom are in for a real treat."

Laid out on the kitchen island were a marbled slab of beef, two yellow onions, and a package of mushrooms. Dinner, if past experience was any indication, was still potentially hours away as Richard made his slow, methodical way through the recipe.

If she hurried, Gin could drive over and be back before her dad put the meal on the table. In the kitchen, she found Richard holding up a mushroom, frowning. "How on earth do I stem a mushroom? All of these already have stems."

Gin laughed. "I'm going to go check my email, Dad. Let me know if you need help."

"I'm offended!" Richard called after her as she went up the stairs.

As she opened the door to her room, something caught her attention—a faint, unfamiliar chemical smell on the breeze that fluttered the lace curtains in the bedroom window. As Gin put her hand on the light switch, she hesitated—hadn't she left the windows closed earlier, because the forecast included a chance of rain? Her heart thudding, she turned on the light.

And gasped. All around the perimeter of the room, random slashes of red paint dripped down the walls. It was still wet, dripping onto the carpet, slopping onto her dresser and the framed watercolors her mother had hung so many years ago. Gin searched for a pattern, but the marks formed no words, no images . . . it was almost as if someone had flung the paint straight from the can.

And then left through the open window. Gin raced across the room and leaned out, her hands sliding in the paint puddled on the sill. Sure enough, there were smudges of paint on the shingles of the dormer—and an empty paint can near the gutter. As she watched, a gust of wind tipped it over and it rolled, almost leisurely, to the edge and then fell with a soft plop onto the lawn below.

Gin hastily wiped the paint on her shirt before realizing that she would ruin it. She ran to the bathroom, her mind racing, anxious to get out of the soiled clothes, to rinse the paint from her hands. The sense of violation was overwhelming. She needed to leave the room, preserve any evidence, call the police, take care not to alarm her father—but first she needed to remove all traces of the vile act from her skin and clothes.

After scrubbing until her hands and forearms were pink and stuffing the ruined shirt into the trash and knotting the bag closed, she took a deep breath and went back down the stairs. Her mother had come home in her absence and was sitting at the counter with a glass of wine, laughing at something Richard had said. Seeing Gin's expression, Madeleine's expression immediately changed.

"What's wrong?"

"Nothing, Mom, everything's fine." Gin forced a weak smile. "But we seem to have had an uninvited visitor."

"What do you mean?" Richard asked, setting down the grater and the hunk of parmesan he was holding.

"It's . . . everything's fine, all right, so please don't panic, but I'm going to call Tuck. I think someone broke into my room."

Madeleine looked aghast. "If that's true, he could still be in the house! Shouldn't you call nine-one-one?"

But Tuck's phone was already ringing, and besides, the upstairs had felt entirely empty and still. Whoever had splashed the paint, he or she had retreated.

"Hiya sunshine, did you miss me?" Tuck answered jovially.

Gin could hear Cherie in the background, singing along with the television. "I'm sorry to bother you at home, and—maybe I should call the station. Someone's broken into the house. My, uh, room actually."

"Where are you now?" Tuck said, his tone instantly hard and terse. "Did you see the intruder?"

"We're downstairs in the kitchen. Dad's cooking." Gin felt a little silly. "It's just a little paint . . . red paint."

"I'm on my way. If you hear anything, leave the house. Don't go back upstairs. I'll be there in ten."

"Thanks, Tuck," Gin said, but he'd already hung up.

"He's on his way," she told her parents, who were staring at her openmouthed. "It's just . . . a prank or something. Kids, maybe. They splashed a little paint."

"Paint?" Madeleine echoed. "Was there a message?"

"No, no message."

"I'm going to check the yard," Richard said, yanking off his apron.

"Dad, please wait for Tuck," Gin pleaded. "Let him handle this." She didn't want to say it, but the idea of her father going up against an intruder frightened her. Richard was in excellent shape for his age, but there was no way to know who had done this.

Someone with an axe to grind. Someone affected by Gin's consulting work—perhaps a relative or friend of a suspect who Gin had helped identify in one of the county's recent forensic investigations.

Or someone trying to discourage her from digging deeper in a current one.

Her mind flashed to the unidentified body in the

morgue . . . to the cabin in the woods where it had been buried. She thought of Jonah, frightened and incapacitated on Jake's floor, and of his father raging in front of the police station.

"Did he go in any of the other rooms?" Madeleine asked, twisting her hands together.

"I didn't check, Mom, I'm sorry. I'm sure Tuck will check them all out." She didn't share her intuition that this was directed solely at her. "Let's just sit down and stay calm until Tuck gets here."

Richard topped off Madeleine's glass of wine and wordlessly poured one for Gin. They'd barely sat down when there was a knock at the door and both Madeleine and Richard jumped up to answer it.

"I'll get it," Gin said hurriedly. "You guys relax."

She opened the door and discovered that it had started to rain in the time since she had been upstairs; Tuck was standing in the drizzle, wearing a windbreaker over the T-shirt he'd had on earlier. His expression was hard. "Show me."

She led him up the stairs; he muttered a greeting to her parents as they passed. The room was just as she'd left it: the curtains fluttering, the paint still glistening in places. She noticed something she had missed before: the vase of cut flowers that her mother had left on the dresser lay on the floor, the water puddling out, the flowers crushed.

Tuck went to the wall and dabbed at the paint, held it to his nose. "Latex, is my guess," he said. "Other than the color, it looks like ordinary paint. It can't have been here more than an hour or so. None of you heard anything? Saw anything?"

"I just got home right before I called you. And mom got here after me. Dad's been in the kitchen—and he's a little hard of hearing."

Tuck nodded. "Go back downstairs. I'm going to clear the rest of the house. You know that technically I shouldn't even be here—but I'll get someone over here to dust for prints. I don't need to tell you it's a long shot."

Gin remembered the can that had rolled off the roof. "The paint can's out on the lawn. Do you want me to bring it in?"

"No, leave it for now." He was already on his phone, and he spoke quietly to the dispatcher as he walked into the hall.

Gin wanted to follow him, but she knew her parents had questions—and worries. Reluctantly, she went downstairs to keep them company.

"Tuck called someone in to see if they can get fingerprints," she said. "They'll be here soon."

"I'm sorry, Dad," Gin said, deciding it was best to acknowledge what they weren't saying. *Obviously I don't know who did this, but given the work I do . . .*

"Makes me wonder if this damn gun turn-in of your mother's is a good idea," Richard muttered. "I'd like to get ahold of whoever did this—"

"Let's not get ahead of ourselves," Gin chided.

Tuck came back down the stairs, looking at his phone. "All clear up there. I took a few pictures but Max will take more when he gets here. So. No thoughts on who it might have been?"

"None," Madeleine said. "I mean, there's a few council members and contractors who I've had words with, but nothing that would spur something like this."

Tuck shot Gin a glance; his meaning seemed clear: they'd talk later, out of her parents' presence.

Richard cleared his throat. "Can I offer you something to drink? I realize you probably won't have wine, but shall I make some coffee?"

"No, sir, I'm fine. I think it's best that we focus on getting this processed and cleaned up so you folks can get some rest tonight."

* * *

Nearly two hours later, Gin finally joined her parents downstairs after cleaning up as much as she could, and putting clean sheets on the bed in the room next door. Tomorrow she would make some calls to get someone in to replace the damaged carpet and repaint; Madeleine had already suggested they take the opportunity to finally replace the old furniture. Glad to see her mother's attention focused on something other than the intrusion, Gin had agreed.

But for the foreseeable future, she would be living in Lily's old room, with the white painted furniture and the sunny yellow walls, the holes still in the walls from the posters that her sister had hung.

Downstairs, lights burned in every room. Her parents

were sitting in the living room, but seeing her, Richard jumped up.

"Sweetheart. Come and relax. Your mother set out some snacks."

"She doesn't want to eat," Madeleine scolded, patting the sofa next to her. Indeed, the platter of cheese, bread, and sliced apples on the coffee table was untouched. "She's been through a traumatic event. We all have."

"Then a glass of wine," Richard said. "Or maybe sherry?"

"Thanks, Dad, but I'm fine," Gin said. "Or I will be, anyway."

"Honey, are you sure I can't fix you a plate?" Richard asked.

"No . . . actually, I think I'm going to head upstairs in a minute. I'm exhausted. I just wanted to say goodnight."

But after she'd kissed them both, washed her face and brushed her teeth, and slipped into an old nightgown she'd found in the back of one of the dresser drawers, she got into Lily's narrow bed and stared at her phone, suddenly longing to call Jake.

She didn't even know exactly where he was staying, only that his client had offered him the use of a corporate apartment near the job site. Gin's fingers hovered over her phone, as she tried to compose a text that would let him know what had happened—but she got stuck when she thought about her motivation for contacting him.

She felt unnerved and scared and needed a friend—but Jake wasn't a friend, exactly. He was both more and less, now that he'd put their relationship on hold, and as much as she missed talking to him, it wouldn't be appropriate to reach out to him now. Not if she had any hope of accepting that it could be ending, that she might have to move on. She'd been hoping that he'd call, even just to talk, to say he missed her; but as his silence stretched, it was starting to feel like he was really gone for good.

There was one other person Gin thought about calling, one other person who knew everything she had been through and had already provided her a measure of comfort. Someone who could help her navigate her emotions and convince her that she was safe.

As she was reminding herself of all the reasons it would be a terrible idea, the phone rang. Gin stared at Tuck's name on the screen, marveling at the coincidence—it was as though she'd summoned the call merely by thinking about him. Finally, after three rings, she answered.

"Hello?"

"Everyone doing okay there?"

"Yes. Thank you again for—for everything. And Max, too. He was so considerate, especially with my parents."

"Yeah. I'm sure he'll call tomorrow if anything comes up from the prints, but I'm not holding my breath."

"Thank you," Gin repeated.

Tuck exhaled audibly. "I'm concerned about you going alone to meet Keith Walker tomorrow night. I think you should call it off."

"That doesn't make any sense, Tuck. We'll be in a public restaurant, with people all around. He doesn't even know my real name."

"Okay. Here's the thing. And don't give me any shit about being sexist or—or any of that PC crap. Can we agree that what happened tonight changes things?"

"I don't see why," Gin retorted, "given that there's no reason to think it's related."

"It's not unrelated. Maybe. Probably."

Gin smiled despite herself. Tuck didn't seem to be aware that concern made him stumble over his words. "That was some very strange logic. You're worried about me meeting a man for a date, in a crowded public restaurant. The worst that could happen is he could throw a dinner roll at me."

"Whatever. The only way you're going through with this if I'm there too."

"That's—I don't—you can't tell me what to do." She tried again. "But if you do insist on showing up, you'd better stay out of the way."

"Gin. I've worked as an undercover cop." Tuck sounded exasperated. "I think I can manage to sit at the bar and drink a beer without attracting attention. I'm trained for this—I could check out your ass all day long without anyone knowing it."

"I guess we'll see." How was it that conversations with Tuck always seemed to end up leaving her feeling unmoored?

"Okay. Well." Tuck cleared his throat. "I hear someone who should be asleep tiptoeing around her bedroom, so . . ."

"Good night, Tuck."

Gin hung up the phone and turned out the lamp on her bedside table. The soft glow of the moon filtered through the eyelet curtains hanging in the window of her sister's childhood bedroom.

When she closed her eyes, she could almost pretend that Lily was asleep next to her.

14

It was only a nightmare, obviously, but while it was happening, it had felt so terribly real.

Lily, at the end of a long tunnel, calling out to her. Gin was trying to reach her, but the faster she ran, the more distant Lily seemed to become, the tunnel twisting and changing, its outlines shrouded in mist. She was cold, so cold, but she knew that where Lily was it was colder still, and she looked so thin and frail in the gauzy white dress that floated around her body. Over and over Lily called her name, but her voice grew more and more distant, no matter how hard Gin tried to get to her.

And then she woke. The room was still dark, and she could hear rain falling gently onto the roof. She glanced at the clock: nearly five. Before long, Madeleine would be up and in the shower; Richard would follow soon after that. Their home would come alive, and Gin would welcome the activity, the proof that they were all still here, all still safe.

* * *

She was pulling into the morgue parking lot by seven thirty, having avoided the worst of the traffic. Madeleine had filled a travel mug with coffee for her and told her not to worry about calling contractors; she said it helped her cope to have a task to throw herself into, and had already arranged to meet with the designer who'd helped her with the kitchen remodel.

"I'll bring back paint chips and sample books for us to look through," she promised.

"Oh, no. Do you think they'll declare a city emergency when you don't show up?" Gin teased, glad her mother had found a distraction.

"They can muddle through without me for a day," Madeleine had declared. "Even the mayor needs to play hooky now and then."

Now that Gin had arrived at work, she too planned to keep herself busy today. Her first stop was a visit to Paula Burkett's office in the forensics lab. For once, she was glad that Katie wasn't in yet.

"I was wondering if I could talk to you . . . privately, for a few minutes," Gin said uncomfortably.

"Of course," the CSI tech said, standing and maneuvering the swell of her belly around her desk so that she could shut the door. "Is everything all right?"

"Yes. I mean mostly. It, um . . ." Gin was uncharacteristically at a loss for words. "Well, I think some past trauma has caught up with me. I'm having nightmares, and a little trouble focusing. And, well, I know you know a lot about this."

Paula had met her partner, Angie, in an IMPACT self-defense class. Among other things, the class was lauded for empowering those who had suffered abuse and trauma, and Paula was pursuing certification to become a teacher.

"I don't know about that," Paula said, "but I'm happy to listen. And of course whatever you tell me will stay between us."

"Okay." Gin took a deep breath, then described the nightmare she had, and her memories of her work in the mass graves. "I think it was triggered by seeing the John Doe left in the ground like—like garbage. I can't stop thinking about his family."

"That makes sense," Paula said, putting her hand on Gin's arm. "What a terrible thing to have gone through. I wonder, though . . . it was a desire to help families that sent you overseas in the first place. Is it possible that that same desire to help might be the key to healing?"

"That's exactly what I've been thinking," Gin said, feeling a rush of relief at being able to talk to someone about it. "I just—with everything going on, I wasn't sure I could trust my instincts."

"Well, I'm no substitute for a qualified therapist," Paula cautioned. "But I'm sure you're familiar with exposure therapy and the theory that facing past experiences in a safe setting can help one move past them."

"My parents probably wouldn't call my current situation 'safe,' unfortunately." Gin briefly described the paint splashed by the intruder. "But I feel that it's more important for me to face this than to retreat, especially because—because," she finished awkwardly. She had been about to say, because Tuck was available whenever she felt threatened, but given the fact that Paula was employed by the county and Tuck had been suspended, it felt unwise to mention that.

"That *is* alarming," Paula said. "Please be safe—and let me know if there's anything I can do to help, okay? And . . . and maybe make an appointment with a therapist. If you don't mind me suggesting that."

Gin squeezed Paula's hand. "That's a good idea. I'll definitely make some calls. Listen, Paula, I appreciate you speaking to me so frankly."

"I'm just happy I was here to listen. I had been thinking of going on maternity leave early, but now with us being so short-staffed, I'm going to stay on as long as I can to help out until they can hire new staff."

"You've got to take care of yourself," Gin said. "For your sake and the baby's as well."

As she walked to her car, Gin paused to look over her shoulder at the building that had been her refuge for the last year, the place where she could shut out everything but her work.

* * *

Gin checked her phone when she got into the car, and discovered that she'd had two missed calls, one from Rosa and one from Jake. Only Rosa had left a message.

She tried to ignore the complicated feelings evoked by seeing Jake's name as she listened to Rosa's message. "Hey gorgeous, wondering if you'd like to stop by for a bit tonight? Mom and Antonio will both be in bed by nine or so, but come over any time."

Gin sent a quick text thanking Rosa, mentioning that she had a date and promising to try to visit afterward, thinking it would be a good way to unwind after the stress of her subterfuge. Then she took a breath and dialed Jake.

"Gin," he said, not bothering with a greeting. "I just talked to your dad. He told me what happened."

"My *father* called you?"

"Yeah, don't be angry with him. He was asking for some advice on how best to secure the house. You know, update the alarm system and the locks. I gave him a name—a guy I've worked with in the past. I'll follow up and ask him to make it a high priority."

"I—wow. Thanks, I guess." Gin was always annoyed when her parents inserted themselves into her private life, but she had to admit that she understood her father's concern. And Jake truly was the best person to give such advice. "I'm fine, though. Just in case you were wondering."

"I don't doubt that," Jake said tightly. "For now. Gin, you are a highly capable woman. Tough, too. But this is getting out of hand. Whatever's going on with that John Doe investigation, you need to stay clear of it."

"Dad should *not* have discussed that with you."

"He loves you, Gin." Jake shot back. "He's worried about you." A second later, in a quieter voice, he added,

"*I'm* worried about you. And there's something else. Now that Baxter's gotten canned, I don't want you anywhere near him. He's reckless at best—and there's no telling how bad this could be, since Wheeler's not talking."

Gin's irritation spiked to fury. "You don't get to tell me who I can or can't talk to," she said. "Not after you walked out on me."

"I didn't . . ."

Gin could hear Jake breathing hard into the phone, and she pictured the way his jaw pulsed when he was angry. "You know what? I think I need to get off the phone."

"Gin . . ."

"No. I know we were calling this a break, but—it's too hard, Jake. You can't just pop into my life whenever you want to tell me what to do. I—I needed you, last night, and you weren't there." She didn't tell him that she'd turned to Tuck instead, that he was the one who'd made her feel safe, who'd given her comfort. "So I think we need to call this what it is—a breakup. Maybe not forever, but until you figure out what you want—until you come *home*—I can't do this anymore."

For a long moment neither of them spoke. Gin's heart felt like it was shattering inside her. She longed to take back the words—to say that she had overreacted, to beg him to come back.

But she knew it wasn't the answer.

"I . . . understand," Jake said, his voice hoarse. "I . . . I love you, you have to know that. Please, if not for me . . . for your family. Please take care and be safe."

"I will," Gin said, tears springing to her eyes. She wiped them away. "I have to go."

She hung up before he could reply.

* * *

At 6:55 PM, Gin walked through the doors of Drake's Tavern, a historic pub that had once served the steel workers and had been lovingly restored, with a popular menu of light fare and hand-crafted cocktails. She scanned the room, looking for the man whose photograph she'd seen on the dating web site. Instead, she saw Tuck sitting at the bar, watching a baseball game on TV and drinking a beer.

She hadn't spoken to him yesterday, though he'd texted her to make sure she was still planning to keep her "date." Gin had sent a terse reply, then spent the rest of the day trying to keep busy with a long run and paperwork.

As she stared at Tuck's broad shoulders, straining against the plaid shirt that was only a slight improvement over his usual off-duty look, she just couldn't believe that he'd done anything to warrant the suspension. She had watched him care for his daughter, heard him cheer as hard as any parent at a middle school basketball game, seen the posters he'd made with Cherie for a car wash fundraiser for the school.

She'd seen the way his eyes grew flinty when he was angry, opaque when he was working on a case, and dark and depthless when he was thinking about kissing her.

"Excuse me—are you Beth?"

Gin turned, awkwardly remembering that she was

185

Beth Conway, a saleswoman who loved to dance and browse art galleries. She smiled at Keith Walker, who looked exactly like his photograph: attractive in an easy-going way, with thinning brown hair and a host of laugh lines, a neatly trimmed goatee, and a hint of a paunch that would probably turn into a beer belly if he wasn't careful.

"You must be Keith," she said, shaking his hand.

"Nice to meet you. I've got us a table over here by the window. Hope that's okay." He had a warm smile, and he stood politely aside for her to pass, then held her chair while she sat.

Certainly not the sort of manners that hinted at a dark side. Keith was a bit stiff, but that could easily be chalked up to first-date nerves; he might also simply be shy. As he took his own seat, nearly knocking over his water glass, she decided it was the latter.

The waiter stopped by the table to drop off happy hour menus, and Gin ordered a Greyhound while Keith suggested a burrata appetizer that he'd enjoyed before. "I know I shouldn't," he admitted, patting his stomach, "but they do a terrific job with it."

Once Keith finally relaxed, conversation flowed easily, and Gin found herself enjoying his company until she remembered that she was here to try to find out if the man across the table knew anything about the body that had been discovered near his land. She steered the conversation to hobbies, and Keith enthusiastically launched into a description of his outdoor pursuits, including hunting and fishing. "I grew up hunting these woods," he said, giving her the entrée she needed. "And I still spend as much time as I can at my cabin."

"Oh, the Pennsylvania countryside is so beautiful," she said. "Is your cabin near a good fishing spot?"

"Yeah, as a matter of fact. I can walk out the front door in the morning and have my line in the water in less than five minutes. My grandfather built the cabin in the thirties—can't even imagine how many trout we've taken out of the stream since then."

"Oh, so the cabin has been in your family all that time?"

"Yeah, though it's just me and my sister now. Well, technically my dad owns it, but he's in a nursing home so unfortunately he's not able to use it."

Gin's ears perked up at the mention of a sister. "Is your sister into fishing as well?"

"Cindy? Hardly," Keith said, smiling fondly. "She's not really the outdoorsy type. Her hobby is garage sales and selling stuff on eBay. Or at least it was until her kids hit their teens—they're giving her kind of a hard time these days, and with her ex-husband out of the picture, she's really got her hands full."

"Oh, I'm sorry to hear that," Gin said diplomatically. "Teens can be challenging."

"Yeah. Well, my niece is okay, she doesn't spend as much time as Cindy would like on homework, but she's a good kid. It's Logan who's got Cindy more worried. Poor kid has always had a tough time fitting in, and once he got to high school, he got mixed up in some bullying. And to make things worse, he goes to North Valley High, and the overcrowding problem is really bad there—it's easy for kids like Logan to fall through the cracks."

"That's really unfortunate," Gin said. A troubled kid could be a possible suspect—and there was a potential connection between Keith's nephew and Jonah Krischer, although Logan didn't attend Jonah's expensive private high school. "Bullying can create such lasting scars. It sounds like Logan could use some specialized attention. Is he involved in any activities that he enjoys?"

A flicker of uncertainty in Keith's eyes made Gin wonder if she'd gone too far. "I only ask because I have a cousin who went through something similar," she added hastily. "But he got involved in theater and found his true passion—and a community that he really enjoys."

"Oh. Well, yeah, Logan's interested in some sort of gaming group. I know he made friends through it, but Cindy's not crazy about it. From what I gather the imagery is pretty violent, and I don't think she likes the other kids very much. Let's just say there aren't any Rhodes scholars in the group, know what I mean?"

The appetizers came, and Gin sampled the burrata. "You're right, this is amazing!" she said, realizing that she hadn't eaten lunch.

"I'm so glad you like it," Keith smiled. "So, Beth Conway, all we've done is talk about me. How about you tell me how a nice girl like you ended up in a place like this?"

15

By nine thirty, Keith and "Beth" had enjoyed a second round of drinks (Gin switched to soda after her first, while Keith ordered a light beer) and a heap of chicken wings in addition to the burrata. Gin had embellished the basic ruse she and Tuck had come up with, adding details that she had no possible chance of remembering. And though they'd talked at length about Keith's family and love of the outdoors, he'd made no mention of the body being found on his land. It seemed unlikely that he had no knowledge of the gruesome discovery, but she had to admit it didn't make for great first-date conversation.

Tuck's plan to gain insight from Keith might be a bust—but Gin had sufficiently charmed him that he'd asked her out on a second date.

She felt terrible telling him that as much as she'd enjoyed the evening, she didn't feel that there was enough of a connection between them to see him again. Keith looked crestfallen, but he thanked her politely and gamely offered to walk her to her car. He shook her hand and wished her the best, adding that if she ever changed her mind, she knew where to find him.

Gin had driven only half a mile or so when a car behind her flashed its brights. She slowed, and Tuck's SUV passed her. He tapped the horn and motioned for her to follow him.

They could have discussed the evening over the phone, especially since nothing had come of the conversation that would be helpful on the case. But Gin had to admit that she welcomed a chance to talk in person, to share her thoughts on what had happened.

She parked behind Tuck's truck in his driveway. He got out of the truck and came back to her car, opening her door for her.

"Hello, Beth Conway," he said, grinning. "You were very convincing. I saw more than one guy in that place checking you out."

"Well, for your information, Keith asked me out for a second date."

"I'm sure he did. Maybe the two of you have a real future together."

As they entered the house, Gin saw a gray-haired woman sitting on the couch, working on a Sudoku puzzle.

"Hello, Mr. Baxter," she said, giving Gin a cool, assessing stare.

"Hi, Mrs. H. This is Gin Sullivan, a friend of mine.

Gin, this is Mrs. Hill, who stays with Cherie from time to time."

"I see. Isn't it a bit late for visiting?" Mrs. H took off her glasses and let them hang from their silver chain, the better to glare at Gin.

She thinks I'm here to hook up, Gin thought, embarrassed. "It's very nice to meet you."

Tuck pulled some bills from his wallet and handed them to the elderly woman, who tucked them into her pocketbook. She picked up her puzzle book and said, "Cherie ate all of her supper and said her prayers. She was no trouble at all." Glaring pointedly at Gin, she added, "I'll see myself out."

Once she was gone, Tuck and Gin burst into laughter.

"I didn't know they made them like that anymore until I met Mrs. H.," Tuck said. "I always feel like she's about to rap me on the knuckles with a ruler. But Cherie loves her, so I can't complain. How about a beer?"

"No thanks. After all those appetizers, I'm going to have to stick to salads and water for a week."

They sat in the living room and Gin shared everything that she had learned about Keith—and his sister and her kids, especially her son's connection to the gaming group. "Sounds like he's close in age to Jonah. It's a stretch, but maybe it's worth looking into."

"Too bad you weren't able to get the kid's last name," Tuck said. "But maybe we can figure it out."

He grabbed his laptop and patted the sofa next to him. "I promise I don't bite. Let's do a little surfing."

Gin moved over to the sofa, deliberately leaving space between her and Tuck. The late hour, the cocktails, the strain of trying to stay in character—and now sitting so close to Tuck that she could smell his aftershave—all of it combined to make her feel extremely self-conscious. Especially after the painful conversation with Jake, her feelings were more convoluted than ever.

"Look," she blurted. "This would be a lot easier if I knew what was going on with you and the department."

"I'm afraid I can't tell you," Tuck said calmly. "I know it's frustrating. I'm sorry."

"That's—you're putting me in a difficult position," Gin protested. She wished she could tell him about the disturbing incident with Katie, but she'd promised Paula to keep it to herself. "Since I met you, you've come under not one but two official inquiries. And there are things . . . people I've talked to, who—I mean, this affects other people. You have to know that."

Tuck nodded. "Yes—it looks bad. Especially since I can't in good conscience say a thing to defend myself. So here's what you need to ask yourself, Gin—given that you've known me for a while now, that we've shared some fairly intimate moments—do you believe I'm capable of doing something bad enough to lose my job? Or of hurting anyone, for that matter?"

Gin held his unblinking gaze as long as she could and then finally shrugged. "No. I don't believe you're capable of something like that."

"Good. Now can we please move on?"

He was already opening his laptop again. He brought up a browser window and logged into Facebook. "I checked out Jonah's page already . . . there, see, he's cleaned it up quite a bit. I'm guessing his dad's lawyer made him do it. There used to be links to a number of things that wouldn't make the best impression on the jury, should Jonah ever be charged on the evidence we have."

"What kind of things?"

"Nothing too racy—a few metal bands, a few gaming sites—but it looks to me like they're trying to sanitize Jonah's social media, make him look like a Sunday school student. See, look at the pages he recently liked—his high school STEM club, the National Parks Foundation, the Carnegie Museum of National History. A few jazz music sites. He's a regular boy scout."

Tuck clicked over to Jonah's friends list and scrolled down slowly. Jonah had almost two hundred friends; not a lot, in Gin's experience, at least compared to Brandon's daughter Olive, who had over six hundred.

"Bingo," Tuck said. "Logan Ewing. Does that ring a bell?"

"I don't think Keith ever mentioned his sister's married name."

Tuck clicked on the link and Logan's page came up. His profile picture was of a scowling young man with pale skin, sharp features, and dyed black hair. Most disconcertingly, he'd altered the photograph so that his eyes were stark white orbs with no pupils.

Gin shuddered. "That's creepy."

"Not as creepy as this," Tuck said, scrolling down his likes. "Hard core gaming sites, slasher movies, anarchy organizations—and Jesus, look at this."

"Who are they?" Gin asked, staring at the page for a group called the First Amendment Strikegroup. It featured a group of about thirty white men of all ages arranged around what looked like a decommissioned Humvee. Many of the men wore black; a few held United States and confederate flags. A man standing on the hood of the Humvee wore a bandana tied over his face under mirrored sunglasses and brandished a sword.

"Short answer is they're a hate group. We've been keeping an eye on groups like this for a while—especially lately, given the rise in clashes between white supremacist and liberal activists. You may not be aware that Pennsylvania's in the top five states for hate groups, because they generally operate under the radar."

"I've seen the news," Gin said. "I just didn't realize it was going on so close to home."

"These guys have been relatively well behaved," Tuck said. "They mostly show up at protests by other, more prominent groups, though they don't really have a coherent mandate—basically they hate liberals, immigrants, anyone of color, feminists. Probably public television and the NEA. They're not very well organized."

"That's awful, but I'm not sure it's relevant."

Tuck had gone back to the friends list. "Look, here's your boyfriend, Keith Walker. Logan's Uncle Keith? And here's Cindy Ewing—his mom?"

"Keith's sister is named Cindy," Gin confirmed. "He told me she's been having trouble with Logan—she's a single parent. So now we know that Jonah and Logan know each other. At least, on Facebook they do."

"They go to different high schools, but they could have met in some extracurricular activity," Tuck said. "Or even online in a game forum."

"So are you going to talk to him?"

"Well, now, that's going to be a little tough given my current status in the department," Tuck sighed. "I hate to say it, but it's probably time for us to share this with Bruce and let him take a crack at it."

"And when you say 'us' . . . you really mean me, right?"

"Unless you're spoiling to have my leave made permanent," Tuck said. "Which would give me more time to campaign for 'World's Sexiest Stay-at-Home Dad,' of course, but probably wouldn't help get this case solved. So yeah, we're going to have to figure out a plausible way for you to tell Bruce about this that doesn't involve me."

"You don't have faith in him . . ."

"Nope. And neither do you, or you wouldn't have agreed to help me out with this in the first place."

Gin yawned, the long day catching up with her. "I'll think about it. I guess one more lie isn't going to make things any worse than they already are."

"I'll walk you out," Tuck said, his voice softening. "Make sure the boogeyman doesn't get you on the way to your car."

"That's . . . I'm not sure that's a good idea."

"What? All I'm going to do is walk out onto my own driveway."

Gin took a breath, but she couldn't quite meet his eyes. "I think we both know it's not as simple as that, Tuck."

He raked his hand through his hair in frustration. "Gin, when are you going to accept the fact that Jake can't give you the attention you deserve? Hell, at the first sign of trouble, what does he do—doesn't stick around to make sure you're okay. No, he heads out of town." He shook his head with disgust. "To my way of thinking, a man's job isn't done until he knows his woman is taken care of."

Perhaps he hadn't meant the double entendre . . . but given the way he was gazing at her, Gin wasn't so sure. She wasn't about to confess that she'd just made their breakup more permanent. "You can't understand what he's been through."

"Not much to understand, the way I see it. Look, I know Jake's been through a lot. So has everyone. I won't bore you with my own sob story, but no one handed me anything in life—I earned it. And I didn't become the man I was until the doc looked me in the face and told me my baby only had a fifty-fifty chance of surviving. So I know a thing or two about grit." He touched Gin's face with a tenderness that belied his harsh tone. "Grit's something I've got in spades, Gin. I take care of what's important to me. I'd take care of you. Just give me a chance."

For a moment Gin teetered on the edge of his invitation. It would be so easy to give in, to lean into his touch, to let go of all the pain from her breakup with Jake. Maybe it was time to try to take her life in a new direction, starting with the kind, strong, undeniably sexy man in front of her.

But the questions that nagged at her were real. She could live with not knowing why he'd been pushed out of the county police, what his role was in the Internal Affairs investigation. But she couldn't deny the impropriety of what they had undertaken together. A cop on administrative leave with a cloud of suspicion over his head . . . a consultant with no legal right to involvement with any police business she hadn't been explicitly hired to address . . . they were on dangerous enough territory trying to get information about the case, much less actively investigate it. Add to that the lies Gin had told to Keith, the subterfuge in setting up the date in the first place, the fact that she and Tuck were secretly pursuing not one but two separate cases—getting involved romantically would be the cherry on top of a series of bad decisions.

"As . . . flattered as I am by your attention," she said quietly, "I think I'd like to keep things as professional as possible between us."

Tuck's only reaction was a slight tightening of his expression, a dimming of the light in his eyes. "Understood," he said gruffly. "For now. Although I sometimes wonder what Crosby would have to do to finally convince you that he isn't man enough."

The words stung, and Gin pushed back against the

emotions they provoked. "Let's just get back to what we were doing, okay? I'll figure out a way to tell Bruce about the connection."

"So . . . you won't date me, but you're still okay with flouting authority and disregarding the law and courting all kinds of trouble with me?"

"Well, when you put it that way," Gin said, forcing a small smile, "how can I resist?"

* * *

Gin glanced at the dashboard clock when she got into her car. Almost eight thirty—still early enough to fit in a quick visit with Rosa. She made the short drive and found a handwritten note on her door that said "Come on in."

Even a few years ago, it would have been unthinkable to leave a front door unlocked in this neighborhood, but the town's renaissance was in full swing halfway through her mother's first term as mayor. Where there had once been cracked pavement, boarded up houses, and empty lots, there were clean streets in good repair, working street lights and even a pocket park with a pint-sized play structure. Neighbors were out enjoying the nice evening, and Gin could smell barbecue and hear laughter and music.

Gin walked into the house and was greeted by the smell of popcorn. She passed through the living room and the bright, scrubbed kitchen, and heard Rosa's voice through the screen door in the back of the house. She went out on the patio and found Rosa and her mother eating popcorn and talking.

"Gin!" Rosa said, jumping up and giving her a delighted hug. "I'm so glad you stopped by."

Gin bent down next to Rosa's mother, who suffered from the early stages of Alzheimer's disease. "It's nice to see you, Mrs. Escamilla," she said, and gave the elderly woman a kiss on her soft, papery cheek.

"You're a very pretty girl," Mrs. Escamilla said, beaming and giving Gin's hand a squeeze.

"You just missed Antonio," Rosa said. "He tired himself out trying to catch fireflies back here. Practically fell asleep while I was carrying him upstairs."

"Antonio is very good boy," Mrs. Escamilla said. "My grandson!"

"Yes, you're a lucky grandmother," Gin agreed.

"I have agua fresca," Rosa offered. "Pineapple and watermelon. We made some earlier to take to the park. Doyle and the kids joined us for a picnic."

"Very handsome boy," Mrs. Escamilla observed. "And from good family."

"Mom sometimes gets Doyle confused with a boy she apparently used to date back in Mexico," Rosa said cheerfully. "I've been trying to get her to tell me if she broke his heart."

"No, no heartbreak," Mrs. Escamilla said, yawning. "Is no good to be sad all the time. Much better to settle down and have nice family."

"Mom, how about we take you up to bed?" Rosa asked. "You look pretty sleepy."

She helped her mother up from the lawn chair,

promising to be right back. Gin poured a glass of the cold watermelon drink from the pitcher on the patio table, and sat down to enjoy the view of a fat yellow moon rising over the neighborhood. The scent of jasmine floated over the hedge, and a woman somewhere nearby called out into the night, "Thomas! Marlon! Time to come inside!"

Rosa came back with a stack of blankets over her arm. "It's getting cool out," she said, handing a blanket to Gin. "Now tell me all about this date you had."

Gin stuck to the truth as closely as she dared, describing Keith and the conversation they'd had, but omitting the fact that she'd pretended to be someone else.

"Did he ask you out again?"

"Yes," Gin admitted. "But I don't think I'm going to go."

"You're not ready yet," Rosa said. "You're still in love with Jake."

Gin shrugged; there was no point arguing.

"Well, we'll talk about something else, then. Has there been any progress on your latest cases?"

Another minefield. Maybe coming to see her friend just now had been a mistake. "Unfortunately not. I did sit in on an interesting autopsy recently, though."

"Oh, tell me all about it!" Rosa didn't blink at the subject change; she was fascinated with Gin's job and never tired of the stories she brought back from her work.

"Well, it's an open investigation, so I can't say anything about the details of how the body came to us, only that it was moved from its initial burial location. But what was interesting—to me, at any rate—was the challenge of establishing an approximate time of death given that the body had been embalmed."

She gave Rosa a quick explanation of the various factors that went into establishing time of death, warming to the subject as Rosa asked thoughtful questions. "Couldn't you identify him by his teeth?"

"Dental records weren't relevant in this case, because the John Doe has implants," she said.

"Wait—I thought you said the guy was in his forties or fifties? Isn't that kind of young to get dentures?"

"Yes, we discussed that. There are a number of conditions that can cause early tooth loss, however, even in affluent communities. In fact, one in five people over forty wear dentures. It's out of the ordinary but certainly not as rare as you might expect."

"Like what, for instance?"

"Well, periodontal disease and tooth decay from poor dental hygiene, for starters. But also severe tooth erosion from gastrointestinal reflux. Factors like smoking and having rheumatoid arthritis or type two diabetes can contribute to tooth loss. And—"

"But you wouldn't lose *all* your teeth with those conditions, would you?"

"Perhaps not, but depending on the extent of the damage, a full implant might make sense, or the patient might choose it for cosmetic reasons."

"Did your John Doe have any of those other conditions?"

"Well, actually, not that I could tell from the autopsy, but keep in mind that his organs had decomposed to an extent that makes it hard to draw firm conclusions. Still, his lungs didn't show signs of smoking, and the condition of his joints didn't indicate rheumatoid arthritis."

"So you have a real medical mystery on your hands."

"I suppose you could say that. The truth is that, in the absence of any of the other factors I mentioned, the only time you see full implants at an early age is in combination with—"

Gin paused, as the germ of an idea formed. There was one condition that could have led to implants, but it hadn't occurred to her because the other telltale sign of the disease occurred in the hands—which had been hacked off.

"I think John Doe may have had ectodermal dysplasia!!"

"Well, you don't have to sound so excited about it," Rosa said, surprised. "It sounds horrible, whatever it is."

"I can't believe I missed it. Although, some of the symptoms are subtle, like the frontal bossing and prominent supraorbital ridge. But the hands—"

"Slow down, Gin. What exactly is this condition?"

Gin took a breath and tried to focus her racing thoughts. "Ectodermal dysplasia is characterized by defects in tissues derived from the embryonic ectoderm, specifically the skin, hair, nails, sweat glands, and teeth. Patients can have any or all of these defects, in a broad range of severity. In the case of the teeth, they can be missing or malformed, and often a full implant is the best course. The thing is, the hands are often the most obvious symptom when the patient is afflicted with ectrodactyly—that is, fingers are missing or fused together, or can have a cleft down the middle, commonly called 'split hand syndrome.'" Something else occurred to her. "Cleft palate also commonly co-occurs, and while our John Doe didn't have that, he could have easily had a microform cleft, which looks like a scar above the upper lip. Given the state of decomposition, if the cleft had been minor, it may have been impossible to detect." She would have to review the photographs again.

"Sorry if this comes out wrong, but I still don't understand why you're so excited about this."

"Oh, sorry, Rosa. It's just that ectodermal dysplasia is rare enough that if our John Doe knew he had it, or if his ectrodactyly was obvious, it might help us track down who he was. Listen, I can't thank you enough, because I never would have figured this out without you—you're a genius!"

"I still don't know what I said but . . . thanks," Rosa said. "I think I'll stick to teaching fourth graders. They can be a pain some days, but at least the only mysterious conditions affecting them most of the time are sniffles, sneezes, and a bad case of talking back."

16

As Gin drove home from Rosa's house, her mind went into overdrive reviewing what she knew about ectodermal dysplasia. There was the hair—often thin and sparse. *Check*. She hadn't noticed any abnormalities in John Doe's feet or toes, but the severe mottling and blistering that she'd chalked up to normal decomposition could also have been the result of dyshidrosis, a blistering of the skin of the hands and feet. It was often treated with topical steroids, which could account for the thinning and resultant rapid breakdown of the skin.

She pulled into the drive and hurried into the house, tossing her purse on the hall table. Light emanated from the study, where she found her father reading one of his beloved thrillers, a snifter of scotch at his side.

"Oh, hi, sweetie, you just missed Mom," he said. "She has to be up early, so she said to tell you—"

"Dad," Gin said, unable to contain herself. "In your

practice, did you ever come across an organization for people suffering from ectodermal dysplasia? Like a support group or something?"

"Not really," Richard said, taking the abrupt subject change in stride. "I mean, there are organizations at the national level, and a pretty active one in the UK, if memory serves. But at the local level, at least in rural areas like ours, I would imagine there simply aren't enough affected people to support the formation of local clubs. In fact, in all my years in Trumbull I can only recall two cases, both men, but one moved away years ago and the other one died just last winter from a heart attack." He snapped his fingers. "One of Mark Krischer's patients, come to think of it— wasn't that who you were asking me about the other day?"

"Wait," Gin said. "You're saying Dr. Krischer had a patient with ectodermal dysplasia who recently died? Do you happen to know if he was buried locally?"

"That is an odd question," Richard observed, "but I suppose experience has taught me not to ask. I don't know the answer, but it should be easy enough to find out."

"Do you remember his name, by any chance?"

"Sorry, honey. I can't remember half of my own patients' names, much less my colleagues'."

Gin was already headed for the door. "That's okay," she called over her shoulder. "Love you, Dad."

She went to her room and grabbed her laptop, then got into bed, leaning back against the propped pillows. She tried various google searches and found dozens of mentions of Dr. Mark Krischer, including photos of him at several fundraisers and galas and articles in several journals to which he'd contributed, but little about his individual patients. Taking a different tack, she tried searching on "ectodermal dysplasia" and "Trumbull", then when she still came up dry, "Allegheny County" and then other nearby towns. Finally, when she tried "Clairton," she was rewarded with a recent obituary of a man named Douglas Gluck.

Douglas Gluck—Beloved husband of Connie Dover Gluck; Devoted father of Kenneth (Jean) Gluck and Cheryl (Fred) Ingram; Caring brother of Daniel. Employed at Harris Carton for nearly forty years, Doug was recognized for several innovations in the industry. Doug enjoyed golf, travel, and music, and belonged to the St. Theresa's men's choir for the last sixteen years. Passed away February 2, 2016 at the age of 56. A celebration of life service will be held at 11:00am, Monday, February 9th at the Ingleside Mortuary, 925 Wayne Avenue, Clairton, PA. Interment will follow in the East Riverton Cemetery. In lieu of flowers, donations may be sent to the National Foundation for Ectodermal Dysplasia.

Bingo. It took her a little longer to find a photograph, but in a 2012 article in an online trade magazine in which Gluck posed with other members of the Harris Carton management team, his hands appeared to have only two or three digits each. The sparseness of his hair, and characteristic facial structure, were far more obvious than they had been in the body's current condition. Gin's excitement grew as she realized that Douglas Gluck had to be the same man whose mutilated body had been discovered. She reached for her phone and tried Tuck, but he didn't pick up. She left a message for him to call her and deliberated only for a moment before calling Bruce. This gave her the perfect opportunity to mention the information she and Tuck had found about Logan Ewing, if she could find a way to work it in.

"Bruce here."

"This is Gin Sullivan calling. I've got a couple of pieces of information for you. Well, one piece of information, to be accurate, and one theory about the John Doe I'd like to share."

"I'm all ears," Bruce said sarcastically. "Did you discover that John Doe has a tattoo with his name on it somewhere where the sun don't shine, that we all somehow missed?"

Gin bit back a retort. "No, but I think I've figured out who he is." She gave him a quick description of ectrodermal dysplasia, its potential effects, and explained how she'd found out about Dr. Krischer's patient, with her father's help. "It makes sense now that I've seen a photograph of him. The hands would have made it obvious, but I might have figured it out from his distinctive facial features, if I'd seen him before decomposition."

"Even teachers' pets like you make a mistake now and then, Gin. Try not to get depressed over it."

Gin seethed. "I'm hardly depressed. I'm only trying to be helpful."

"So what's your margin of error here? Is this a slam dunk or just a hunch on your part?"

"My confidence is quite high," Gin said stiffly.

"Okay, well, I'm going to make a few calls, see if we can—oh, shit."

"What?"

"I just googled Gluck. Dude looks like a giant elf. An old, giant elf."

Gin winced. "Patients with ectodermal dysplasia have to deal with unpleasant side effects already. Insensitive characterizations of their appearance hardly help to—"

"Jeez, ease up, Gin, okay? Guy's dead, he can't hear me. Listen, I'll add him to the list. Guess we'll have to take a look at his grave, see why no one noticed it was robbed. Not sure how we'll explain that to the grieving widow. 'Hello, ma'am, about your husband . . .'" He laughed. "I'm sure that'll go over well."

"But you *are* going to look into this, right? I mean, at the very least you could take a look at his grave and see if it's been disturbed."

"Not that it's any of your business," Bruce said. "But yes, I'm inclined to pursue this. Let me remind you that once you step out of the morgue, you're just an ordinary citizen, Gin. So while I appreciate this fascinating little tidbit you've shared with me, it doesn't entitle you to tell me how to run my case. Now what was the other thing? You said you had two things to tell me?"

"Oh—right." Gin had gotten so caught up in the discussion of Gluck's condition that she'd nearly forgotten. "It turns out that the owner of the cabin where Douglas Gluck's body was found is a friend of a friend." True enough, if Gin considered her alter ego, Beth Conway, a 'friend.' "I understand you spoke to the owner's son, Keith Walker. What you may not know is that Keith's sister has a son, Logan Ewing, who is the same age as Jonah Krischer. I looked at his Facebook page—he 'liked' a lot of pages of radical groups that promote white supremacist interests, as well as violent gaming culture."

Bruce snorted. "You're a super sleuth now, Gin? Thought you'd do a little *investigating*?"

Gin reminded herself to stay calm while she roiled on the inside. "I was only trying to help. It just seems to me that it might be worth seeing if Logan is involved somehow."

"What, just because he's got a hard-on for shoot-'em-up video games? Hate to break it to you but it's the same with half the pimply kids who couldn't get a date to prom."

"These aren't just ordinary first-person shooter games," Gin argued. "The one he's most into—it's called Dead Lands 2—the imagery is truly disturbing."

"Oh yeah? Try me."

Gin took a breath, reluctant to even describe the horrific depictions of murder and torture she'd found while investigating Dead Lands 2. "There are graphic depictions of dismemberments, disemboweling, decapitation . . . there are characters who rip out their enemies' organs and eat them, characters who are slowly pressed to death by massive weights. There is one character who kills his victims by peeling off their skin and leaving them to die."

Bruce snorted dismissively. "Nothing worse than the stuff me and my buddies used to talk about. Besides, haven't you ever heard about teenage angst, Gin? Or did they not have it at the country club where you grew up? Never mind that—did Logan even go to the same school as Jonah? Any evidence that they were friends anywhere but online?"

"No," Gin admitted. "Not that I've found so far, anyway. But don't you think it merits looking into, given the rise in violence committed by hate groups like the ones Logan is interested in? Especially given the atypical nature of Gluck's appearance. I'm not saying I know what motivated someone to tamper with his body, but all through history there have been those who were repulsed—or fascinated—by physical deformities to the point that they attacked and even killed people and populations affected by them. Eugenics is only the most recent example."

"Now you're stretching so far, I can barely follow the connection you're making. If I understood you right, you're saying that Gluck had this disease that freaked people out to the point that its victims got hunted down and murdered? Sounds like fantasy to me. Unless you're claiming that the kid killed him in the first place, I don't get—well, actually, I don't get it at all. Why would a kid dig up a corpse afflicted with a condition that, in your words, repulsed and fascinated him, only to re-bury him somewhere else? Unless he was doing some sort of Dr. Mengele experiments on him . . . but I didn't exactly see evidence of that in the autopsy room."

"Look, I didn't say I had it figured out," Gin said, flustered. "Only that I thought it was worth talking to him."

"Listen, Gin, I'm writing this down, okay? And if it makes you feel better, go ahead and shoot me an email with everything you found about this kid—links to his social media, these so-called hate groups he's into, et cetera, et cetera. I'll try to take a look at all of it, but as you may have noticed, we're understaffed and underpaid and under the gun to keep this from blowing up in some sort of media frenzy." He paused. "That was pretty good, huh? *Understaffed, underpaid, under the gun.* I'll have to use that with Wheeler. Anyway, have a good day, Gin."

"Wait! Are you going to let me know what you find out?"

Bruce sighed audibly. "Remember the part where you're an ordinary citizen? Think about that for a minute."

There was a click and Gin realized that he'd hung up on her. She stared at the phone in frustration. But Bruce was right—not only was she merely an ordinary citizen, Tuck wasn't much better off at the moment. Even if they were right about the identity of their John Doe, anything beyond a casual visual investigation of his grave would require a warrant, and there was no way Tuck would be able to secure one while on leave.

But . . . there was one other person who might be able to help.

Before she could change her mind, she dialed Liam Witt's number.

"Hey, Gin," he answered.

"Hi, Liam. I'm sorry to be calling you at home. But something's come up that I could use your help on. But I know it's a bit . . . unorthodox for me to be making this call at all."

"I'm intrigued, Gin."

"All right." She explained the situation to him, from her findings at the autopsy, to her realization that they added up to a diagnosis of ectodermal dysplasia, to what she had learned about Logan Ewing, to her frustrating conversation with Bruce. "I wish I had confidence he would follow up on this," she ventured. "But I'm afraid that if he delays, this will be forgotten, and it will go nowhere. We could end up never knowing who was responsible for tampering with his body."

"Yeah, I can see that," Liam agreed. "But it's easy enough to make a few calls. I can't promise anything— this could go either way. Look, I'll drive by the cemetery and take a look first. If there'd been anything obvious, like a big hole where the headstone used to be, someone would have reported it by now. But assuming that the grave site is intact, we'll need to get a warrant to dig. It's rare, but it's not unheard of. And if we get a sympathetic judge, he could put it through right away."

"We could also wait for a DNA result to identify him— but that could take weeks."

"Yeah, no, I think we'll want to move on this quickly. I

mean, it won't look good if the family finds out we had a lead on his identity that we didn't bother to follow up on."

"I don't mean to cause trouble between you and your partner, though. Will Bruce be upset that you went over his head?"

"Eh, Bruce isn't so bad. I mean, I know he has a problem with women—taking direction from them, anyway—but with me, I've just learned how to manage him. The trick is getting him to think things are his idea. I'll just tell him that we ran into each other up in the city. That we got talking and I dragged it out of you, the stuff about your John Doe theory. And then I'll ask for his opinion, you know, make him feel like he's schooling the newbie. Like, 'Hey, Bruce, I've never run into anything like this before. I don't even know where to start.' Trust me—that's all it'll take.'"

"You're a genius," Gin said, impressed. "Remind me never to play poker with you."

17

The next morning, as she was working on the classroom grant proposal at the kitchen table, Gin got a call from Bruce.

"So, I've made some headway on this whole clusterfuck," he said, sounding considerably more upbeat than he had the day before. "I snagged Judge Amador and he was more than happy to help. He shares my opinion that this shouldn't wait. So, I'm headed over there in a few minutes to pick up the paperwork and then I'll drive over to East Riverton to take a look at the grave and talk to whoever's in charge. Wheeler's talked to the family, and they've given their permission. They obviously didn't know shit about Gluck wandering away from his grave, and they want answers as much as we do. With any luck, we'll get a shovel in the ground today."

Gin ignored the remarkable shift in Bruce's tone.

Clearly her talk with Liam had paid off. "I'm glad to hear that."

"I'm going to need you to come along. Can you clear your schedule?"

"You mean—right now?"

"Yeah. You're our decomp specialist, right? So we might as well make use of you."

"Funny how yesterday you didn't consider me a bona fide member of the department," Gin couldn't resist pointing out. "And as a private citizen—those *were* your words, weren't they? I've got no obligation to help. However, I'm committed to doing whatever I can to get to the bottom of this."

Bruce snorted. "Yeah, I'll bet. Don't take too long putting on your lipstick or whatever—we'll probably be paying the gravediggers time and a half."

* * *

The East Riverton Cemetery wasn't the largest in the area, but Gin had always thought it was the prettiest, with a gentle slope bordered by rows of stately trees and an ornate iron fence that dated back more than a hundred years. Her own grandparents were buried there, near the crest of a ridge with views of both the river and the beautiful grounds of the country club they'd belonged to for over half a century. She had worried that visiting the cemetery might trigger more anxiety as well as memories of those other graves, half a world away. Instead, she found herself feeling motivated—almost excited, even—to get to work.

Maybe there was something to the "exposure therapy" that Paula had referenced. Whatever the reason, Gin was glad she hadn't let the incident with the intruder put her off the case. Here in the sunshine and balmy weather, the scent of fresh-cut grass mixing with blooming jasmine and lilies, it was almost impossible to believe anything threatened her or her family.

Gin had planned to stop in the office to find out the location of Gluck's grave, but when she drove through the gates she spotted a county cruiser parked on the lower, newer area of the cemetery. Standing nearby were four men, two of them wearing orange vests.

As she came closer she saw that one of them was Bruce. He was talking to a man in a suit, ignoring the two men in vests a few paces away. One of the men had his hand on a large sheet of plywood, holding it upright, and the other held the handles of two shovels.

"Ah, there she is," Bruce said. "None other than the doc herself. Gin, this is Mel Pinkston, he's in charge around here. Mel, this is Dr. Gin Sullivan."

"Pleased to meet you," the man said, shaking her hand gently, as though she were delicate. "My official title is actually Managing Director of East Riverton Cemetery. We are, of course, extremely distressed at the possibility of any disturbance of an interment space."

"That's what they call graves here," Bruce said.

"I . . . believe I would have figured that out."

"So, this is it," Bruce said, pointing at the ground behind him, where there was an unplanted area of dirt roughly ten by four feet, at the edges of which a few weeds had sprouted. A small metal marker had been installed flat on the ground, but there was no headstone. "Mel here says that if we'd come two weeks from now, it would have been sodded over."

"Should have happened already," Pinkston said anxiously, looking around as though he expected someone to come out of nowhere to complain. "But the thaw came so late this year, we're behind. At this rate we won't be caught up until the fourth of July."

"So a winter burial means the plot stays like this—raw dirt—until conditions are warm enough for planting?" Gin asked.

"Yes. And it's even worse than that. In a bad winter, like the one we just had, the ground freezes solid to a depth of four feet or more. Used to be we couldn't dig at all until spring, and we had to keep the bodies in the receiving vault until after the thaw. You can use a jackhammer hooked up to an air compressor, but it still takes a really long time to get down through the frost. A few years ago we invested in frost teeth for the backhoe—it's like a big two-tined fork that breaks up the dirt—but they came out with something this year that's really made a difference. It's a large warming blanket that you hook up to a generator—leave it overnight and the next day the ground's soft enough to dig. It adds to the price, of course, but if a family chooses it, as in Mr. Gluck's case, we do our best to accommodate their wishes." He cast a respectful glance at the grave. "We find that our families appreciate it. They don't like to think about their loved one waiting."

"Like purgatory!" Bruce said. "Right? Neither heaven or Hell."

Pinkston frowned but said nothing to contradict Bruce. "Shall I have the gentlemen begin?"

"They're just using shovels?" Bruce said dubiously. "Isn't that going to take forever? Can't you use a bobcat or something?"

Pinkston tented his hands and managed to look even more serious. "The soil depth is not actually as great as you might assume. The days of digging 'six feet deep' are long gone—today's burial vaults are strong enough to withstand a great deal of weight, and don't shift under the soil, so there's no need to go that far."

"Burial vault?" Bruce echoed.

"It's an outer chamber for the casket," Gin explained. "Generally they're made of concrete or fiberglass. Their use is why you don't see depressions in the soil where the earth has caved into the casket, like you sometimes see with older graves."

"And, of course, they offer additional security for the casket, creating a sealed environment that is resistant to the elements."

"No shit? Nice. Okay, let's get moving."

Pinkston signaled the workmen. One laid the sheet of plywood next to the grave, while the other began digging, piling the dirt on the plywood. He'd only moved a few shovels full of dirt, however, when the shovel's blade plunged deep into the soil, as if it were loose grains of sand rather than densely packed earth. Even stranger, the soil began to cave in on itself, as though there were a hollow space underneath.

"What the . . . hang on there, George," Pinkston said. "Can you see what's down there?"

The larger of the two men knelt next to the hole and used a hand spade from his tool belt to widen the hole until it was roughly a foot across, opening into . . . blackness.

"What the *fuck* is going on?" Bruce demanded. "Anyone have a flashlight?"

"I have one in the shed," the other man volunteered.

"Why don't you go get it, Angelo," Pinkston said. "Detective, doctor, I must ask you to stay back until we figure out what is going on here. We can't have you getting hurt, heh."

"No shit," Bruce said.

"Would it be wise to get a crime scene team here to photograph this before we go any further?" Gin asked, trying to conceal her frustration. She'd been surprised Bruce hadn't made the arrangements already, though she could guess at his reasoning: the mortuary would insist on using their own staff to dig; the process would be routine; and most importantly, there was no reason to expect something like a hollow space above the vault where the dirt should have been. And finally, since there was no guarantee that Gin's hunch was correct regarding the identity of the John Doe, it would be a better idea to wait until there was confirmation of grave tampering before assigning valuable resources.

As if echoing Gin's thoughts, Bruce snapped, "Well sure, Captain Obvious. I was planning to just as soon as we confirmed that there was actually something to your theory. Gotta admit, I didn't expect this—I sort of thought you were full of shit." He turned to Pinkston. "I don't suppose you've got video surveillance of this area?"

"No, only the gates and the offices. Our grounds are simply too large, and there are too many areas obscured by trees and buildings."

Bruce turned to George. "What about you guys? Did you dig this one back when he was buried? You didn't notice anything strange?"

"No. We dug the hole and filled it back in same as every time."

"And what about after? You must drive by here what, every day, two at the most? I mean come on, this place is big, but it's not *that* big."

George shrugged. "It was winter, man. We don't mow, we don't do much of anything with the lawns."

"They use the winter months to prune and do routine maintenance on the equipment and facilities," Pinkston said, sounding slightly peeved. "Mr. Gluck was interred in February. That month they were painting the interior of the restrooms, and if memory serves they were also doing fence repairs—"

"So you don't even bother to take a look?" Bruce said

incredulously. "I mean, you have to drive your golf cart by here to get to the restrooms when you need to go. Don't you look around, take stock, make sure there isn't vandalism, trash, whatever?"

George shrugged. "It's always the same, every day. I don't see nothing different."

Angelo came jogging back, holding a large flashlight. He was out of breath from the effort.

"I'm sure you know this already," Gin said hastily, "but given that we don't know what is under there, you could be putting yourself in danger of injury."

"From a little hole in the ground? Come on," Bruce said. "I mean, seriously, does this guy look like he's going to get hurt in a hole that's only a few feet deep?"

Gin resisted rolling her eyes. "In Srebrenica," she said tersely, "we sometimes encountered pockets created by the way the bodies fell. There were several occasions where our colleagues whose job it was to move the earth were injured, sometimes seriously, when they couldn't anticipate the ground giving way. I'm sure we don't want to risk injury to George and Angelo."

"Okay, Gin, way to be a buzz kill," Bruce said sarcastically, as the two workers glanced at each other. "Okay, look. I'll call for CSI support. I'm sure Wheeler will move the pegs around on the board, given the shit show this is turning into. Jesus, with Paula barfing every five minutes, I don't know who she can get out here, but she'd damn well better find someone."

"I can be safe," Angelo said. "I'll lie down on my stomach, like this?" he gestured to show that his body weight would be well distributed.

"How long until your team can arrive?" Pinkston asked Bruce.

"I'll know in a few, buddy," Bruce responded, his phone pressed to his ear. "Oh hey, Captain, listen, we got a situation here."

As he walked a few paces away to speak to Wheeler, Pinkston nodded at Angelo, who crawled gingerly onto the earth. He shone the light into the hole, then reached down into it, his arm disappearing nearly all the way to his shoulder. He inched forward a little more and peered in, immediately turning his head away. "It—it smells awful," he said, visibly shaken. "Sorry. Just give me a second." He took a deep breath and tried again, shining the light in the hole. After a moment he drew back on his haunches and expelled the breath he was holding.

"It's . . . it's a big box," he said. "Like a refrigerator box or something. And—and I think there's a body in it."

18

By the time two technicians arrived in a Westmoreland County van forty minutes later, Pinkston had ordered his staff to set up additional plywood to protect the manicured lawn around the grave. While the CSI team was suiting up and unloading their equipment, George came over for a quiet word with Gin. "Thank you, you know, for what you said before. Most people don't think much of what we do, but we really try to show respect and make it easier for the families."

"I'm sorry for the detective's choice of words," Gin said. "Naturally we are all focused on understanding what happened here, but it is also important to remember that we are in a sacred place."

"You really did that? Helped out with those mass graves over there?" George shook his head. "Man, I can't even imagine."

Gin removed a card from her purse. "If you are ever

interested in serving in a similar capacity, please call and I'll tell you more about the program. It's thanks to the hard work and sensitivity of people such as yourselves that we can honor the dead in these war-torn countries."

"Okay, if you two are done exchanging recipes, the team is ready for you," Bruce called.

The CSI technicians, who'd introduced themselves as Bill Bromwich and Lorna Fuller, worked efficiently alongside George and Angelo. After taking photos from several angles and collecting samples of the soil near the surface, the four began removing the dirt, loading it into a pile on the plywood. In twenty minutes they'd cleared the top of what was indeed a large box, though smaller than a refrigerator. Gin estimated the top was about six by four feet and made of a hard fiberboard that had begun to disintegrate in the damp conditions, which explained why it had caved in so easily. The smell had also grown stronger. Gin knew that the odor was due to a decomposing body, and she assumed the others probably knew it too.

"We'll need to test this whole surface for prints," Bill said, while Lorna took photographs. "but I'm not too optimistic, given the conditions."

"Do you have to do it while it's still in the hole?" Bruce asked.

"We've got a drywall saw in the van," Lorna said. "We could probably take the whole top off. Take it with us."

She went to get the saw while Bill got an awl from his tool box and created a small hole. "This stuff's ready to give," he said. "It's really thin. I'm surprised it held the weight of the soil."

Lorna returned with the saw and knelt at the edge. The cutting went quickly, the damp material giving way to the tool's sharp teeth, and in a few moments she and Bill were able to lift the top of the box, though it collapsed along the hole in the center as they moved it to a tarp. The odor was much stronger now.

Inside the box, a body lay in the corner, tucked roughly into a fetal position, its face obscured by an outstretched arm. It appeared to be male, with thinning, matted gray hair and soiled, worn clothing. It had only one old, worn leather shoe and no socks; the flesh of the exposed arm was swollen and discolored, the feet blistered and peeling. Insects had burrowed their way in and done their work, as well. Gin noticed beetles and *conicera tibialis*, commonly known as "coffin flies" for feeding on human flesh.

"That is certainly not Mr. Gluck," Pinkston said, visibly shaken.

"I hate to ask the obvious question, but where's the coffin?" Bruce asked. Of everyone gathered, he seemed the least surprised at the discovery.

"It would be underneath," Pinkston said, recovering his composure. "Directly under the box will be the vault—I believe Mr. Gluck's family chose the Tribute series, which is constructed of reinforced plastic infused with polyethylene structural foam. It's lightweight and very strong."

"So whoever did this just dug to the top of it and put

the box on top? Then they covered the box with a foot of soil and no one ever knew?"

"Is there any way someone could dig that all out in one night?" Lorna asked the workmen.

"A couple of guys could," George said. "Or what I would do, it was me, I'd do it over a couple of nights, real early in the morning when there's no one around, not even kids messing around. Use a series of boxes if I had to. Dig out like a TV size box the first night, and cover it back up. Then do a little more, uses two boxes maybe. Work my way up to this big box."

"Yeah," Angelo agreed. "You'd have to wait until the ground thawed, though. No way you could do it without special equipment in the winter. And we would have noticed that."

"So where's all the dirt?" Bruce asked. "I mean, even just what you dug up just now, that's a pretty big pile."

Both men looked off into the woods. "Wouldn't be too hard," Angelo ventured. "Just bring a wheelbarrow in your truck. Dump it out there."

"Could you walk with me later?" Lorna asked. "Show me where you'd take it if it was you?"

"Sure," George said.

"Let's get photos and then get him out," Bill said.

He retrieved more equipment from the van while Lorna did the photography work, and then they both got down into the box. It was difficult to maneuver in the small space, but they worked methodically through the collection of evidence, taking scrapings of the box material, fibers and other matter that had accumulated on its surface, and insects and casings.

Gin hung back with the others while the two technicians worked. She was relieved when Bruce wandered away, evidently finding her uninteresting, and from her vantage point it looked like he was badgering Pinkston, because the cemetery director looked distinctly uncomfortable. A handful of cars arrived, and their occupants gave curious glances their way before moving on to visit their own loved ones' graves, but otherwise the team was able to work in peace.

When the evidence collection was complete, Bill and Lorna retrieved a stretcher from the van and maneuvered the body onto it. Gin didn't expect to learn anything additional at this point, but felt obligated to stay anyway: since she was already involved with this case, and was also certain to be called in to the autopsy, she wanted to make sure she didn't miss anything during this stage of the investigation.

Bruce joined her again as the investigators maneuvered the stretcher out of the box and onto the ground, an intermediate step before they climbed out and carried it to the van.

Up close, the odor emanating from the corpse was strong; despite the great care and attention Lorna and Bill used, moving the body had caused the flesh to split in several locations, fluid seeping out. The face was a grotesque mask; the flesh around the mouth had sloughed partially away, and the nose showed evidence of insect feeding.

"He sure does have a case of the butt-ugly," Bruce said, whistling. "Any chance he's got the ecto-whatever thing?"

"I really shouldn't venture any opinions until the autopsy," Gin said stiffly.

Most of the body was clothed, other than the extremities and head. The clothing would be removed at the morgue and delivered to the forensic analysts, along with the samples Bill and Lorna had collected. It was too early to draw any conclusions, and Gin certainly wouldn't share them with Bruce if she had, but if pressed she would say that the man had been living outdoors, possibly homeless, and that he had not been treated at any hospital immediately before death.

"Might want to stick around a few more minutes," Bruce said. "Once they get the box out of there, assuming the casket's underneath, they'll open it up. Who knows what they'll find in there, now that this whole thing has become one giant freak show?"

George and Angelo maneuvered the heavy box out of the ground, revealing the ivory plastic lid of the burial vault. The lid was considerably easier to lift, given the molded handles along the sides.

There was no sound other than the clicking of Lorna's camera as she photographed the polished dark wood surface of the casket. Some of the earth slid onto the casket from the sides of the hole, but it held its shape remarkably well. Gin could practically feel the collective intake of breath as George stepped gingerly down into the narrow space between the casket and the wall of the vault, and gave one of the brass handles an experimental tug.

"It's empty," he said. "I can tell from the weight of it."

Bruce rolled his eyes. "How about you indulge me and open it anyway."

George bent down and uncoupled the ornamental brass fittings and lifted the lid.

Inside, the pristine white silk was dusted with a bit of soil. Other than a faint depression in the silk head pillow, the interior of the casket looked like it had never held a body at all.

19

"I picked up a Sweetie Pies take-and-bake," Gin told her mother several hours later. "I knew you'd be getting ready for the city council meeting, and I figured neither you nor Dad would feel like cooking."

"You're right about that," Madeleine said as she came through the door and set down her briefcase, which was bulging with reports. "I've got twenty-four hours to come up with a convincing argument for additional state funding for heavy metal contamination remediation along Industry Avenue near the old plant. Speaking of your dad, have you seen him?"

"Actually, I've only been home for a few minutes myself, but he left a note saying he was going over to the garden." Richard was an avid member of the community gardens near the banks of the river, where he grew heirloom vegetables in his carefully tended plot. "I'm about to head out myself—I want to get a run in before dinner."

Madeleine glanced at her watch. "Okay, I'll wait an hour or so before I put the pizza in—that'll give you time for a shower, and I can make a few calls before we eat. And maybe your dad will bring back some snap peas."

Gin grabbed her water bottle and tucked it into her waist pack, then headed out into the late-afternoon sun. As she started out at an easy pace along the ridge road, she gazed down at the town below, the river glinting in the sun, the traffic moving lazily along the edge and over the bridges.

Running was Gin's favorite way to center herself, to let her subconscious mind wander freely, making the connections and leaps that her conscious mind could not. Especially when she was under stress, or working on a confounding case, solutions often came to her paradoxically when she was thinking nothing at all, just focusing on the rhythm of her feet on the trail, her arms pumping at her side, her lungs filling with air and releasing it.

But she'd only gone a few blocks when she realized that today, she would not achieve that serene state. Something was nagging at her brain, a break in a pattern, a piece that didn't fit the puzzle. Finally, as she left the paved road for one of the many trails that crisscrossed the ridge above the town, she gave up and began to talk herself through her thought. It was one of the advantages of these seldom-used trails that there was no one to hear her.

"Douglas Gluck, dead of natural causes, laid to rest—then disinterred. Not clear when.

"Second John Doe, unknown cause of death, found in Gluck's grave.

"Marnie Crosbie, dead from presumed overdose."

"Jonah Kischer . . ."

Here she got stuck. Jonah was connected to Gluck in two ways: Gluck was a patient of his father's—and Jonah had discovered his body. Coincidence? Maybe.

"Keith Walker. Cindy Walker Ewing. Logan Ewing."

She had crossed Keith off her mental list, but maybe that was premature. Could his nice-guy persona be faked? On the other hand, she knew nothing about Cindy other than she was having trouble with her son, who was involved in some frightening interests. And Logan was the right age—and temperament, perhaps—to have made a connection with Jonah.

But it still seemed like a stretch. Still, she had nothing else to go on. The autopsy of the body found in the grave might reveal more, but for now, Gin wanted—needed—to act. The sense of urgency that had followed her since her disturbing nightmare had only grown.

She stopped for a rest at the top of the ridge, taking a moment to watch the sun slipping down to where the horizon met the sky. Even the natural beauty failed to calm her, though, and she took out her phone and tapped out a Google search. It took a little poking around, but in moments at least one of her questions was answered.

Cindy Walker Ewing. Nurse's assistant at a dialysis center in Greenport, where she also owned a condominium. Formerly employed by the Sears distribution center that had closed last year. Divorced a little over two years.

If Logan was involved somehow with the body discovered near the family cabin, would Cindy know?

Was it possible that Cindy was involved herself?

It made little sense—but right now there was nothing else to go on, at least until the newly discovered body was identified. Greenport was only a ten-minute drive. It was doubtful that there were any answers waiting for Gin there . . . but as beautiful as it was high on the ridge, there were definitely no answers here.

She tucked her phone back into her pocket and began running down the path toward town.

* * *

By the time she showered and changed and drove to Cindy's condo development, at the end of a narrow access road leading off Route 837 through a desultory thicket of scrub trees, the sun had set, and a chilly mist had set in along with the darkness. The towns along the river were in the grip of an unseasonably cold and gloomy spell where the sun shone for only a few hours here and there. Soon summer would arrive, heralding backyard barbecues and Sunday drives and ball games, but for now the intermittent rains were encouraging the wildflowers and coaxing new growth along the river banks.

Cindy Ewing's condo development probably didn't look like much in the best of days, but with a light rain beginning to fall on dumpsters spilling over with trash, puddling on the cracked asphalt, and dripping from the

curling roof shingles, it looked little better than a tene-
ment. Gin found Cindy's condo, a plain gray two-story
unit wedged between four other identical ones, and parked
in a visitor space out front.

She'd come up with a plan on her short run home.
She'd grabbed an old jacket of her father's and dressed in a
wool blazer and coordinating pants. She planned to intro-
duce herself as one of the counselors at Logan's school and
ask if Logan was home. She was counting on neither Logan
nor his mother knowing the entire counseling staff at
North Valley High—with over three thousand students in
the school, that was certainly plausible. She would say that
he'd left his jacket behind, and since they were on her way
home, she thought she'd drop it off.

The ruse was a shaky one, and it would probably gain
her little more than a glimpse into the home, a short conversation with a harried mother. Nothing that would
implicate either Logan or his mother in wrongdoing—and
nothing to clear them of suspicion, either. But with no
other ideas, Gin simply hoped to get a sense of whether
Logan was as troubled as his Facebook page implied.

She got out of the car, clutching her father's jacket, and
raced through the mist to the front porch, where she was
protected by a listing metal overhang. She tried the door-
bell, but when no one answered, she resorted to knocking.

In seconds the front door was flung wide open. A thin
woman with limp, brassy hair and an inch of gray roots
glared at her. She was dressed in a stained scrub shirt with
a pattern of stethoscopes on a pale blue background,

matching blue pants, and white nursing clogs. Cheap plastic reading glasses were pushed up on top of her head.

She looked Gin up and down and crossed her arms over her chest. "What do you want?" she snarled. Behind her, a girl of thirteen or fourteen peeped around the corner, then raced past and up the stairs.

"I—I'm Jennifer Miller," Gin stammered.

"I know who you are, and I know what you're up to. But I don't have to say one damn thing to you. Mary Harper is a vicious old bitch with nothing better to do than spy on me all day long, and the last time you people were out here I *proved* to you that she was lying. Logan's had his troubles but he isn't a thief and I have *never* laid a hand on him. I'd like you to find one house in this whole place where no one's ever raised their voice. Bunch of fucking hypocrites."

Gin took half a step back, unprepared for Cindy Ewing's outburst. "I—I'm not who you think I am."

Cindy gave a short, bitter laugh. "Right. All you DHS do-gooders look exactly alike." She eyed Gin's handbag. "It's pretty easy to judge for you, isn't it? I know they don't pay you enough to dress like that. I bet you're married to a doctor, right? Investor? Wait until he leaves you high and dry with your kids and no way to pay the bills before you think you know anything."

Then she slammed the door inches from Gin's face.

Gin stood, immobile from shock, for several seconds before turning and running through the rain back to her car.

She'd learned something about the little family, that

was for sure. But she wasn't sure if it made them more or less likely to be connected to the string of bodies.

*   *   *

Gin was distracted enough as she drove toward the main road that she almost ran over a large branch that had fallen across the road. She looked up at the overhanging trees and sighed; the rain and wind had taken its toll, and the ground was littered with twigs and branches. The one in the road was dead; it had probably been ready to fall for quite some time and now extended across both lanes. She could probably drive around it, though the shoulder looked soft and slanted sharply away from the road, but she knew she ought to move it before some other motorist ended up damaging their undercarriage on it.

She put her blinkers on and put the car in park, then got out of the car. Rain pelted her face and trailed down her neck as she rounded the branch and took hold of the end. It was heavier than she expected, and she grunted from exertion but only managed to move it a few inches. She set the branch down, wondering if there was some way she could tie it to her bumper and drag it out of the way.

Something soft wrapped around her face. Gin clawed at it, startled, thinking it was a cloth carried by the wind, but there was a guttural sound behind her and a hand clapped it against her eyes. Before she could react, a pungent smell—like lemon floor cleaner—filled her nostrils.

And then there was nothing.

20

Something cold was pressing against her cheek.

Gin moaned and rolled over. Her body felt unmoored, as though the cartilage and sinew weren't holding her limbs together properly. Her mind was foggy, her thoughts a tangle.

She tried to sit up and a wave of dizziness felled her. Wherever she was, it was so dark that she couldn't see anything at all. Lying on her back, she used her fingers to explore: the floor felt slick, like linoleum; her face was inches from a wall with a plastic baseboard. She took a breath and couldn't detect any smell other than her own body. How long had she been here?

She forced herself to lie still and concentrate. Slowly, it came back to her—the branch in the road, the cloth wrapping her face, the sound of someone behind her. The smell, like lemon-scented cleaner, one that Gin was familiar with from her medical school days.

An inhalational anesthetic—probably sevoflurane, which was less pungent than some but highly effective. She'd probably been out from between four and twelve hours, depending on the concentration and how much she'd inhaled.

Panic threatened to build inside her, and Gin squeezed her eyes shut and focused for all she was worth. "Stay calm," she instructed herself. "You can do this."

In a few minutes she felt a little better and managed to sit up, then stand, with only a little nausea and trembling in her hands. She felt her way around what turned out to be more of a closet than a room; there were shelves on one wall, and a mop bucket on wheels in a corner. As she was exploring, a thin band of light suddenly appeared along the floor.

A door. Gin lurched the few steps to it and started banging as hard as she could on its unyielding surface. "Help!" she screamed, but it came out as a hoarse croak. She tried again, pulling off her shoe and using the heel to pound harder.

It occurred to her that whoever had turned on a light could very well be the same person who had put her in here. But the darkness pressing around her was making her panic: it was like the nightmare, the feeling of being in that long, narrow tunnel with no end.

"Who's there?" A woman's voice—gravelly, like a smoker's—sounded on the other side of the door. "Who is that?"

"I—I'm stuck in here. I don't know how I got here. Please, can you let me out?"

Silence.

Gin pounded again. "*Please!*"

"I don't have a key," the woman said doubtfully. "I'll have to find Mr. Holt."

"Please, hurry. Don't leave me here."

It seemed an eternity but was probably only moments before another voice came through the door. "Ma'am?" a man's voice said, and there was the sound of metal on metal, a key being tried in the lock. A moment later the door swung open. Standing in the hall were a tall, stooped man in a dark green uniform and a woman in a matching green shirt. On the pockets of both was stitched "Pierpont Farms."

Somehow, Gin had ended up in the chicken processing plant.

* * *

Ten minutes later she was seated in a break room a floor above. A clock on the wall read nearly three thirty—in the morning, as Gin confirmed with her rescuers. It turned out that she had been locked in an unused basement closet of the old plant headquarters. "I don't even know why they have us clean in here," Marla, the cleaning woman who had discovered her, said. "Hardly anyone uses it anymore."

She had made three mugs of instant cocoa in the

microwave, but Mr. Holt, her supervisor, hadn't touched his; he was on the phone with the police.

The Pierpont Farms plant was in the Clairton police jurisdiction, and from Holt's side of the conversation, Gin knew they'd be here soon. She had driven by the old plant hundreds of times when she was growing up; in the last few years, the plant had been expanded and modernized. State of the art equipment and record earnings had gained Pierpont the gratitude of a community still struggling to re-emerge from the collapse of its steel economy. Gin would guess that many of Cindy Ewing's neighbors—just a few miles away—were employed here.

Though she didn't plan to tell the police that. Or anything about her adventure, for that matter. She'd just say she'd been picking up Thai food for her and her parents; she knew there was a popular Thai restaurant in Greensboro. She'd say it was her father's favorite to explain why she'd made the drive.

As for the rest . . . the truth would have to do.

So much for staying under the county police radar.

* * *

Madeleine came to pick her up. Her car had been towed; the plan was for Madeleine to drive her to claim it from the impound. Gin knew that Tuck would be angry when he found out that Gin hadn't called him immediately—but she figured that the last thing he needed was to show up uninvited while he was on suspension.

"They would have given me a ride," Gin protested, but Madeleine's expression sufficed to make her drop it.

"Mom . . ." she began, when they were both in Madeleine's Lexus. It was almost eight o'clock in the morning, and Madeleine had clearly not slept. Her face was drawn and there were purple circles under her eyes. She and Richard had spent the night frantically making calls, trying to find her.

"We were terrified," Madeleine said. "After what happened in your bedroom—and all these unidentified bodies—"

"I'm so sorry." Gin reached for her mother's hand. "I hate that you were worried. But I wasn't hurt, and I would have been found. Whoever drugged me didn't mean to kill me. Only to frighten me."

"Well, they succeeded in frightening your mother," Madeleine sighed, then started the car.

They rode in silence, Gin's head growing heavy as sleep threatened to overtake her. Pulling up in front of the house, she wondered if she had ever been happier to be home. Richard came flying out the front door and practically pulled her out of her seat, then held her tightly, murmuring her name.

"Come inside," he said. "You need to rest. Are you hungry? Thirsty? Do you need some Tylenol?"

"Dad," Gin laughed, as she followed him into the house. "I'm fine, honest. They took a blood sample at the station to see if they can figure out exactly what I was drugged with, but you don't need to treat me with kid gloves—as you very well know!"

"I suppose I can't talk you into staying home until this case is solved, now that we're getting this fancy new security system," Richard said hopefully. He'd led them into the kitchen, where they all automatically took their usual seats.

"Dad . . ."

"I know, I know. Honestly, you're as stubborn as your mother."

"Hey!" Madeleine interjected.

"Just—can you let the police handle it from here? Things are bound to settle down soon."

Gin changed the subject. "I think I'm going to try to get a few hours of sleep. You guys should too, don't you think?"

Madeleine frowned and looked at her watch. "Definitely. After I just call a couple of—"

"*Now*, honey," Richard said. "I've rescheduled the security guy for tomorrow. I think we've all had enough excitement for today. And Madeleine . . . those calls can wait."

"Oh, all right," Madeleine said, covering a yawn. "Are you coming up?"

"In a minute."

"Listen, guys . . . I've got plans tonight that I don't want to break, so I won't be here for dinner."

"Shouldn't you stay home and rest?" Richard objected.

"They'd better be purely social," Madeleine said. "Second date with the mystery man?"

"N—um . . ." Gin had been about to come up with an excuse when she realized that Keith Walker would make a good alibi, since tensions were still high from the night before. She didn't like lying, but she reasoned that it would only upset her parents to know the truth—even though she wouldn't be in any danger. Probably. "Yes, actually. He's a nice guy."

"Oh, honey, you deserve to relax and have a wonderful time." Madelyn touched Gin's cheek, clearly relieved. "I know you've been nursing a broken heart, but I promise you that it will heal."

"Thanks, Mom." Gin wasn't sure that she completely agreed, but she wasn't going to argue. "I'll be home early."

"See that you are, missy," Richard said, as if Gin was sixteen again.

* * *

She hadn't been lying about going to the city. When she'd reviewed Logan's Facebook account with Tuck, she'd seen that he was planning to attend a rally in Pittsburgh at Market Square, a public outdoor space downtown. Loosely organized around what its promotors claimed was "first amendment freedom," the event page featured stark black and yellow imagery of eagles and closed fists, and slogans like "Down with White Genocide" and "March to Reject Degeneracy."

After her encounter with Cindy Ewing, Gin had decided she needed to be at that rally as it presented an opportunity to catch Logan unawares. She felt certain that her attacker had followed her car last night, but she wouldn't put herself in harm's way again tonight. Even if someone were to manage to follow her to the city, she would be in a crowd. She dressed in comfortable, dark clothing and carried a cross-body bag that left her hands free. She felt a little silly packing mace, a flashlight, and a small first aid kit, but similar rallies across the nation had resulted in a distressing number of casualties, and she was trained to be prepared.

Before getting on the road, Gin called Tuck, glad for the privacy of her car. He must have found out the news—from whom, Gin couldn't be sure—at around lunchtime, because he'd called every half hour since. She'd slept through the first few calls, then ignored the rest since her parents had been hovering.

"Hey," she said when he picked up.

"What the *fuck*, Gin?"

"Do *not* yell at me, Tuck Baxter. It's not like I was walking down the street asking for someone to knock me out."

"Yeah? What were you doing in Greensboro, for God's sake?"

Gin hesitated. "Picking up Thai food . . . ?"

"Don't lie to me," Tuck said, his voice a contained roar. Gin could hear a children's television program in the background and pictured him making dinner with Cherie nearby. "I know that Logan Ewing lives in goddamn Greensboro."

She knew he was angry—but she also knew she hadn't

done anything he wouldn't have done himself. And that his anger was probably masking fear. Fear for her safety.

Which felt oddly comforting. More than comforting, but she didn't want to examine the rest too closely.

"You're right. He does. With his mom, who thought I was a DFS agent. She was terrified I was there to take her kids."

"Really? On what basis? Is she abusing them?" Instantly the anger in his voice was replaced by steely interest. Gin smiled to herself—in some ways, they were two of a kind; neither could walk away from this case.

"No, I don't think so—but the stress of raising those kids alone with too little time and too little money is wearing on her. Not to mention that the place she lives is as bad as anything in the worst areas of Trumbull. She's probably worn out just trying to keep them safe."

"You don't know that, Gin. She wouldn't be worried about DFS unless she had a reason to be. Did you see Logan?"

For a moment Gin wavered; now would be the perfect time to tell him where she was going. But given the fact that he was already on the brink of a lecture about what had happened last night, she wasn't about to give him the chance to interfere with her plans. She could just see him forbidding her to go. Between her parents and Tuck, Gin felt like she was dodging one obstacle after another.

"No, he wasn't home. Listen, Tuck . . . I'm pretty tired.

Can we finish this conversation on Monday? I'm going to spend tomorrow with my parents." Not a lie. More like an omission.

"Yeah. Okay. Look, call me first thing, okay? And it better not be from the inside of a shipping container."

"Ha," Gin said, hanging up with a smile—his crude humor was growing on her.

Traffic was light for a rush hour, and Gin arrived in plenty of time to find parking in a well-lit, attended lot and make her way to the plaza. Police had set up barricades along the edge of the public space, but it didn't look like they'd be needed: about twenty mostly male protesters—far fewer than the hordes predicted on the event page—milled about the square, with no clear direction or leadership, while a group of counter-protesters marched peacefully along the edge of the square, holding signs saying "Unite Against Hate" and "All Are Equal in the USA."

Gin took up a post under the awning of the nearby historic Oyster House, and pretended to be looking at her phone while she scanned the protesters. They wore mostly black and camouflage clothing, or T-shirts bearing images of the confederate flag. Many of their signs were crude and homemade, but one long printed banner read "Diversity=White Genocide." Men in sunglasses and black hoodies held up either end, standing as still as statues, while others marched half-heartedly in circles around the center of the square mostly refusing to look at the counter-protesters.

She spotted a tall, thin teenager wearing a gray T-shirt

with no logo or slogan on it, and a pair of frayed jeans. He had the longish dishwater blond hair in the same ragged cut that Logan had on Facebook, and—at least from a distance—the same narrow, pinched features. He looked not so much angry as uncertain and uncomfortable. He stayed close to two other young men who were pumping their fists and jeering at the counter-protestors, but they seemed indifferent to his presence.

Was it Logan? Gin couldn't be sure. She shuddered to see one of the young men unfurl a red flag bearing a swastika in its center. Amid cheers and hooting from the protesters in the square, another chant began—just a lone voice at first, but soon joined by others.

"Haters go home! Haters go home!"

The counter-protesters edged closer and increased their pace, moving like a drunken beast, the stragglers at the edges dodging and darting back and forth. A couple of news cameras tracked their movements. A small, peaceful march didn't make for good news, but Gin knew that if violence were to break out, it would be covered by every outlet around.

She moved out from under the awning and toward the news crews, skirting the scattered groups of observers. As she stepped over someone's backpack that was lying on the ground, she heard the sound of broken glass. A second later, shouting began rocketing back and forth.

"He threw a bottle!"

"Watch out for glass—"

"Jesus, they've got bats!"

"Oh my God, they're going to smash that shop window!"

Gin rushed forward, straining to see, just as one of the counter-protestors was knocked down by men rushing past. The counter-protestor was an elderly woman, and she dropped the cane she'd been leaning on; her purse spilled its contents on the ground. In the next second Gin's view was blocked by people rushing toward the plate glass windows in the shops lining the plaza.

She ran toward the woman, as the crowd swelled and heaved like a living thing. By the time she managed to push her way through, she was confronted by an unexpected sight: the boy she'd been watching—the one she thought might be Logan—was on his hands and knees, picking up the contents of the purse, while several of the counter-protesters helped the old woman to her feet.

"Stop him!" she yelled, her voice high and cracking. "He's stealing my purse!"

One of the counter-protestors, a man with a long gray ponytail, ran forward and grabbed the purse out of the boy's hands, then gave him a hard shove on the shoulder, sending him crashing to the ground on his side. Gin was close enough to hear him grunt with pain.

"Get a cop, that fuckin' Nazi's going to get away!" someone yelled.

"Not if I can help it," came another voice, as a burly, bearded man charged forward. He was about to deliver a kick to the fallen boy's back when Gin leapt between them.

"Stop!" she cried.

"*You* stop! That asshole's a thief."

"I wasn't . . ." the boy protested uncertainly, as he tried to stand.

"I'm with the county police," Gin snapped, an exaggeration if not an outright lie, but she didn't know how else to stop another senseless act of violence from being committed. "I'll take care of this. Get up."

The boy's eyes rolled up at her dubiously, but he didn't argue.

"Where's your badge?" the bearded man yelled at her.

"Just walk with me," Gin muttered under her breath.

The boy looked even younger up close. He limped silently alongside Gin as she led him in the direction of where she had parked. He didn't even look back at the crowd of protesters now engaged in a shouting match with the police who had moved to block them from the shop windows.

Gin waited until they'd crossed the street, moving in the opposite direction of the protest, to speak again. "Are you Logan Ewing?"

The boy's mouth fell open. "How did you know?"

"Mmm. I'll explain later. I'll give you a ride if you'll agree to answer a few questions."

"Are you a reporter?"

"No."

"But you're not really police."

Gin sighed, deciding that the truth was the best option at this point. "No, I'm not. I'm a pathologist. Semi-retired, actually, but I do some work for the county police, so . . ."

Logan shrugged, looking neither impressed nor relieved.

"Does your mom know you're here?"

The glare she got in response told her what she wanted to know.

"Just out of curiosity, where did you tell her you were going?"

He still didn't answer, staring straight ahead in stony silence.

They had arrived at Gin's car, the old Range Rover that had belonged to her parents. Gin unlocked the door and motioned for him to get in. When he did so, she breathed a sigh of relief; she didn't have a plan for what to do if he'd bolted.

She went around the car and got in on the other side. "I'll make a deal with you, Logan—"

"You already made a deal. You said I could have a ride if I answered your question. What is it you want to know, anyway?"

"Okay, I'd like to *amend* the deal. I'll buy you a burger, and I won't tell your mom—or anyone else—that you were here, but I've got more than one question."

Logan gave a small, desultory nod.

"I know you live in Greenport, so how about the Applebee's right off Route 51?"

This time, all she got was a shrug.

Gin decided she'd wait until Logan had some food in him, in case that made him more talkative. There was little traffic, and Logan seemed perfectly comfortable with silence, leaning against the passenger door and staring out at the night.

At the restaurant, he surprised her by holding open the door. The hostess seated them in a booth near the window, with a view onto the highway, the cars going by a blur of taillights. The protest suddenly seemed a thousand miles away.

"I've got one question for you, before we get started. Where were you last night? At around six fifteen?"

He stared at her, understanding dawning in his eyes. "That was you, wasn't it. That came to our house? Pretending to be a caseworker?"

"I never said—"

"What I was doing last night was getting reamed by my mom," he said angrily. "After you left she lost her shit. Drove over to my friend Mason's house and chewed me out in front of his whole family, then made me come home and study for like four hours. What were you trying to do, anyway? She's already terrified we're going to get taken away. I mean, not me, because I'm like an adult already, but . . . DFS keeps checking on Tiffany."

Logan's voice softened when he said his sister's name. His mother clearly wasn't the only one trying desperately to maintain some semblance of a normal family. He could be lying, of course . . . but Gin suspected he wasn't.

The waitress approached before she could respond, and Gin decided to change the subject.

"I'm curious, Logan," Gin said after the waitress had taken their order—bacon barbecue burger for him, chicken

Caesar salad for her—"why are you interested in that protest?"

He looked at her gloomily. "I'm not a racist," he said. "I don't care what you think, but I'm not."

"Um, well, I hate to tell you this, but I think most of your friends back there are."

"It's stupid," Logan said, plucking a packet of soda crackers from the basket on the table and crushing them in their wrapper, between his fingers. "It was supposed to be about jobs. *American* jobs. About how they're moving all of our jobs overseas and giving the ones here to illegal immigrants."

"I see," Gin said, though she didn't, really. The flawed rhetoric coming out of the boy's mouth couldn't have been parroting his father, since—according to Keith Walker—the father had been out of the picture for quite some time. And it certainly wasn't coming from Keith, the boy's uncle; he'd impressed Gin as thoughtful and moderate. "Are you worried about finding a job when you finish high school?"

Logan chewed on his thumbnail, looking out the window. Finally he glanced at Gin and said, "You never said how you knew who I was."

"We'll get to that. Just tell me what brought you to that rally first. I know you're involved with some controversial gaming groups, and that you write fan fiction for Dead Lands 2."

"Oh, *God*," Logan said. "I'm not *involved* with anything. I like the game, is all. The fan fic's a joke, kind of.

And I like the art. I used to like to draw . . . but I suck at it. I suck at pretty much everything I do. I dropped out of wrestling, even. I'm just trying to get through my senior year so I can start trade school and get a halfway decent job and move out of this stupid town."

Jobs, again. Gin took a chance, softening her tone. "Logan, are you upset because your mother lost her old job when the distribution center closed?"

Logan stared at her with his eyes wide. "Wouldn't you be? She had seniority, she was being paid well there. I mean, now she makes half as much and her new boss is a goddamn Paki, he treats her like shit. She missed a couple days because her back was bothering her and she couldn't afford to go to the doctor again so she couldn't get a note, and he threatened to fire her. Everyone knows that those towelheads can't deal with women. And then they hired some other Indian guy to take her job."

His eyes had gone shiny with emotion, and he gripped the packet of crackers so hard that the seam split, raining crumbs down on the table. Logan didn't appear to notice. He grabbed a paper napkin and rubbed his eyes savagely, cursing under his breath.

"I'm really sorry to hear that your mother lost her job," Gin said. And she meant it. So many of the young gang members who ended up on her table in Chicago had been like Logan, disenfranchised by poverty, angry at the world, and yet underneath it all, possessed of an oddly naïve, almost childlike sense of injustice at having been born into a class that couldn't seem to get ahead. "No wonder you're so angry at people who you perceive as having taken opportunities from your family."

"I'm not a racist," Logan mumbled. "I told you that. I don't know why you won't believe me."

"All right. Let's say, for now, that you aren't." Here was Gin's chance to segue to the matter she'd come here to discuss. "Do you have friends who are from families who are better off than you? Kids with wealthy parents . . . maybe lawyers, doctors?"

Logan glanced up at her but didn't answer.

"I guess I'm wondering about one friend in particular. Jonah Krischer. How did you and Jonah meet?"

"I—I don't know him. I mean I know who he is. We were in an SAT prep class together. But I don't like *know* him."

"Which SAT class was it?" Gin asked, wondering how his mother had afforded it.

"Tri-valley Academy," Logan said. "My uncle gave the class to me for my birthday. He thought maybe it would help me get a scholarship or something."

Gin decided not to ask if the class had helped him improve his score. Since bringing up Jonah's name, Logan had become agitated, though he was clearly trying to cover it up.

The waitress brought their food and set the plates in front of them. "Careful, they're hot," she advised. Logan mumbled a thank you.

Gin waited for him to dig in, but after dipping a fry in ketchup and nibbling at it, Logan seemed too nervous to eat more.

"Speaking of your uncle," she said, not wanting to spook Logan by forcing him to talk about Jonah, "do you ever get to fish with him at the cabin?"

This time he couldn't help himself. He sat up straight her and regarded with what looked an awful lot like fear. "How do you even know about the cabin?" he asked. "Or Jonah or my uncle or—or any of this?"

Gin kept her expression neutral, but it was time to turn up the heat a little. "I was telling the truth when I said that I do some work for the county police department. I have a specialty in disinterment and decomposition cases. That means bodies that have been buried, often for a long period of time, under a wide variety of conditions. It turns out that science can tell us a great deal about a person's death, if we know what to look for."

She was taking a gamble, playing her ace. Mentioning the body meant that she couldn't disguise the reason for her interest. Not only was she unsure if it was sound investigative practice, she wasn't sure it was even legal.

When acting as a paid consultant for the office of the medical examiner, Gin was bound by the contract she had signed, which included a sweeping non-disclosure agreement. In short, she was not to discuss the details of any autopsy in which she was involved, nor the identity of the body, unless given explicit permission or compelled to do so in court.

But Gin and Tuck had found the body on their own. The discovery had been made outside the official investigation, even if they had then dutifully reported it to the proper authorities. And more importantly, Gin's instincts told her that it was key to getting Logan to open up. He struck her as confused, frightened, and lonely . . . but not dangerous. Even though Gin had trained herself to ignore any preconceived notions about the people she came into contact with through her work, the sum of her experience—encounters with dozens, perhaps hundreds, of criminals and victims over the years—had given her a certain amount of insight into human behavior.

And she needed to gamble on that now.

Logan was clearly unsettled by her words. "I don't know what you're talking about."

"I see. All right, that's interesting, especially because the discovery of a body on your family's land has been reported on the local television news programs. The police aren't releasing any details yet, and of course I can't discuss the particulars of an active investigation, especially one that's moving as fast as this one is. But I think we both know more than we're saying on this subject."

Logan looked terrified, confirming Gin's suspicion that her vague insinuations had had the desired effect of convincing him that he was under scrutiny. Logan knew something about the body discovered near the cabin. The trick would be to get him to tell her. Right now, he thought that lying was his best option; she needed to find a way to convince him that telling the truth would work in his favor.

"So let's talk about Jonah."

"I already told you, I don't know him."

"Not well, you said. But surely you have impressions, opinions, perhaps casual encounters that gave you some insight into who he is." Gin smiled encouragingly, trying to defuse some of the tension in Logan's eyes. "It's just human nature that we form impressions of everyone we meet, even if it's a brief encounter. Studies have shown that in the first ten seconds after we meet someone, we form opinions on as many as two hundred distinct qualities. And not just superficial things like gender, race, and physical characteristics, but far more subjective things like whether the person is kind or intelligent or generous. People even feel confident in making guesses about things like whether a person has siblings, is in a relationship, or earns a good income."

"But nobody can know all that," Logan protested. "Not from just meeting someone. And if they think they do, they're wrong."

Gin nodded, pleased that she was getting him to engage in the conversation. "You're absolutely right. But what's interesting is that taken in aggregate—that is to say, when you add all of those impressions together—some people tend to be highly accurate in their guesses. And it makes sense, if you think about it—these guesses come from the accumulation of all the experiences a person has had, encounters with people who might be similar or opposite. People who are highly observant and empathic obviously do the best; these qualities correlate with sensitivity and intelligence. And Logan, it's pretty clear to me that describes you."

Logan had been about to take a bite of his burger, but he set it down instead. "You don't even know me," he said, so bleakly that Gin's professional barriers weakened. This, she thought, was one unhappy kid.

But she wasn't here to diagnose him, so she set aside her emotions and pushed harder. "Well, I also have the advantage of having read your file."

She waited to gauge Logan's response to this lie. When he looked frightened, she pushed forward more assertively. "We know that you score high on intuitive reasoning and emotional intelligence. Given that advantage, you must have some impressions of Jonah. Especially if he might be involved in something illegal, I hope you'll consider sharing them with me—with my guarantee that this is off the record."

Again, Gin was staying within the parameters of truth, though perhaps not the entire truth.

"I don't know," Logan said. He picked up the burger again and took a bite, giving himself time to think. After washing it down with soda he said, "Jonah is smart and he works hard. He got like the highest score in the class. I get the feeling his dad expects that from him. That he pushes him hard, you know? And, his mom left. Jonah says she told his father that she couldn't deal with him. With Jonah. So, I mean, that would hard, you know?"

"I see. How was he with the other kids? Is he someone who gets along with people?"

"I mean . . . I guess. As much as anyone, anyway. We were all just thrown together, there were kids from all these different schools." He paused, thinking. "He knew some kids from the private schools, I think he probably knew them from the country club or something."

"What were his interactions with them like? Friendly? . . . Competitive?"

Logan shrugged. "Normal, I guess. He kind of kept to himself."

"Did you ever talk to him about Dead Lands 2? Because that's something you have in common."

Logan looked at her warily, and Gin guessed he was trying to figure out if she already knew the answer, if she was trying to test him.

"Yeah, a couple times," he finally said. Bingo. "I'm pretty active on the forums, so he asked me about that. And we're two of the only players to have gotten to Skull Boss. So we talked about that. But I never actually *saw* it. I kind of had the feeling he was making it up."

"Skull Boss," Gin repeated. "Is that a level of Dead Lands?" She'd looked the game up after viewing Logan and Jonah's Facebook pages. Half a dozen parental advisory groups had called for the game to be banned for its extreme content.

"It's an unlockable. Like where you have to reach a certain level in a certain amount of time, and then you have to do it again with this like random handicap." Another shrug. "It's almost impossible if you don't play professionally. But that's not like why I play or whatever. I know I'll never make pro. I just like the strategy. And the art."

"What about Jonah? Did you get the impression that

he enjoyed the violence for its own sake?" Gin chose her words carefully, speaking gently and maintaining eye contact with Logan. "Do you think he might be capable of violence in real life?"

Logan stared at her with a troubled expression, his eyelashes fluttering, his hands twisting his napkin much as he'd unwittingly destroyed the packet of crackers. For a moment she was certain he was about to speak, but then he changed his mind.

"How would I know?" he whispered hoarsely. "I didn't know him."

* * *

Soon after, Logan declared that he was tired, and Gin had no choice but to drive him home. A single light was burning in an upstairs window. Gin wondered where Cindy thought he had been this evening. Or whether, when she returned home from her low-paying job, with her abusive boss, she'd had energy left to do anything but get Tiffany her dinner and then crawl into her bed.

"Listen, I want you to have my phone number. Can I text it to you now, just so you can call me if you ever feel like it?"

"You said that tonight was confidential. That nothing we said would go further than our conversation."

"Yes, I did. And I stand by that."

Logan must have detected the slight hesitation in her voice—Gin had meant the promise when she made it, but if she was asked in an official capacity—if she was ever under oath, or if the investigation went in a direction that required corroboration on her part—how could she keep that promise? Why had she even made it in the first place? Gin mentally kicked herself for being out of her depth. Her work had been instrumental in solving dozens of murders, hundreds if you counted the war crime victims, but she had never interrogated the living, only the dead.

And the only promise she'd ever made to the dead was her silent one that she had learned and adopted from her boss in Chicago, Chief Medical Examiner Reginald Osnos, who over the course of his long career had made a practice of beginning each autopsy with an unspoken promise to honor and respect the journey that had brought the person to the table while attempting to find all the answers that science could provide.

But only two nights ago she had also lied—deliberately, brazenly—to a man who only wanted to get to know her better. She'd violated her contract by speaking about an active case. And she'd colluded with Tuck in an investigation he was not legally allowed to conduct. Oh, and she'd knowingly manipulated Liam Witt, to get him to lie to his supervisor.

There were so many violations of her own code of ethics, if not outright breaking the law, that Gin couldn't keep track any more. Her involvement had begun innocently enough, then been complicated by Jake's misguided desire for vengeance, then somehow morphed into something much more personal. Somehow, she had to bring closure to the families of the two dead men—maybe as much for herself as for them. And if the intruder in her home, her kidnapping and imprisonment, weren't enough to dissuade her—then nothing was going to stop her now.

For better or worse, Gin meant to see this through to the end.

"Look, you seem like you could use a friend," she said, making one last try. "What's your phone number?"

He opened the car door and got out. Then he leaned down and rattled off the number.

"Good night, Logan," she said, as the boy got out of the car and slammed the door shut without looking back, and then she texted him quickly while she still remembered the number. Call me any time—this is Dr. Gin Sullivan

She let the car idle while she watched Logan dash up the front steps and let himself into the house. A moment later a second light came on upstairs. The curtains rustled in the window, and she thought she saw Logan's face briefly peering out, before the curtains went still.

The small, shabby row of townhouses was silent and reproachful, hunkered down at the edge of a town that, like its residents, seemed to have lost its urge to thrive. While Trumbull embraced change a few miles up the river, turning its shuttered mills into workspaces and upscale eateries, Greenport succumbed little by little to decay, until it seemed that it would end up like the abandoned houses in the flats, choked with vegetation as they were slowly reclaimed into the earth.

Gin eased the car out of the drive and headed back toward Trumbull, following the meandering path of the river, an inky blackness out her window. She was home in no time, traffic nonexistent this late at night.

A powerful melancholia had her in its grip, and she was exhausted, having only managed a few hours of sleep earlier. The light in her parents' window winked out as she gazed at the house from her car; they had turned in for the night.

A text chimed just as she was about to get out of the car. She checked the screen and saw Stephen Harper's name.

Wheeler wants rush on autopsy for cemetery guy. Can you make 10:15 Monday morning?

Gin sighed. It looked like work was going to continue to be her solace for the time being.

Yes, I'll be there. Goodnight, Stephen.

Then she got out of the car quickly, so that no more trouble could find her tonight.

21

After spending Sunday relaxing, helping her father in his garden and taking a long walk with her mother, trying to reassure them that she was taking no risks, Gin was ready to return to work on Monday morning. She was blow-drying her hair in the yellow-tiled bathroom adjacent to her room when there was a knock at the door. She opened it to find Madeleine, dressed for work in a tailored beige linen suit, holding two mugs of coffee. She handed one to Gin.

"You have a visitor," she said, one eyebrow arched. "He promises not to take too much of your time."

"Jake?" Gin asked, her heart stuttering. Was he back in town? Had their last conversation changed his mind?

Madeleine frowned slightly. "No, it's Tuck."

"Oh." Gin winced, hoping her mother wasn't worried by his presence. Evidently, Tuck had expected her to call the minute she woke up, and when she hadn't, he'd taken matters into his own hands. "Mom, look, I—"

"Despite my obvious reservations about the work you're doing, I happen to think Tuck has been roundly mistreated," Madeleine said crisply. "I have access to certain information in my role as mayor, and suffice it to say, there is no solid evidence of any substantive case against him. So while I of course expect both of you to uphold the highest professional standards, and for the love of God stay out of harm's way, I don't see any harm in speaking to the man. Besides, I made him some toast."

"Mom!" Gin looked down at herself in dismay. She hadn't brought her bathrobe home with her, so she was wearing an old swim team robe that she'd found stuffed in the bottom of her dresser. It barely grazed her thighs. She was going to have to make time to go back and get the rest of her things soon. "I don't have time to change if I'm going to get to Pittsburgh in time—"

"I'm sure he'll understand," Madeleine said sweetly, turning and heading back down the stairs.

Gin followed, fuming. If she didn't know better, she would think her mother was encouraging her decidedly inappropriate relationship with the chief of police. But she was probably only hoping that Tuck could provide Gin with an extra measure of safety.

Tuck was seated at the head of the table with a half-eaten slice of buttered raisin bread toast in his hand. "Thanks, Mads," he said. "this is amazing."

"*Mads*?" Gin echoed incredulously.

"We have a good working relationship," Tuck said, shrugging. "What can I say?"

"Gotta run," Madeleine said, setting her mug down in the sink. She kissed Gin's cheek as she passed by her. "Good luck today, honey."

Gin took a seat at the table, awkwardly tugging the hem of her robe to make sure it didn't slip up.

"Sorry to stare," Tuck observed, grinning.

"Perhaps you could stop, then." Gin aimed for a stern tone, but came up a little short. "What are you thinking, coming here? I told you I'd call you. Anyone who drives by could see your SUV in the drive—"

"I came on my bike," Tuck said mildly. "Cherie and I have started biking to school when it's nice out. Might as well take advantage of my little compulsory vacation. Hey, I don't suppose you'd fry me up some bacon to go with this, would you?"

"Tuck," Gin said, exasperated. "I have to be at an autopsy in less than an hour. Wheeler called a rush on it."

"Yeah, I know."

Gin stared at him. "*How* do you know? And what's so important that you had to come over here at this hour?"

"On the first question, my answer isn't going to change, Gin. I don't want to talk about who I'm getting my information from. Suffice it to say that I'm up to speed on Gluck's grave, and the new body . . . I need to know what you learn today at the autopsy as soon as you get out. How about you meet me at that bar in Squirrel Hill after?"

Gin blinked in surprise. She'd accompanied Tuck to a seedy little tavern in Squirrel Hill, a section of Pittsburgh, once before. That time he'd introduced her to an ammunition specialist who lived above the bar. "We're going to see Dusty?"

"Not this time—but we're guaranteed privacy."

"You couldn't have asked me this over the phone?" she demanded.

"Yeah, I guess, but then I wouldn't have gotten a chance to have breakfast with the mayor—or to see you in that thing, for that matter, which is going to fuel months' worth of daydreams—and most importantly, I wouldn't have been able to give you this."

He pulled a tiny Tupperware container from his pocket and snapped off the lid. Inside was a mound of foliage—feathery leaves and sturdy stems with a single, slightly crushed flower with white petals and a purple center. It resembled a wildflower Gin had often noticed on her runs.

Gin took the box and examined it carefully. "Was this found near the burial site?"

Tuck looked bemused. "No, actually. It's just the first thing to bloom in our yard. Cherie picked it herself. She specifically wanted you to have it." He stood and carried his cup to the sink. "I don't have much of a green thumb, Gin. Consider that an invitation to teach me."

After he left, Gin floated the little flower in a drinking glass filled with water, and carried it up to her room, where she set it on her nightstand.

* * *

Gin pulled into her parking spot with moments to spare, and raced through the building to the morgue. No one was in the sink area, but Gin still took care to scrub completely and gown up. Years of habit did not allow her to take any shortcuts.

She made it through the doors at 10:19. Immediately she was confronted with the noxious odor of a decomposing body. Stephen was poised over the table, and to Gin's surprise, the only other person in the room besides the autopsy assistants was Captain Wheeler.

"Good morning, Gin," Wheeler said. Her face was obscured by the mask, but her silver hair showed under her cap, and her expressive eyes flashed behind her stylish red glasses. "Thank you for agreeing to sit in."

"Hi, Gin," Stephen said. "Was traffic bad?"

"No worse than usual—and I'm sorry to be late," Gin said, glad that the mask would obscure her blush. "Especially since you've had to deal with the smell."

Wheeler shrugged. "I put some peppermint oil in my mask. It helps, some. But how do *you* deal with it? You're around this a lot more than me."

"I know this sounds odd, but you kind of get used to it," Gin said. "I mean, it's never pleasant, but it's just part of the job."

"I don't even use Vicks or oil or anything anymore," Stephen said. "I just try to get in the shower before my wife gets home."

Wheeler raised her eyebrows. "Well, I'm impressed. And grateful. Douglas Gluck's wife is demanding that we release her husband's remains for reburial. Naturally, we would like that as well, and as soon as possible. I want to shield the department from any negative exposure on this one. So far we've kept the existence of the second body out of the press, but it's imperative that we process this with haste."

"Will Bruce be joining us?"

"He had another obligation this morning," Wheeler said. "But I'll be sure to fully brief him as soon as he is free. And, of course, he'll have access to Dr. Harper's notes and the lab results, which Morgan King assures me they will process as quickly as possible, given the circumstances. I expected fingerprint results this morning, but given the staffing situation, it seems they're delayed."

Gin turned her attention to the body, and immediately noticed something shocking: there was already a Y-incision similar to the kind made in an autopsy in the dead man's torso. It had been sewn shut using what appeared to be shiny red nylon cord, the type used for crafting or gift wrap. It was a serviceable job, other than the materials used and the size of the stitches.

"Yeah," Stephen said in a tone of confusion. "Got to say I've never seen anything like this before. Never even *heard* of anything like this before."

"Neither have I," Gin agreed, bending down to take a closer look. Without any means of preserving the body, the incision area was badly degraded, but otherwise surprisingly precise. The end of the cord had been neatly knotted below the final stitch.

"Do you think this was done by someone with training?" Wheeler asked. She didn't appear to be put off by the sight, and Gin remembered that she had come up through the ranks of homicide herself.

"Hard to know, though the stitch is different—we don't typically use an overcast stitch. So I'd say no. Just to catch you up to speed, Gin," he added, "analysis of the post-mortem blood sample showed heroin and alcohol."

"Signs of chronic use, I assume?" Gin asked, basing her assessment on faint track marks visible near the wrists and telangiectasia, or prominent cutaneous blood vessels of the face, evident even despite the swelling and decomposition of the skin.

"Yes, and we'll get a better read from tox, obviously, for what it's worth."

"You'll be able to determine if this was an overdose?"

"No, unfortunately," Stephen said. "The levels won't necessarily reflect those at time of death, especially since we can't pinpoint when it was."

"But given their presence at detectable levels, it's reasonable to assume he was intoxicated."

Stephen nodded. "Other than that, there is ample evidence of chronic exposure. These open lacerations on his ankles are from untreated varicose veins—they probably burst days before death. Here—these squiggly lines— that's from a parasitic infestation. And this ulcer on the ear is an untreated carcinoma. Oh—and here, you see, he's lost most of his toenails—he's got damage to the soft tissue and nerves consistent with immersion foot." He glanced at Wheeler. "That's common in the homeless."

"I remember," she said grimly. Like, Gin, she'd probably seen too many exposure deaths while working the streets.

"Now it's hard to be certain, but I'm seeing indications of possible strangulation." He pointed to dark, bruise-like marks on the throat. "Because of the condition of the body, these aren't distinct enough to be sure, but the discoloration here could be from asphyxia. Then again, it might not—and in half of strangulation deaths, there are no external marks at all. So it's problematic."

"But how else would you explain that?" Bruce demanded, pointing at the patchy ring of apparent bruising.

"I agree, it's a strong possibility that he was strangled—I just can't offer any guarantees."

"Noted."

"Okay. Moving on . . ." Stephen appeared to visibly steel himself, picking up a small pair of angled dissecting scissors. He snipped every few stitches carefully and removed them with tweezers, dropping the bits of cord onto a tray. He then used forceps to carefully lift the flaps of flesh on either side, folding them out of the way. Finally, he lifted the chest plate, which was typically removed in one piece during autopsy.

It fell apart in his hands.

"What the . . ."

Gin moved automatically to help him, then stopped

herself. Instead, one of the technicians took one piece so that it didn't fall back into the cavity and set it aside, while Stephen did the same with the other. Usually, bone saw or electric saw was used to cut each rib, and then the connective tissue was snipped away, and the entire plate removed in one piece with the cartilage and muscle attached. Then it was returned in one piece before the body was sewn closed.

But in this case, cuts seemed to have been made in several places, using a rougher tool that didn't leave a clean edge.

"It was as if whoever did this didn't know where to start," Stephen said. "They may have—what the hell?"

He reached into the cavity, plucking out tissue that had come free of the ribs. Underneath were several round, purplish objects.

"What is *that*?" Wheeler asked.

"I don't . . ." Stephen reached for a pair of forceps and carefully lifted the first object, laying it on the steel tray.

It was a plastic bag, the common kitchen zipper-top variety rather than the kind usually used to return the organs to the body cavity after they were examined and weighed. The contents looked like spoiled meat, swimming in viscous purple fluid. Stephen lifted out three more bags, each similar to the first, and laid them on the table. "That's it," he said.

"Are those his organs?" Wheeler asked.

"Not sure." Stephen teased open the first bag's zippered

tops and upended its contents. The noxious odor in the room deepened. "It's a heart, anyway, but . . ."

"I don't understand," Wheeler said.

No one spoke as Stephen opened the other three packages, all of which contained nearly identical organs.

"Four hearts," Stephen said. "Obviously, decomposition is advanced, and liquification has begun."

"Those aren't human," Gin said, breathing through her mouth as she leaned closer to the table. "I think they're pig."

"How can you tell? I mean, I haven't seen a lot of them, but they look the same," Wheeler said.

"Here," Gin said, pointing to a large vessel to the rear of one of the hearts. "The cardinal vein in a pig is notably larger. Also, the shape is slightly different—more rounded, and the muscle is coarser, and kind of crumbly."

"So someone took out this man's organs, and replaced them with four pig hearts?"

"We'll do further testing to be sure," Stephen said.

Something was nagging at Gin's brain, as she processed the horror of what was in front of her. "I've seen this before," she said. "Or not this, but . . . something."

"Well, I can say with certainty that I have never seen anything like this, ever." Stephen appeared visibly shaken.

"Me either," the technician said.

"Something ritualistic?" Wheeler asked. "There wasn't anything like this in Douglas Gluck's autopsy, was there?"

"No, in his case the original incision and the stitching

that closed it were undisturbed. I don't think he had been tampered with."

"And you can't draw any conclusions about the cause of death, I assume?"

"Not in the condition the body is in. It could have been any number of things. Without the internal organs, it's anyone's guess. Is there anything else you'd like to see, Captain?" Stephen asked politely.

"No, I think that'll do. But do copy me on all reports relating to this case."

"Of course."

"And Gin, that goes for you too. I know I eventually see everything you turn in, but please consider this a priority. When can you have your report back to us?"

Gin thought fast. She'd hoped to spend time at the school today, but she could arrange to work on her proposal over the weekend. "I can get it to you by this evening."

"That will be fine. And I am sure I don't need to remind either of you to keep this information to yourselves."

Stephen offered to walk out with Gin, as the techs began photographing and weighing the matter that had been bagged and placed in the body cavity. "I know you'll want to get started on that report, but do you have time for lunch?"

Gin deliberated; she'd promised to text Tuck when the autopsy was over, but she welcomed the chance to brainstorm with Stephen. "I'm afraid I can't do lunch, but I could squeeze in a quick cup of coffee."

They decided to go to a popular little coffee shop

nearby on the Strip. As they walked in the late morning bustle, enjoying the sunshine, Stephen shared that the morale around the offices had been terrible.

"Not only is everyone anxious about the internal investigation, but no one knows what to make of Wheeler getting involved like this. I mean, obviously, this case presents a challenge for her election chances, so that part's clear. But like today—she's been showing up all over the place where she doesn't make a habit of going. I heard from my friend in Narcotics that she's been showing up at their daily briefing on a regular basis. I don't remember that ever happening before."

"Do you think she could be trying to conduct aspects of the investigation of her own? Like maybe she or her superiors don't feel they are getting sufficient traction on the internal probe—the official one anyway—and they've elected to keep parts of it out of her subordinates' hands and have her on the ground directly?"

"Well, if that were true, you could make a case that she's investigating *me*. Because she's never come to one of my autopsies before and I have to tell you, Gin, I kind of hope she doesn't make a habit of it. I was so nervous in there . . . I was sure I was going to make some spectacular mistake and you were going to have to bail me out."

Gin saw an opportunity. "Actually, speaking of bailing people out . . . Tuck once told me that you got him out of some hot water years ago when he was a sergeant."

"Oh, that." Stephen chuckled. "He way overstates my contribution to that case. I just noticed the inconsistency on the report, that's all. A shooting victim's family insisted that the responding officers let him bleed out on purpose, but I was able to determine time of death as *preceding* the officers' arrival. Honestly, I think he could have defended the officers' actions pretty easily if it had ever made it to court. He's got—had, anyway—a pretty solid reputation. He just demands too much from himself, if you want my opinion. *He's* the one who couldn't accept that he hadn't been able to resolve it himself."

"But you and he became close . . . at least that's what I took away from the conversation."

Stephen shrugged. "Sure, he's a great guy. But I mean we don't get together outside of work or anything. Don't get me wrong, if there were more hours in the day, I'd love to get together with him for a bike ride or a few beers, but he's got his daughter and I've got the wife and kids, and, well, that's a luxury that's going to have to wait until things settle down at home."

Gin was disappointed—it didn't sound like Stephen was the source Tuck had been unwilling to name, after all. They'd arrived at the little coffee shop, and Stephen bought two lattes and two macaroons, which they carried to an iron table in the tiny outdoor seating area. As they were sitting down, Stephen's phone rang. He glanced at his screen. "Sorry, Gin, I'd better get this—it's the Westmoreland County guys."

He answered and exchanged a quick greeting, then listened for a few moments, then said a terse goodbye, hung up and let out a breath. "Well—we've got a fingerprint ID match. That was Paul Singh, he's a records officer over there. Our special guest this morning was Brian Dumbauld, age sixty-four, and not only has he been homeless for the last six years, he's got a sheet as long as my arm dating back well before then. The last few years it's been mostly minor stuff, vagrancy and public intoxication, and crimes of opportunity—purse snatching, shoplifting. One scuffle with another homeless man that sent the other guy to the hospital."

"Where did all of this take place?" Gin asked.

"Mostly McKeesport and Denton, it sounds like, but I'll have the full report in the next half hour. I'll forward it to you as soon as I get it."

"So whoever removed Paul Gluck from his grave left a homeless man there in his place, after performing a disembowelment and replacing the organs with four pigs' hearts." Gin thought for a moment. "I don't think we're any closer to understanding what happened and why than we were before. Any brilliant ideas, Stephen?"

Stephen popped the last of the macaroon in his mouth, thinking while he chewed. "Nope, not a one," he finally said. "Luckily, that's out of my pay grade, anyway. And I have to say, on days like today, I'm pretty happy about that."

"I know what you mean," Gin said, wondering what Stephen would say if he knew how deep she'd gotten involved in this case. Remarkably, news of her kidnapping—and even the home break-in—didn't seem to have made the rounds here yet. But that would change the minute one person got wind of it: the grapevine was spectacularly efficient.

Gin and Stephen threw away their trash and started walking back.

"Listen, there's something I should have said before, when we were talking about Tuck. I know that you and he have become friends," Stephen said, "and I just want to tell you—well, I guess I wanted to say that, for what my opinion is worth, there's no chance that he's guilty of the things people are saying he did."

"Thank you, Stephen, but I try not to listen to gossip. All I know is that he was forced to step down." At the mention of Tuck, Gin glanced at her watch. "Stephen, I'm sorry, but I'm meeting someone and I should probably get going. Let's do this again soon—my treat next time."

"Sure thing, Gin. Maybe one of these days when things slow down, we can talk about something other than work."

"I'd love that," Gin said.

But she suspected that they both knew that day was unlikely to come.

22

Gin texted Tuck that she was on her way, and drove through Schenley Park, past the Botanical Gardens, to the historic neighborhood known as Squirrel Hill. She parked near the top of a street on the considerably less gentrified edge of the neighborhood, where shabby old houses lined blocks anchored with corner markets and bars. She had been here once before, and knew that the unmarked brick building between an apartment building and a body shop housed an old-school tavern.

She opened the door and took a moment to adjust to the darkness and the smell of stale beer, and was greeted with a wolf whistle.

"Hey, pretty lady, wanna car date? I've got cash."

Gin spotted Tuck sitting at the bar in front of a huge pile of chicken wings on a paper plate, and sat down on the stool next to him. The bartender who'd been there last time gave her the same bored, indifferent nod, and she ordered a soft drink.

"Did you pick this place to deliberately embarrass me?" Gin asked, as the bartender slid a glass in front of her.

"What, do you mean Chuck? He doesn't listen to anything anyone says. And there's nobody else here. Dig in, I got plenty of wings. They're from a joint down the street—best in town."

Gin sampled a wing, grabbing for her water glass as the spicy sauce made its way down her throat.

"I should have mentioned they're a bit spicy," Tuck said, taking a drink of his beer. "If you don't mind me thinking you're a wimp, the ones on this side are mild."

"You did that on purpose," Gin accused, gasping from the heat of the sauce.

"Who, me?" Tuck smirked. "Anyway, you first. What have you got for me, Inspector Gadget?"

Gin told him about her interaction with Logan, emphasizing his evasiveness and underplaying the violent end of the protest, but Tuck still chided her.

"What the hell were you thinking, Gin? People have *died* at those damn protests. Do you think that just because you managed to get out of that closet some lunatic locked you in, suddenly you're bulletproof?"

"I was never in any danger," Gin protested, knowing it wasn't true. "And if I hadn't been there, I wouldn't have had an opportunity to get Logan to open up."

"You drove him in your personal car. That's a huge risk, Gin, and a liability to the department, too."

"I—I can't believe you're saying that." Too late, she realized he was messing with her. "Besides—when have you ever cared about the department's exposure?"

"But that's me. I'm armed, I'm trained, I'm tough. You're a—a cupcake in a lab coat."

"Wow, thanks. For your information, I gained Logan's *trust*. I learned more from him than anyone else has."

"You just keep telling yourself that. But if you do something like that again, I'm going to make sure you're grounded. Now tell me about the autopsy."

Gin tried to ignore the mixture of anger, frustration, and other, more confusing emotions his words provoked, and filled him in on the details of the autopsy in as clinical language as possible. She skipped over the more routine parts, describing the puzzling contents of the body cavity and the amateur incision and stitching.

"Damn," Tuck sighed, pushing the plate of bones away. "Gotta say, that's a little tough to stomach, even for me."

"So you've got no idea what that might have signified."

"Nope. Sometimes the criminal mind eludes me."

"I have to say . . . I know this will sound weird, but it reminds me of something."

"That *is* weird. Maybe you need to take a break from your job—go get your hair done or buy shoes or something."

"Wow, Tuck, every once in a while, I start to think you're evolving, and then . . . besides, what's wrong with my hair?"

"Nothing, as far as I can tell. But you know women."

He shuddered in mock horror. "Actually, the hair thing is on my mind because Cherie and I have . . . well, it's a little complicated. The visit to the specialist is kind of a tough thing for her. All the tests, the questions . . . anyway, a few years back I started bribing her. Made a deal with her that after it was over, she could pick a special outing, anything she wanted, within reason. We've gone to the zoo, the movies, ice skating."

"Sounds like a good way to reduce the stress of a difficult situation."

"Yeah, except this year—well, there's no other way to say it. She wants to cause me as much suffering as possible, I guess. We're going to the spa. Hair, nails, the whole nine yards."

"Oh, Tuck," Gin laughed. "That's wonderful. I'd offer to go with you, but I'd hate to deprive you of the full experience. You should get a pedicure, at least."

This time, his horrified recoil looked real. "I'd sooner have someone pull my nails out with pliers. Look, at first I thought it was a dumb idea, but Cherie's noticed that a lot of the girls are beginning to experiment with makeup and nail polish and so forth. And she wants to get her hair cut like Olive's. I don't know . . . I guess there's a part of me that wishes I could shield her from all that."

"I understand the impulse. But I think it's great that you're helping her fit in as she's getting older."

"And then I'm on the hook for dinner at Shady's," Tuck added, naming a family restaurant popular with kids, with an expansive arcade and a menu featuring pizza and burgers.

"So you're having wings for lunch? Sounds like you're spoiling for a heart attack," Gin teased. "Maybe you should see if Cherie wants to run a 5K with you next."

"Hey, Sullivan, there's nothing wrong with my heart," Tuck growled. "I'm ready to prove it to you any time—just say the word."

"I'll have to take a rain check," Gin smiled. "Some of us still have to work."

Funny thing, how his risqué teasing didn't offend her as much as it once had. Only because she was tired of scolding him, Gin told herself.

But as she sipped at her soda, she wondered if it was time to accept that she enjoyed it.

*   *   *

Tuck and Gin had agreed that she should pre-emptively offer to share everything about the autopsy with Bruce in an attempt to see if he might open up to her about any new developments in the investigation, rather than waiting for him to review the report, but it was the end of the week before he got back to her after she left him several voice mails.

"Hey, Sullivan, you called?" he said, as though days hadn't passed.

Gin felt her face warm, wondering if it was possible to speak to the man without becoming frustrated. "Look, I was calling because—well, because I have concerns about this case."

"Which part? Dead guy number one? Dead guy number two? I read the report, by the way—that's some freaky shit. Or are you still hung up on Jake's junkie mom?"

"All of it. The connections between them. I'm glad to hear you at least think they're all connected somehow."

"Oh, I didn't say that. Far as I'm concerned, Marnie Bertram might as well have put a gun to her own head when she ate that bottle of pills. Douglas Gluck was already dead, so the only question there is why somebody decided to interrupt his eternal rest. And Brian Dumbauld? I looked into his case history after I got the report. He isn't exactly going to get a key from the city for his contributions to the community. Look, I hate to be blunt here, Gin, but I'm not sure where you think I'm going to find support for following up on this guy, given that we're running on empty in the manpower department. I mean, yeah, the case is open, but I can't justify throwing resources at it. I'm sorry to say it, but dead junkies aren't very high on anyone's list."

"Yes, but you're a *homicide* investigator," Gin said, exasperated. "And at least one of those was likely a homicide. I haven't exactly heard about any other new murders that could be taking up your time, so . . ."

"Gin. You want me to spell this out for you? You'd have to be living under a rock not to know how serious Wheeler is about her upcoming campaign. Everyone's expecting her to make the official announcement next week. She's heavily favored to win, and then Goldman will be promoted to captain to take her place, leaving a big fat hole where Special Ops lieutenant used to be." He paused, and Gin could imagine the self-satisfied smirk that was his signature expression. "See where we're going with this?"

"You're hoping to be promoted to that post," she said.

"Which means that I need to show I've got the chops for it. The *leadership* potential."

"I haven't exactly noticed," Gin said drily.

Bruce snorted. "If you did more than play in the corpse sandbox, you'd know that I've been heavily involved in the narcotics investigation. The one that *has* caught the public's attention. The one that Wheeler's going to be talking about at her announcement speech."

"Thank you for making this all crystal clear," Gin said. "You're worried about how you're going to look up there at her side, and to hell with everything else on your plate." She couldn't remember the last time she'd been provoked enough to curse at a colleague.

"Everyone you mentioned—they're *dead*," he said flatly. "They don't care. And they don't have loved ones to care, either. Look, Gin, I'll probably never convince you of this, and I don't know why I even give a flying fuck, but I care about my job. I do good work. Ask your buddy Tuck if you don't believe me. And I'm going to be able to do a lot *more* good once I'm running Special Ops."

Could he be telling the truth? Or was this evidence of a dark, manipulative side of Bruce—a man who seized opportunities wherever he found them, regardless of the cost to others?

"Let me see if I can change your mind," Gin said instead.

"I doubt you can, but sure, give it your best shot."

Gin described her conversation with Logan, explaining how she'd been studying his social media. To her relief, he didn't seem to care that she'd endangered herself by attending the protest, and seemed intrigued by Logan's relationship with Jonah and their shared fascination with violent computer games.

"This Dead Lands 2," Bruce said. "I'll look into it, but even if it's as violent as you say, it's just a game. If we had to check into every kid who's hooked on first person shooter games, we'd never do anything else."

"The point is that there's data to support a link between violent gaming and increases in aggressive behavior, and just as important, a decrease in prosocial behavior, empathy, moral engagement—in other words, the sort of profile behind a lot of violent crime. Add to that Logan's family's economic woes, his social disenfranchisement—"

"Yeah, you've got yourself a little serial killer, right? Sorry, Gin, that's sounding a lot like a Hollywood movie."

"Don't you think it's relevant that he and Jonah were friends?" Gin asked in frustration. "It never made much sense that Jonah would simply stumble on a body ten miles from where he lived. This suggests he was at the cabin for some other reason. Meaning that at the very least he lied about how he discovered it—and suggests that the boys were involved somehow."

"And this means . . . what, exactly, for me?"

"I think we should talk to Jonah again. At the very least, he might be able to give us some insight into Logan's activities. And I know where he is tonight—the jazz band is playing at the senior center."

"Right." Bruce barked a laugh. "His dad will be thrilled with us showing up. Pluck his kid right out of a sanctioned school activity—nice. Besides, Gin, I realize you probably spend your Friday evenings watching masterpiece theater and reading medical journals, but I'm off the clock in about ten minutes. And I've got a really, really important date."

Gin squeezed her eyes shut in frustration. "Bruce . . . please. This could be an important opportunity—and I can help. If Jonah has information he's reluctant to share, I've had psychological training, I can—"

"If I wanted assistance from a professional, why wouldn't I just call the departmental psychiatrist?" Bruce interrupted her. "Sorry to have to point it out, but you don't get a lot of practice with head shrinking since all your patients are dead."

Progress, Gin thought—he hadn't flat out refused. "Because, in the first place—it's Friday night. Like you said, Dr. Tanenbaum probably has a date with masterpiece theater and her medical journals. And in the second place—you traded away your chance to nail Jonah for the drug charges, which would have fit right into Wheeler's campaign—and this might be your chance to bring him back in. If we can show that he's involved with the grave tampering or the death of Brian Dumbauld, the immunity deal's off, and you can focus attention on the opiate crisis. Which in turn will help your own chances for advancement."

Bruce didn't reply for a moment. Gin could hear his slightly adenoidal breathing. "Hang on," he said abruptly. "I've got another call."

Gin waited; as the moments ticked by, she wondered if Bruce had actually hung up on her. After what seemed like ages, he finally came back on the line. "It's your lucky night," he said. "My date canceled on me. So I find that I've got a little free time."

"You're not going to regret this," Gin said.

She desperately hoped she was right.

23

As Gin was buying two tickets from the parent volunteers manning the desk at the senior center, Bruce came up beside her. The parking lot had been full of cars, and parents and friends chatted as they waited to buy tickets.

"Enjoy the concert, you two," the cheerful middle-aged blond said, handing Gin her change.

Gin realized she thought she and Bruce were a couple. He was still wearing his work clothes, though he'd removed his jacket and loosened his tie. He wasn't a bad looking man, but his manners were so offensive that Gin had to resist the urge to correct the ticket taker's mistaken impression.

"So, we'll approach him after the concert?" Gin asked as they entered the auditorium.

"Fuck that—I didn't give up my Friday night to listen to a bunch of screeching and wailing. The band's just going to have to deal with being a man down in the horn section. Come on, this probably leads backstage."

Gin followed Bruce through a door, up a ramp and into the backstage area, where teens milled around warming up and tuning their instruments. Girls and boys alike wore a uniform of jeans and black shirts, some of them accessorizing with outlandish ties and hats and Mardi Gras beads.

"There's our boy," Bruce said, not bothering to keep his voice down. Gin had spotted him too. He was standing in a corner by himself with his arms folded over his chest, and the expression on his face could only be described as a smirk as he watched the other students milling around. He looked arrogant, unapproachable—far different from the first time she'd seen him, when Jake had dragged him home.

Bruce didn't bother to keep his voice down. "Hey, Jonah, how about you hang up the sax and come with us for a chat?"

"What do you want?" Jonah asked, plucking a sheaf of sheet music from a nearby stand. "I already told you guys everything I know. My dad's lawyer says I don't have to talk to you anymore."

"What's this about?" a thirtyish man with a lot of product in his hair asked as he approached them. "Who are you?"

"Detective Bruce Stillman, Allegheny County Police Bruce flipped his badge with an air of boredom, then nodded in Gin's direction. "I brought her along in case things get out of hand. She's a real pit bull—I wouldn't give her any reason to get cranky."

Imagine that, Gin thought. Bruce had a sense of humor.

The badge seemed to have done the trick. "You can't come back here," the band director said, uncertainly. "We're moments away from the performance."

"And I'm sure it'll be memorable," Bruce said. "Maybe there are some talent scouts in the audience and you'll be playing Carnegie soon. Don't worry, we'll find some-where quiet to talk."

Jonah had dropped the aloof manner and was packing his saxophone into his case. To Gin, it looked like he might be considering bolting. Bruce seemed to have drawn the same conclusion. "We can do this the easy way, or the hard way," he said cheerfully. "I'll give you a clue—the easy way is you coming with us before that hot flute player over there figures out we're not here to give you a scholarship to Juilliard."

Jonah hefted the case and scowled. "Can we please just get this over with?"

Gin and Bruce filed out with Jonah between them, through the gauntlet of the curious gazes of his peers. He stumbled twice, and Gin couldn't help feeling sorry for him.

"So what now? Are you dragging me to the station again?"

"I've got a better idea," Bruce said. "I thought we'd go

visit the cemetery. We can go in my car—county picks up the tab for gas, and nobody's going to hassle us."

Gin said nothing. The cemetery was an inspired choice—*if* Jonah actually knew anything about how Dumbauld's body ended up in Gluck's grave, and Gluck ended up near the cabin. They rode in silence, Jonah silent in the backseat. Several times, Gin turned to look at him, trying to decide if he was angry or frightened or some combination of the two, but he'd resumed his implacable smirking. She tried to imagine him having the wherewithal to follow her to Greensboro, set up an obstacle, drug her, and somehow transport her to the plant, and decided the idea was ludicrous; he was still a kid, plagued with acne and nervous around his teachers.

The gates of the cemetery looked more imposing at night. One of the lights near the offices was burned out, intensifying the foreboding atmosphere. As Bruce cruised slowly along the paved cemetery road, a parked car started up and hurriedly exited. Kids, Gin figured, using the cemetery for a little privacy to make out or get high.

Even knowing exactly where they were going, the grave site was still a grim shock. The area was still ringed with crime scene tape, the surrounding lawn rutted and torn where the CSI team had set up. The small mound of dirt the two workmen had excavated still sat on the plywood sheet. Since their visit, a tarp had been stretched over the open grave. As they followed Bruce to the edge of the hole, Gin could see that it was empty, the weak moonlight battling the black void.

"Take a good look," Bruce said, in a friendly tone. "I know that pile of dirt doesn't look like much, but the gravediggers showed me where most of it ended up, in the woods over there. You know, you don't realize how hard it is to move that much dirt around, especially with soil being damp. My pops used to make me and my brother help him out with his rental houses on the weekends—we replaced a whole foundation when I was thirteen. Jacked that fucker up on piers while my dad yelled at us. Damn, that was a shit ton of dirt, too."

Jonah said nothing, his hands jammed in his pockets, looking around the cemetery.

"Nothing like you guys have it now," Bruce went on. "Playing for the stiffs on a Friday night—and then, what, an after-party at some kid's house? Get your hand up that redhead's skirt, from the way she was looking at you. You hit that already?"

"Don't be disgusting," Jonah said. Gin had to admire Bruce's ability to provoke a response from him.

"Yeah, you're right," Bruce said. "Got to keep your nose clean, you're probably going to spend the weekend studying for the SAT, right? Daddy's got plans for you. Nothing but the best for his kid."

"You're wrong about him," Jonah muttered. "My father doesn't love me. He only wants to change me."

"Jonah," Gin said, deciding that it was time to change the course of the conversation. "I talked to Logan Ewing. He shared some . . . disturbing things."

Jonah lifted his head slowly, his mouth set in a tight

line. "Logan? The kid from my prep class? He's a freak. He's the one you should be talking to, not me. Whatever he said about me, it's probably just part of his pathetic need for attention."

"But you're here and Logan isn't. Humor us, Jonah—if you know anything about the body you discovered near the cabin, now's the time to share it."

"Is this where you scare me straight or something? If I don't toe the line, I'll end up here, something like that?"

"Why, would that convince you?" Bruce asked.

"Probably not. My dad's been telling me I'll end up in jail or dead before I'm twenty, so I've had a chance to get used to it." In a quieter voice, he added, "It would almost be a relief."

"Why a relief?" Gin asked, while Bruce rolled his eyes. "Are you saying you sometimes think about harming yourself?"

"You sound like my shrink," Jonah said, in possibly the most empty, despairing tone Gin had ever heard.

"Before you decide you're too angsty to live, consider what happened to that guy," Bruce said. "That body you took us to, at the cabin? Poor guy was minding his own business, being, like, *dead*, and somebody came out here and dug him up. This is his address, right here." He pointed at the hole. "He was all nice and fixed up for the funeral, and whoever took him out messed that all up. He isn't a pretty sight any more, believe me."

Jonah was trying to maintain his attitude of defiance,

but Gin could see his composure slipping. He looked rather queasy, actually.

"Was he . . . uh, like, rotting?" he asked.

"Well, you saw him, didn't you?"

Jonah shook his head emphatically. "All I saw was the part of this black trash bag that wasn't buried, and the . . . the arm sticking out. With no hand. I only went close enough to make sure it really was, you know, what it looked like. And then I . . . uh."

"Ran away, right?" Bruce said with disgust. "Couldn't handle it. Probably cried like a girl all the way home."

"Bruce," Gin cautioned him with some exasperation. "I'm not actually sure how this line of questioning is helping . . . ?"

Bruce brushed her comment away. "Just getting the lad softened up. Making you more receptive to what we have to say. Right, my friend?"

"Whatever," Jonah mumbled morosely.

"The thing I don't get, that maybe you can help me out with, the whole time your dad's pushing the ivy league thing, you're trying to set yourself up as some kind of baller, right? Stealing his prescription pad, writing scripts, selling that shit to your friends. But that wasn't enough for you. What happened, did you get bored? Because cutting into someone else's territory, going up against established dealers—don't you watch TV? You didn't think about what happens to dealers who try to take over someone else's corner?"

"I only sold pills," Jonah protested. "Not street stuff."

"Oh, so you only dealt with a discerning clientele," Bruce scoffed. "Thing is, you die with a silver spoon up your nose and a stomach full of hydrocodone, you're just as dead as the poor asshole who could only afford a little cheap smack. I know you managed to convince yourself that you're not responsible for Marnie Bertram's death. I thought maybe if you came out here, where a lot of addicts just like her end up before their time, it might bring it home to you."

"You might think that the addicts who were desperate enough to buy from you weren't worthy as human beings," Gin said, trying to take a more empathetic tack in order to get Jonah to see things her way. "But what you may not realize is that virtually anyone can get addicted to opiates. I've seen all kinds of people die from abuse of prescription drugs—housewives, ministers, kindergarten teachers."

"Oh, boo hoo," Jonah said. But clearly the conversation was taking a toll on him. His shoulders slumped, and he was tugging nervously at the hem of his shirt.

"I'm not naïve enough to think that getting you to stop selling drugs is going to have any effect on the problem of overdose deaths," Gin said. "Someone else has undoubtedly stepped in to take your place. But you can still help out in another way. I believe you know more about the body you found than you're letting on. And there's a disturbing pattern underway." She couldn't tell him about the gruesome contents of Brian Dumbauld's body, but she could at least try to force him to see the victims as human beings. Gin suspected that Jonah was far more sensitive than he'd let on, and that the key to his cooperation was the guilt she felt sure he was carrying below the surface.

"I believe that you really do feel badly about Marnie Bertram, Jonah," she said gently. "I think you actually feel terrible about it, that it hurts every day to know that you can't undo what happened. And maybe you think that it doesn't really matter that Douglas Gluck's remains were disturbed, since they'll soon be returned here and given a respectful reburial.

"But here's what you don't know, Jonah." She paused to let the full impact of her words sink in. "There was another murder. When Mr. Gluck's body was removed from this grave, it was replaced with the body of a homeless man who had the misfortune to cross paths with the killer. He was murdered and tossed in that hole like a piece of trash. And it's entirely possible that there will be more, if we can't identify and stop the killer."

Jonah seemed at the very limit of his composure. His lower lip trembled and he was trying to look anywhere but at the hole.

"But I don't know for sure," he mumbled. "I mean, because if it was him, maybe I could have stopped him."

"Stopped who?" Bruce said. "Gonna need some more details, son."

"He—he seemed okay at first. He was just someone to talk to while we were waiting for our rides."

"Logan Ewing?"

Jonah nodded. "We were always the last ones waiting.

Dad thought it would force me to talk to the tutor after class, but she was out of here practically before the time was up. And Logan . . . sometimes his mom never came at all, and we gave him a ride."

"Your dad didn't mind?"

Jonah snorted. "Of course he minded. He minds everything that inconveniences him even a little. And he says *I'm* lazy—he says it's the reason that my mom left, but I think it's because of how he treated her. But he couldn't leave Logan waiting there at ten o'clock at night, and besides, Dad loves to act like he's some big do-gooder, and this way he could brag to his friends about how he helped this poor kid out."

"That was it?" Bruce said. "Your whole connection to this kid—a few rides?"

"It would have been," Jonah said, "except one night I mentioned to him I'd picked up a copy of Dead Lands 2. He told me it was, like, his favorite game. That night he texted me a bunch of links—unlockables, cheats, and hacks. They're on the internet, the coders wrote them in but they're not in any of the documentation or anything."

"I've read about those," Gin said. "Gamers are obsessed with them."

"Yeah, they're cool, kind of." Jonah looked embarrassed. "I mean they're stupid, they're not worth anything, but people collect them and then they brag about them so if it's something you're into, you can try to get some of the rare ones and then people are like really happy to play you."

Gin suspected that it went even further than that, that the virtual badges were a form of social capital for awkward kids.

"How many do you have, Jonah?" she asked gently.

"I don't know, like ten or twelve," he admitted, not looking at her. "But Logan had, like, forty or fifty. And some of them were really bad. I told him I didn't believe him about some of them, so he sent me screen shots. He had Stone Face, and Claw Hand, and Triple Saw—that's super hard to find. But the one . . . God. The one that I never heard of anyone else finding was Blood of the Enemy. He's kills his victims by suffocating them and then eviscerates them and pulls all their entrails out and . . . this is disgusting, but in the game he eats the hearts. Like, raw, with blood dripping everywhere. The most anyone ever got to was four."

"No shit," Bruce said, not bothering to keep the excitement out of his voice. Here it was, the first real clue they had connecting Logan to the disturbing contents of Dumbauld's—a detail that had not been made public. "What does this online character do with the bodies?"

"I don't know," Jonah said, looking green around the gills. "I blocked Logan after that. He, uh, scared me. I'll admit it."

"So what really happened, at the cabin? How did you find out about the body?" Gin said.

Jonah's eyes darted back and forth, as if searching for a way out. "He, uh, came to the house one time a few weeks later. He had his mom's car. It was a Saturday; my dad was playing tennis. I thought it was a package delivery or something, but I opened the door and he was standing there, looking crazy. He was pissed that I'd blocked him, and he said he had something really cool to show me. It was weird, it was like he was going back and forth between mad and trying to be friends . . . I was kind of thinking he was losing it."

"But you went with him anyway," Gin said. "Why would you do that, if you were afraid?"

"Because he—he said he'd post all these things online, about how I was a Castrato. That's like the worst thing you can be in Dead Lands 2—it's a troll that's had his balls cut off because he snitched."

Bruce laughed. "You were afraid he'd call you that online? That would be like someone posting on Facebook that I'm a Vulcan. Sticks and stones, you know?"

"You don't get it."

"I think I might," Gin said. "You were afraid of what people would think of you for playing the game at all. That he would out you as a social pariah, a geek."

Jonah lifted his face, affirmation in his expression. "It would be the last straw, okay? I'm already the kid whose dad makes him play in the jazz band. And enter all these speech and essay contests. And I've never been allowed to play sports because Dad's convinced I'll be a surgeon and he's worried about my hands. He might as well have put a big sign on me saying KICK ME." He'd begun to quietly cry. "Do you know how often I got beat up my freshman year? They hate me—all the popular kids. I've never been invited to a party. I—I've never kissed a girl. And if Logan did what he said he was going to, I never would. So yeah, I went. I figured it was going to be something about the game . . . but he took me down by the creek and . . . and, yeah."

"How did he explain the body being there?"

"He said he just found it. That it just showed up. But I figured he did it—from the start, I knew it was probably him."

"Why didn't you *say* something?"

"Because Logan said that if I told anyone about it, he'd make it look like I killed the guy. He . . . he liked having it there. It was sick. He said he was conducting experiments on it. He said he cut off the hands because they had some sort of deformity that made them look like the Claw Hand character from the game."

Gin tried to hide her reaction—Jonah could easily be describing the "split hand" effect in some ectodermal dysplasia patients. "But you did take us to it."

"Don't you get it? I *wanted* you to see it. I just didn't want him to know I was the one who showed you. I thought maybe Jonah would think it was just someone out walking their dog or whatever. I didn't know it was embalmed, that he just stole the body out of the grave. Honestly, if I had, I probably would have turned him in. Because at least he wouldn't have killed the guy." He brushed a tear from his eye impatiently. "I had no idea there was another one. I keep thinking—I keep wishing it was last year. Last summer. Before all of this happened, when I was just thinking

I had to get through one more year of high school and then I could leave, I'd be free of this forever."

He wiped his nose on his sleeve and cleared his throat. "Are we done here?" he said angrily. "Or do you guys want to beat me down or something, make sure I never forget all these important lessons you taught me tonight?"

"We're just getting started," Bruce said, taking Jonah's arm and steering him toward the exit. "You're going to come down to the station and tell that whole story all over again. Don't worry, we'll tell Daddy he's got to stay in the waiting room." Jonah tried to jerk his arm away, but Bruce tightened his grip. "I'm going to go pay your pal Logan a little visit. After we make sure that every last thing you said tonight checks out, we'll put that bad boy away for a long, long time."

"I know this is hard," Gin said, shooting Bruce a dirty look as she fell in step with Jonah. "You were brave to tell us everything."

"Ignore her, son," Bruce interrupted. "Gin, you need to remember you're just consulting on this thing. Glad you could come to the party tonight though—you can send my thank you note to the office."

No one spoke on the drive to the station. As they pulled into the parking lot, Bruce glanced over his shoulder at Jonah. "Tell you what—I might just forget to call your dad for a bit here—given all the excitement. That okay with you?"

"Thanks," Jonah mumbled. He shot Gin a desolate

look as he got out of the car, and then the three of them entered the building.

* * *

Bruce emerged from the interview room an hour later with a smirk on his face, and plopped down on the vinyl sofa in the lobby next to Gin. "He remembered a few more things," he said. "Wrapped this thing up like a Christmas present."

"Did they find Logan?"

"Yeah, had to drive around for a bit, but he was out with a few of his skinhead friends, skateboarding. They'll be here in twenty minutes."

"And Jonah's dad?"

"Screaming like a stuck pig—even though his kid's off the hook. At least we bought Jonah a little time. I'm kind of wondering if we should do him a favor and lock him in the holding cell."

Gin sighed. It hardly seemed fair for Jonah to have to go back to his unhappy home life after he'd helped crack the case. "I think I'll head out, then. I've worried my folks enough in the last few days."

"Hey, before you go, I'm curious—are you banging Baxter?"

"I—I'm going to pretend that you didn't ask that," Gin stammered.

"Don't get all offended, it's just that there's so many people hooking up at work these days. Liam and Katie, Reggie and Wheeler—"

"Wait," Gin said. "Reggie Clawitter, in Narcotics? And Captain *Wheeler*?"

"Well, I don't have any proof of that one," Bruce said. "But I saw him let himself into her office last Thursday night when I went back to get some files I forgot. It was almost eight, and it's no big thing for *her* to work late, especially with all this political bullshit she's working, but what reason would Reggie have to stay past his shift?"

"I don't actually know him that well. I only met him at Douglas Gluck's autopsy. But Bruce—*how* would he let himself in?"

"I guess she gave him a key. But that's another thing—why were he and Serena at the autopsy?"

"Um . . . because it was a suspected OD? Because it happened at a location they were already watching? Because they've become laser-focused on the opioid crisis?"

"Yeah, sure, all true. But there's something else you don't know. They've been hooking up in records."

"*What*?" Gin had seen the records department on a tour of the county offices when she accepted the ongoing consulting role; it was a grim, windowless space in the basement of the county office building, with dingy walls and old metal cabinets literally bursting with files. While much of the building had been updated, the move to a digital filing system was taking longer than expected to complete, which only added to the problem of tracking weapons that had led to the current problem of missing guns. "Why would you think that?"

"Well, obviously they can't use her office, right? With one whole wall of it being glass? But hardly anyone ever goes down to records, not when they can scan things into the archives. Hell, most of the time it's locked up since most of the staff is working at the new space. But I come into the building that way sometimes when I ride my bike to work—I don't like to leave it outside, so I keep it in the boiler room—and I've run into Reggie down there in the hall three or four times, and he acted all flustered. I'll bet you anything he was waiting to give Wheeler the all-clear, so she could come out."

"But even if you're right about him having an affair—he could be taking anyone down there. Just because he was in her office a few times, why would you think it's Wheeler?"

"Because I've figured out their code. I can see his desk from where I sit. You know how on the phones, there's all those keys no one uses anymore because everyone would rather just use their cell?"

"Yes . . ." There was a phone in Gin's office that lit up and even rang occasionally, but she'd never used it; none of the consultants did.

"Well, back when we actually used them, you could dial a shortcut to someone's number by the first letter of their last name. So if you wanted to call me, for instance, you'd hit 'S' and then a number—I was two. So my code was S2."

"And . . ."

"And Reggie always goes straight for the 'W'. Get it?

And then ten or fifteen minutes later, off he goes—right down to the basement."

Gin stared at Bruce, a shocking realization dawning. But apparently he mistook her expression for admiration, because he reached across the center console and gave her knee a squeeze.

"Yep, S2 . . . give it a try sometime. And we don't even have to go down to the basement—my office doesn't even have a window."

"I . . . will keep that in mind," Gin said shakily, pressing herself against the passenger window, as far from Bruce as she could get. Not only was Bruce offensive and out of line, but he apparently wasn't even as smart as she'd given him credit for.

Because Captain Wheeler wasn't the only person whose last name began with W.

* * *

"Nice night for a booty call," Tuck said when he opened the door. "Lucky for you, my little princess fell asleep admiring her glitter nails, so the coast is clear."

Despite the urgency of her visit, Gin smiled. "How was the spa trip?"

"Horrible," Tuck said, glowering. "Hellish. They brought me tea in this frilly little cup. The place smelled like burning hair and cheap perfume. A woman in a bathrobe old enough to be my mom pretended she couldn't find the treatment room so she could flash me her boob." He shuddered. "But Cherie loved it, so . . ."

"So it was all worth it," Gin said. "Next time maybe I'll come with you. We could get side-by-side facials."

"Are you asking me on a date, Gin Sullivan?"

"No chance," Gin said. "Is Reggie Clawitter behind the gun thefts?"

The shift in Tuck's expression was comic—and brief. His eyebrows shot up and he looked like someone had sucker punched him for all of two seconds before he composed himself and managed to look bored. "Can't confirm," he said. "Can't deny. I'd be interested in knowing why you ask, though."

"Because Bruce Stillman is possibly the worst detective I've ever met," Gin said. She described his theories about Reggie and the captain, his frequent visits to the basement. "Will you at least tell me if you think he's working with someone else?"

"And why would I do that?"

"Because I think I might be able to tell you exactly who it is."

"This has suddenly gotten a lot more interesting," Tuck rose and opened a cabinet above the fridge, coming back with a bottle of bourbon and two shot glasses. "I think you need a little more skin in this game. You think you're onto something—and I think you're full of shit. What are you willing to wager?"

24

Several days later, an urgent knock at the door woke Gin from a dream. In it, Lily had returned. She was back in the tunnel, still wearing the strange, diaphanous clothing, still beckoning to Gin to come closer.

But something was different this time. Though she was far in the distance, she wasn't receding any further. In fact, she appeared to be walking slowly *toward* Gin. Her lips moved and Gin had strained to hear what she was saying, but there was only a gentle rushing of wind . . . until the knock at her door.

Madeleine entered, dressed for work and carrying her laptop.

"May I sit?" she asked.

"Good morning, Mom," Gin said with a smile.

"Good morning. Didn't I say that already? Sorry, I've got to be in the city in an hour." Madeleine was attending a hearing regarding Tuck's actions since arriving in Trumbull, and while it was mostly a formality given the arrests of Reggie Clawitter and Liam Witt in the IA investigation, Madeleine was a big believer in tying up loose ends. "But I thought you'd want to take a look at this. Your pal Melanie Carter posted it online, so don't get too upset because it wasn't big enough news to make the print version."

"Mom, whatever it is, no one reads the print version anymore anyway!"

"But it'll get buried under the bigger stories, is the point." She hesitated, and Gin took the laptop out of her hands.

"Oh," she said in dismay. There, under the headline "Trumbull Top Cop Off the Hook," was a picture of Tuck Baxter on the steps of the municipal building, leaning in close to speak to Gin. The angle of the photograph made it look like they were kissing. Underneath, a caption read "Baxter celebrates exoneration with consulting patholo- gist Dr. Virginia Sullivan, daughter of Trumbull mayor Madeleine Sullivan."

"Other than the photo, it's mostly just a summary of the case against Detectives Witt and Clawitter," Madeleine reassured her.

"Yeah, if anyone reads that far," Gin said, handing the laptop back. "Thanks, Mom. At least I'll know why I'm avoiding the press."

"It'll blow right over." Madeleine kissed her fingertips and touched them to Gin's forehead. "Be back soon."

"Mom, I'm fine, really," Gin called after her retreating form.

Now, though, she had a reason to get up. It might be too late to prevent Jake from seeing the photo before she talked to him—but she owed him a call nonetheless. She had been on the phone almost non-stop since Tuck called Wheeler and she ordered the internal comms records be cross referenced with the records logs. Overwhelming evidence of Liam Witt's involvement became undeniable fact when the tech support team located a spreadsheet in a folder shared between the two men, detailing every missing weapon going back six months. The file, amusingly, was named OfficeFootballPool.

She dressed, poured herself a cup of coffee and took it out onto the screen porch, then took a deep breath and made the call.

As it rang, Gin tried to think of the right words to tell Jake how sorry she was. But what was she sorry about? He was the one who'd left her behind. She'd done nothing wrong.

But a part of her still felt like they were bound together. And it was going to be a long time before that feeling went away.

"Hello?"

"Jake. It's me."

There was a brief pause, one she might not have even noticed had she not been so finely attuned to this conversation, and then he said, "Gin, it's good to hear from you. How have you been?"

"I—I'm fine. Keeping busy."

For a few moments they made small talk, Jake inquiring after her parents and describing the state of the retreat center as it entered its final phase of construction. "With any luck, we'll be able to schedule the ribbon cutting for the Independence Day weekend."

"I'm really happy for you," Gin said. With the on-time bonus, Jake would be able to begin his next project with a nice cash cushion.

"I see that kid's uncle hired him a lawyer," Jake said. "I'd feel a lot better knowing he's off the street."

"You and everyone else," Gin said. "I assume you've seen the headlines? They're calling him the Dead Lands Killer, even though they still don't have enough evidence to hold him. And apparently sales of the game are at an all-time high."

"That's disheartening, but it doesn't surprise me. People are fascinated by events like these."

"I know. I just feel terrible for his family. They claim they never had any idea it was going on." She tried not to think about what Keith Walker must be going through, and whether he had figured out by now that 'Beth Conway' had never really existed. "Meanwhile, Jonah Krischer has been exonerated, but his father is still pushing ahead with a lawsuit against the department."

"Yeah, I saw him on TV. What's with that guy? He's gotten everything he wanted. His kid's off the hook. And he wouldn't answer any questions about his son stealing his prescription pad so he could sell drugs—it's like he conveniently wrote that out of the story."

Something was nagging at the back of Gin's mind.

Something about the prescription pads. The drugs . . .

"Jake . . . I'm so sorry, but I think I need to go."

"Is everything okay?"

Thoughts collided and swirled in her head, beginning to resolve into a picture, a realignment of facts that wouldn't quite come into focus.

"Yes . . . I'm fine, it's just—Jake, I'm sorry, I really need to get off the phone. I promise I'll explain later."

"I don't understand—"

"It's nothing to do with you, it's—it would take too long to explain. Jake . . ." There was so much to say, and no way to say it—now, and possibly ever.

But it would have to wait.

"I'll talk to you soon." Gin hung up before giving Jake a chance to respond. She might regret that later, but for now, she had to figure out if the idea that had just come to her was solid.

Jonah had stolen his father's prescription pad and used it to get drugs: Adderall—(or so he'd claimed; they had never actually found it in his possession), Vicodin, and Ativan. They were operating under the assumption he'd sold Vicodin to Marnie Bertram and Brian Dumbauld—and, possibly, the unidentified third victim he claimed he'd killed weeks earlier.

But he'd never claimed to have sold Ativan to anyone, even though he'd had it with him. That was surprising— thirty percent of overdose deaths were due to a deadly combination of opiates and benzodiazepine like Ativan; and benzo abuse was on the rise. If Jonah wasn't selling it—it was because he wasn't offering it for sale. Which begged the question—who was taking the Ativan he'd had with him?

There was one possibility that she had never considered. What if *Jonah* had been taking it? Over and over, Gin had observed him having trouble with balance—the many times he'd tripped or stumbled—which was a telling side effect of benzodiazepine use.

Benzos were prescribed as anti-anxiety, anti-seizure, anti-depressant . . . and anti-psychotic.

Jonah's father had been keen to make the case against his son go away from the very start, even after Jonah had been cleared. What if Mark Krischer had instructed his son to take the medication to address sociopathy—because he feared what Jonah was capable of? Or, worse yet—what if he *knew* what Jonah was capable of—and had been trying to treat him without anyone finding out?

All of the puzzle pieces were arranging themselves in a new and terrifying way. Things Jonah had casually mentioned were taking on a whole new meaning.

My mother couldn't deal with me.

My father doesn't love me.

He's always trying to change me.

And now Dr. Krischer was determined to see someone else put away for the string of murders. Even if it meant that an innocent person paid for the crimes.

Viewed through this lens, what Gin knew about Jonah's personality took on a different light. His frequent shifts in mood, his ability to be charming when he wanted, or to evoke sympathy or concern in adults. Was it all a ruse, a manipulation? Then there was the fascination with the macabre, which—though he claimed it was all Logan—was reflected in his interests, especially his gaming. And then there was his drug dealing: his willingness to sell to the most vulnerable addicts signaled a lack of empathy for others, a failure to take responsibility for his own actions,

Could he be a classic sociopath?

Jonah had been lying all along. He'd been playing her, playing everyone—covering up his true intentions with a persona that he'd put on like a mask. And his father had known.

Gin had been all too ready to accept that he was simply a teen driven by unreasonable parental expectations and social pressures to act out, that he never intended to harm anyone, that he was unnerved and even frightened by Logan's behavior.

He'd made sure that all the pieces lined up—claiming that Logan had pressured him to play Dead Lands with him, the discovery of the body that would implicate Logan, right down to the gruesome detail of the pig hearts. But all along he'd been orchestrating events from inside his own disturbed mind.

He'd robbed a grave, only to disfigure the body—probably to satisfy his own twisted needs, though Gin would defer to psychologists to interpret his actions.

He'd killed and brutalized a homeless addict for no reason that Gin could ascertain, other than the satisfaction he got from the act.

He'd implicated Logan so easily and dispassionately that Gin could only imagine he was unable to experience empathy for another human being. Jonah did not care about Logan's suffering, using him to ensure that he got away with his crimes.

And now that Logan was the only person who could implicate Jonah, how far would Jonah go to keep him quiet?

Gin dialed Tuck's number with shaking hands, only to reach his voice mail.

"Tuck . . . call me, please. It's urgent. I think that Jonah was guilty all along. Of everything. I don't have time to explain now, I need to warn Logan. Just—just please call as soon as you get this."

Then she tried Logan's number. It rang and rang, finally reaching a generic voicemail notifying her that the person she was trying to reach was unavailable at this time. Quickly, with a growing sense of foreboding, Gin texted him.

Logan, this is Gin Sullivan. I need to speak with you right away. Please call me back.

Gin paced the kitchen floor, her mounting fear making it difficult to focus. She tried looking up Cindy Ewing online, but there was no phone number to be found. Finally she decided that she would go to his house; maybe he had turned his phone off, or hadn't bothered to look at it.

She had barely gotten into her car when a text chimed.

Hi Dr Sullivan

A few seconds later:

Whats going on are they coming to arrest me

Gin thought for a moment, worried that she might spook him before she could talk to him.

No nothing like that. I do need to talk to you though. Can you tell me where you are?

I didn't do what they said I did

I know that now, Logan. We can talk more in person. Please tell me where you are.

I've been trying to stay off the radar. There's this cabin near my uncles no one is using it so I've been staying there. Take the dirt road after my uncles road on the right. Go a quarter mile, You have to park get out of your car at the sign that says no Trespassing walk past it you will see a path that leads to the cabin.

Gin was typing her response when another text came through:

I'm just glad someone finally believes me

Gin finished her text, her heart pounding.

Stay where you are. I am on my way. I will be there in twenty minutes or so.

Then she copied Logan's text and sent it to Tuck, adding that she was headed there now.

*   *   *

The dirt road was exactly where Logan said it would be, but it was rutted and overgrown with weeds, and Gin nearly missed the rusted, faded No Trespassing sign nailed to a tree. She parked and locked her car and headed down the path, her feet getting tangled in weeds, her arms scratched by branches. She'd gone about four hundred yards when she saw what was more of a shack than a cabin, a leaning one-room structure supported by crude posts hewn from logs. One window was missing, the other cracked.

She mounted the porch, taking care to avoid the rotted and broken boards, and tried the door handle. The door swung open, creaking, and she blinked to adjust to the darkness inside the small, cramped space.

A single chair sat in the center of the room. Logan was tied to it, his fine blond hair plastered to his forehead with blood, his mouth taped shut with silver duct tape. When he saw Gin, he began making urgent sounds, his eyes wild with fear, rocking violently in an effort to free himself.

Before Gin could react, something fell over her head

and torso, like a scratchy blanket. She pawed at it, trying to free herself, but it was pulled tight around her arms, binding them to her sides. A second later something encircled her lower legs and jerked sharply, causing her to fall. Unable to use her hands to block her fall, she landed hard on her shoulder and hip, and cried out in pain.

"Shut the fuck up," a voice said. *Jonah*.

More ropes were tied around her, at her neck and her knees, and then her head was lifted off the floor as Jonah grabbed the cloth and pulled up. She heard a ripping sound and suddenly she could see; he'd sliced open the fabric in front of her face, the blade of his utility knife coming within a fraction of an inch of cutting her.

A light came on. Gin looked wildly around the shack, which was empty except for the broken, rusting springs from a mattress, and an old linoleum kitchen table.

Jonah regarded her with undisguised contempt. "Welcome to my workshop," he said, lifting something from a collection of objects on the old table.

He went to Logan's side and Gin realized with horror that the object in his hand was a scalpel. He yanked on the tape binding Logan's mouth and sliced through it, then ripped it from his face. Logan screamed, dots of blood appearing around his mouth.

"Shut *up*," Jonah repeated and, holding the scalpel loosely by the blade, bounced the handle off Logan's face.

"I can't believe I didn't put this all together sooner," Gin said furiously, awkwardly maneuvering herself into a sitting position, the ropes digging into her body painfully.

"You mutilated Douglas Gluck's body. You strangled Brian Dumbauld, didn't you? Just like in the game."

Jonah smiled. "Not without help. My good buddy Logan was there, too."

"I didn't help!" Logan protested, his voice hoarse. "I told you to stop!"

"You did," Jonah conceded, raising an eyebrow. "I was disappointed in you. You turned out to be a frightened little nothing."

"He told me he knew somewhere we could go to buy weed," Logan said. "I swear I didn't know what he was going to do. I—I just wanted to try it. The man . . . the homeless man, he was just lying there, behind the warehouse. I think he was passed out, but he woke up when—when—" His words dissolved into hiccupping tears.

"When I wrapped my hands around his neck," Jonah finished the sentence. "I was going to let you do it, before I realized what a coward you are."

He walked to the table and set down the scalpel, his hand hovering over the rest of the objects. Now that the light was on, Gin could see that there was a variety of knives, pliers, and a sewing kit with wicked looking curved needles. There was also a collection of little plastic figurines holding various weapons—the characters from Dead Lands 2.

"That bum was my second," he told Gin with a note of pride in his voice. "My first was two months ago—nobody even investigated it. It was so easy—I just held his coat over his face until he stopped kicking. I guess the cops thought he died in his sleep from exposure or something. Man, there's no rush like that."

"Why did you bother to bury him, then?"

"Why not? I had the grave opened up anyway. I only needed one body for insurance, to hold over Logan here. I figured I might as well stash it in Gluck's place."

"But—I don't get it. If you only needed to incriminate someone else for your crimes, why even go to the trouble of digging up the grave when you had easy access to the homeless?"

Jonah paused, frowning at her. "I'm disappointed you don't see it. Those bums—they're all alike. Disposable. But Mr. Gluck was different. Ever since my dad told me about him, I wanted to see for myself." He picked up a figurine of a muscular figure with human features except for his long, lupine snout and razor-sharp teeth "Like Shiva here—born different, with a power that he was too timid ever to use. I wanted to study him. To understand him, his essence."

"But all you did was dump him behind that cabin."

"Yeah, well, he turned out to be a disappointment," Jonah muttered. "Spent his whole life trying to cover up the only thing that made him special, until he drained his power away. Such a waste. I won't make that mistake again."

Gin shuddered, realizing the extent of Jonah's madness. Whatever he had been searching for in Douglas Gluck, he would never find—but that wouldn't stop him from trying again. From killing again.

"I told Chief Baxter where I was going," Gin said. "He'll be here any moment."

Jonah laughed. "Yeah, that's a good one. I know you didn't call him, or anyone else—you wanted to bring in Logan all by yourself. You wanted everyone to know—you can't stand to share the spotlight, can you? See, I know how doctors are. You're all megalomaniacs like my dad, drunk with your own power. But the crazy thing is, you don't really have any power at all. You try to heal people, but most of the time you fail. *I'm* the one with the real power!"

He was wandering off topic, growing increasingly manic and excited. He picked up a large adjustable wrench and swung it in a lazy arc.

"Let him go," Gin said. "I'll stay—I want to hear what you have to say. I do. But Logan isn't worth your time." She closed her eyes, hating the ruse she was about to play. "They won't cover the death of a poor kid from a bad part of town, not like they would if something happens to me. If you pick me instead, I guarantee it will be in the news for weeks."

Jonah looked at her thoughtfully, testing the wrench's jaws on his thumb, squeezing gently. "Yeah, I see what you're saying. But why should I let either one of you go? I'll do him first. Then you and I will go on a little drive tonight, up to the old fire tower. With any luck the rangers will find you first thing in the morning. By the time Jonah turns up, he should be a real mess—nice and disgusting, rotting away in that chair. What's left of him, anyway."

He turned to face Logan. "Who's the second most feared character in the game, old pal? Huh? Don't feel like talking?" He sighed and picked up a little plastic figurine, an ogre wielding a small dagger with a blood-red handle. "Necrotto, that's who. And we both know why, don't we?"

Logan began to cry harder, mumbling "No, please, no."

"Because he cuts his victims up little by little," Jonah said patiently, as though speaking to a child. "First the toes. Then the fingers, one by one. Then the feet, the hands . . . you get the picture."

He dug something from his pocket and knelt in front of Logan, then removed his shoes almost tenderly. Logan's whimpers turned to screaming as Jonah pulled off his socks. Ignoring the screams, Logan manipulated his toes into the object he was holding—a pink foam pedicure toe separator.

"I'd think you'd be more appreciative," Jonah said, standing and wiping his hands on his pants. "You should have seen the look on the clerk's face at the drugstore when I bought these. Not to mention the latex gloves I bought for updating your bedroom décor. That clerk acted like I was some sort of freak or something."

"You were the one who broke in and threw the paint on our walls." Fury threatened to overtake Gin's terror. "Were you the one who locked me in at the plant, too?"

Jonah bowed mockingly. "One of my finer accomplishments, though you made it difficult. I'd been keeping an eye on my little buried treasure in the cemetery, but I just about shit myself when I saw you and the cops roll in. I'm just lucky I happened to stop by that day."

"But how did you know I'd be visiting Cindy Ewing?"

"I didn't. I followed you all day—do you know how hard it was to keep up with you on your run without you seeing me? I almost grabbed you when you came out of your house, but some old guy came out of his across the street and acted like he was going to call the cops or something, just because I took a short cut through his backyard. And then after you went and talked to Logan's mom, I figured I'd better do something."

"And you just happened to have inhalational anaesthetic in your possession . . . ?"

Logan shrugged. "Sometimes having a doctor for a father pays off. I like to keep it handy."

"Were you planning to leave me there to die?"

"Well, it would have been nice. You've turned out to be a real pain in the ass. But no, I just wanted to scare you enough to back off."

Logan kicked helplessly as Jonah went to the table and picked up a small garden lopper, its curving blades glinting.

"Logan, no—" Gin cried, but Jonah moved so quickly that he'd jammed the blade between the littlest toes on Logan's left foot before she could complete her sentence.

And then he jerked the handles together.

Logan's screams became frantic as blood spurted from his foot. The little toe fell to the floor and rolled several inches, as Jonah inspected the blade.

"You don't have to do this," Gin pleaded, her vision clouding with fear and revulsion.

There was a sound outside—a footfall on the old porch. There was no time to react before the door burst open, slamming into the wall. Tuck followed, gun in hand.

"On the floor! Right now, get on that floor with your arms up or I swear I'll put one through your heart!"

"Yes, Mister Big Shot Cop," Jonah said, a curious smile twisting his lips. Very carefully, he held his hands out to the sides, letting the plastic figurine fall to the floor, but he didn't drop the wrench.

"*Now!*" Tuck roared.

Jonah began to lower himself to the ground—and then he leaped up, arm high overhead, ready to bring the heavy wrench crashing down on Logan's head.

There was a single shot, and Jonah crumpled. The wrench glanced off Logan's scalp, the force significantly diminished, but his head fell forward anyway, and he went still.

The only sound in the cabin were the wheezing grunts coming from the floor. From Gin's vantage point, not four feet away, she watched the crazy light leave Jonah's eyes, and he was transformed into a boy again—a frightened, dying boy. His hands clutched weakly at his chest, from which blood was seeping, and his eyes rolled up into his head. "Hehhh," he said, a final, gentle breath.

And then he was gone.

Tuck raced forward and put two fingers to Logan's neck. "Come on, come on," he said.

"Is he alive?" Gin croaked.

"Yes. I think he's just knocked out, but his pulse is irregular." He pulled out his phone and dialed. While he talked to the dispatcher and sent the location coordinates, his voice was clipped and emotionless, but as soon as he hung up, his neutral expression fell away.

"They'll be here soon," he said, kneeling and checking Jonah's pulse. He was motionless for several seconds, then he shook his head. "Gone," he muttered. "And I'm not going to pretend I'm sorry."

He pulled out his own knife and carefully cut away the ropes and netting that bound Gin. Only when he pulled the fabric off her and the blood began to return to her limbs did she realize how tightly she'd been bound. She rubbed her arms and attempted to stand, but it took two attempts because she'd lost feeling in her lower legs.

Tuck helped her to her feet and gathered her into his arms. "Are you all right?"

Gin pressed her face against his chest, feeling the first waves of shock that would hold her in its grip for quite some time. She concentrated on her breathing, inhaling the comforting scent of him.

"Thank you," she mumbled. "Thank you for coming for me."

Tuck stroked her back and pressed his face into her hair. For a while he said nothing, holding her against him, letting her cry. When he finally spoke, his voice was rough with emotion.

"I've been coming for you for a long time, Gin. And this time, I'm not letting you go."

EPILOGUE

Six weeks later, Madeleine Sullivan threw a party.

"Gin, honey, could you please get some more ice?"

Madeleine handed Gin the silver ice bucket that she'd received as a wedding gift almost thirty-five years ago, polished just this morning to a shine. The matching tongs sat precisely between the cocktail napkins and a uniform row of delicate faceted cups, next to the crystal bowl brimming with the champagne punch that had been a mainstay of Sullivan parties for generations.

"Sure, Mom," Gin said with an indulgent smile. As barbecues went, the ones Madeleine threw could be a little over the top—but everyone seemed to be enjoying the brisket Richard had been smoking since before dawn, as well as the platters of salads and side dishes the caterers had prepared.

Gin watched the two dozen guests chatting and

enjoying the pleasant evening in the backyard. The garden had never looked prettier, abloom with flowers of every color. Gin's contribution were the strings of fairy lights strung from the trees that she had spent the morning hanging.

The party was the first since Captain Wheeler held a press conference naming Jonah Krischer in three murders as well as tampering with Douglas Gluck's grave. Jonah's father had finally broken down and confessed that he'd suspected his son of psychotic acts of cruelty and violence for years; in addition to a jar containing the severed hands of Douglas Gluck in formaldehyde, investigators found animal skeletons and human and animal teeth on a shelf in Jonah's closet, and—in the back of the freezer wrapped in a bread bag, a human heart that was being tested for a match with Brian Dumbauld.

Logan had been released from the hospital after being treated for a concussion, the severed toe, and a laceration requiring thirty stitches on his scalp. Social services had been called in to ensure he had the support he needed to recover from his trauma, and his mother was also receiving therapeutic support and job training and placement assistance.

Madeleine had invited some of her staff as well as friends from the county offices, including Maureen Wheeler, who had taken a break from stump speeches and was enjoying being simply a civilian tonight in bright red Bermuda shorts and a sailor striped top. She was talking to Paula Burkett, whose pregnancy bump was on display in her knit tank dress, while Paula's partner Angie brought plates piled high with brisket and salad, since she finally had her appetite back. Several of Madeleine's support staff were sampling the tamales Rosa's mother had prepared, while Rosa and Doyle filled their plates along with Brandon and Diane.

All of the important people in Gin's life were here . . . except for one. Jake had been invited, but he had begun a new project in downtown Clairton several weeks ago in early July, the complete renovation of a round midcentury hotel with spectacular views of the river, and couldn't get away. They'd spoken several times in recent weeks, though the conversations had been formal and slightly stilted. Gin was still processing the end of their relationship in her own way, but as Madeleine had advised, perhaps the passing of a little time would allow them to be good friends.

Gin walked through the house to the garage, where Richard had stowed the extra bags of ice in the freezer. She gave an involuntary yelp of surprise when someone stepped out from behind Richard's Audi.

"Easy, girl, it's only me." Tuck Baxter had a bit of a sunburn and a fresh haircut, and a faded Nittany Lions T-shirt that couldn't have possibly fit him any better back when he was an undergrad at Penn State. "Any idea where your dad keeps the croquet set? He wants to set it up for the kids."

Richard had gone up in the attic earlier in the day and brought down the old horseshoes set for Olive, Austen, and Cherie. He was enjoying their company so much that he'd made a pointed comment to Gin in passing, about his 'future grandchildren' and how she shouldn't wait too long to have them.

She certainly wasn't going to mention that now.

"Um, I think it's on the bottom shelf of his work-bench," she said, squeezing past Tuck, hoping he couldn't see her blushing. After bringing her home from the hospital, he'd visited half a dozen times, bringing flowers, a bag of peaches, a set of dominoes that they'd all played at the kitchen table while drinking beer. On his last visit, he'd asked if she was sufficiently healed to be granted shore leave. "Not that I don't enjoy your parents' company," he'd said, "but I was thinking one of these days we should do something, you know, just the two of us."

Naturally, that was the moment her mother decided she needed Tuck to reach something from a high shelf, so Gin hadn't had a chance to respond to his invitation.

As she bent down to pull out the croquet set, Tuck whistled.

"I'm sorry to be a jerk, but that's a hell of a view," he said.

Gin stood up and tugged at the hem of her white shorts. She tried to look stern, but the comical leer Tuck was giving her made her laugh.

Then he turned serious. "Gin . . ."

He took a step toward her, and took the box from her, setting it on the workbench.

"I've been trying to get a moment alone with you for weeks," he said, taking her hands in his. "I haven't worked this hard to get a girl's attention since Janie Baker in third grade. Walked her home for half the school year."

"How did that work out?" Gin said, her playful tone covering the pounding of her heart.

"She threw me over for a fourth grader. And she's an attorney in Philadelphia now, so . . . definitely out of my league."

"And I'm not?" Gin said, though it was getting harder by the second to keep up the playful patter, especially because he was so close . . . and his hands were stroking her forearms in the most distracting way.

"Oh, for damn sure you are, Gin Sullivan. But for some reason, you seem to be falling for my dubious charms anyway."

Then he kissed her. It was only a gentle brush of the lips, over much too quickly.

"Is this all right?" he asked, all humor gone from his voice now. "Because I'm losing my mind here. If you turn me down, I'm going to throw myself in the river."

"Can't have that," Gin murmured back. "Because I'd have to jump in after you."

This time, the kiss lasted considerably longer.

When they finally broke away, Gin's back was pressed against the workbench and her arms were tight around his neck. "Dad's going to come looking for you if we don't get back to the party," she whispered.

"Too true. Think I need to tell him I intend to sweep you off your feet?"

"I'm a grown woman, Tuck Baxter."

"That you are." Tuck tucked her hand in his and hefted the croquet set in his other arm. "But I'm not going to give up until you're *my* woman."

Gin allowed him to lead her back toward the house. At the door, she remembered the ice. "Go on ahead," she said. "I have to get ice for Mom. Plus . . . it might look a little funny for us both to come out of here at the same time. I'm not quite ready to scandalize the whole town."

Tuck gave her one last sizzling, lingering look and went into the house.

Gin opened the freezer and, for a moment, let the cold air wash over her overheated skin. She had no idea what she was doing with Tuck, or where their relationship was headed. But maybe it was time to simply trust fate to lead the way.

Gin had spent her entire life trying to keep her life under strict control, never able to forget the devastating loss of her sister, the grief that had followed her to Chicago and taken up residence there. Since coming back to Trumbull, she'd worried that she might always be aimless, tossed and turned on the currents of the passing days.

But she'd been wrong. Giving up control didn't mean losing her chance of a future after all. Once she'd loosened her grip, things had started to fall into place as though they'd been meant to be all along.

Gin dug into the freezer and hefted the bag of ice, and headed back to the party. There was punch to serve, toasts to make, life to celebrate. And she didn't want to miss a minute.